To Ro, Alan, Emma & Jo
   with love and best wishes.
      Bernard

The Far Side of Nowhere

by

Bernard Stocks

authorHOUSE®

AuthorHouse™ UK Ltd.
500 Avebury Boulevard
Central Milton Keynes, MK9 2BE
www.authorhouse.co.uk
Phone: 08001974150

© 2007 Bernard Stocks. All rights reserved.

No part of this book may be reproduced, stored in a retrieval system, or transmitted by any means without the written permission of the author.

First published by AuthorHouse 9/4/2007

ISBN: 978-1-4343-2374-3 (sc)

Printed in the United States of America
Bloomington, Indiana

This book is printed on acid-free paper.

This book is a work of fiction. People, places, events and situations are the product of the author's imagination. Any resemblance to actual persons, living or dead, or historical events, is purely coincidental.

By the same author

The Guardians
The Tennage Pensioner
The Lannan Project

INTRODUCTION

I brought the lifeship down to the surface of the planet as gently as I could. From a hundred or so feet up the view from the visiscreen showed a level surface covered in short grass, but good though the definition of the picture was I knew that appearances could be deceptive. What I believed was grass could simply have been a covering of vegetation over a lake, bog or quicksand and I wanted to be ready to lift off again quickly. A slight bump told me I had touched land and I held my breath. Thankfully there seemed no indication that we were sinking, but I waited a full ninety seconds before switching off the drive. A glance at the clock calendar above my head showed the time as 6.45 p.m.

A quick stretch to ease cramped muscles and I was ready to face my passengers. I opened the door of the cabin and stepped forward into the main body of the lifeship. Twenty seats, in five rows of four, confronted me. They were filled with a mix of men and women, middle-aged and young, plus three children under twelve, all from the one family, who sat on the laps of three of the adults. The occasion merited words of great impact, but I couldn't think of any.

"Well, everyone," I stated simply and without emotion, "we're here – wherever here is."

A florid faced middle-aged man in the back row stood up. "Do you mean to tell us you don't know where we are?" he queried with an edge to his voice.

This one's going to cause problems, was my unspoken thought. I answered him in as mild a tone as I could muster. "I'm afraid that's exactly what I mean."

"Surely you've got charts on this vessel? And if you haven't you're an experienced officer in the Space Service. You must have some idea."

I looked at him thoughtfully, weighing up my reply. I didn't want to cause a panic among the group, but at the same time there was no point in hiding the truth from them any longer.

"Unfortunately immediately after the collision the 'Caledonian Sunrise' was deflected through a black hole into an uncharted area of space. We could be anywhere in the universe. You all probably know that our knowledge of black holes and where they lead is exactly zero."

"Will that affect our chances of rescue?" This came from a youngish woman sitting right in front of me.

"There's no point in raising false hopes," I responded. "To my knowledge at least three spaceships have vanished into black holes in the last five years. No trace has ever been found of the ships or their complements. We have to work on the assumption that we will never be found."

There seemed to be no one willing to pursue the point, so I became brisk and businesslike. "I know that you're all dying to stretch your legs properly, but I'm afraid I must ask you to remain inside for at least the next half-hour. Although the preliminary tests I carried out prior to landing suggest that this planet will support life I now have to make a detailed analysis of the atmosphere, water and soil before we can venture outside. You can move about the compartment for exercise and use the toilets if you wish. I think too that this would be a good time to dole out the daily rations. Could someone give me a hand, please?"

"I will." The offer came from a tall, slim girl with long curling brown hair who was sitting at the end of the second row. She looked to be in her mid to late teens. I beckoned to her to follow and led the way through the rear door of the passenger compartment, closing it behind us. The stores, such as they were, were kept in a locked cupboard towards the rear of the lifeship. All they consisted of were vitabars and plastic containers of drinking water. Vitabars had been staple fare since long distance space travel became a reality. About five by three inches and half an inch or so deep and tasting a bit like strawberries in a chocolate coating, each bar provided ample nourishment for twenty-four hours.

I unlocked the door and then turned to my companion, noticing for the first time that she had hazel eyes under long lashes. "What's your name?" I asked her.

"Susan," she replied. "Susan Forrest in full. And you're Mr. McNeil, aren't you?"

"I am, but I'd rather you called me Matt."

"We are going to be all right, aren't we Matt?" she asked somewhat plaintively.

"I won't lie to you, Susan. It all depends on the tests I'm going to do. If they prove that the atmosphere isn't breathable or the water's poisonous then I'm afraid we're in real trouble. But please don't say anything to the others."

I counted out twenty-three vitabars, slipping my own one into my pocket. I also put out five one gallon water containers and re-locked the door. "Pass them around and tell everyone I'll be back once I've run the tests." She nodded and went forward as I moved across the corridor and into the lifeship's small laboratory. I activated the sampling devices, then sat back to ponder the events that had brought us to our present predicament.

CHAPTER ONE

The slow development of Man's venture into space after Neil Armstrong's historic moon landing in 1969 had gradually eroded the interest and excitement the event had generated. The huge costs and the dangers involved had greatly restricted further exploration as nations concentrated on satellite technology and the profits that could be made therefrom. The various unmanned probes to the far reaches of the solar system raised little enthusiasm among the general public. Dreams of colonies on the moon and on Mars quickly faded as they were revealed to be impracticable. Research continued, but at a snail's pace. The overriding constraints were that Mars could not sustain more than a handful of colonists and the relatively slow speeds of space craft prohibited ventures outside the Solar System. The manned mission to Mars in 2035 was hailed as a qualified success in that the ship and the six-man crew returned safely, but the physical and psychological effects of long periods of weightlessness on all six men were viewed with grave concern.

Little happened for the next thirty years. Then two inventions within the space of fifteen months reawakened the outward urge. The lesser of these occurred early in 2064. An international team of scientists working in Russia perfected a device that provided normal gravity for any ship going into space. But the really big breakthrough came in October 2065 with the creation of the Gonzales-Mallan drive. Manuel Gonzales was a brilliant Brazilian physicist, Irishman Padraig Mallan an equally gifted mathematician. The two of them had met some three years previously at a convention in New York and taken an immediate liking to each other. Mallan quickly moved to Brasilia and the two men began a research programme at the Gonzales laboratory. Both were interested in astronomy; both wanted to further the course of space exploration. Within three years they had perfected their invention.

I doubt if anyone other than the two proprietors understood the workings of the Gonzales-Mallan drive in detail, but having been thoroughly tested and found to be safe and workable and even more importantly cheap to manufacture the space race started again in earnest. In some way the two men had found a way to use the latent power of a vacuum as propulsion for a vessel. A tiny quantity of basic rocket fuel was sufficient to activate the drive, from which it could then attain speeds of over ten million miles per hour. The only other fuel requirement was during the orbit of and landing on a planet. At last the far reaches of space could be opened up. A ship could be out of the Solar System in just over ten days and distant galaxies could be reached in a matter of months. With normal gravity provided by the Russian device the crews and passengers would suffer no harmful after effects. By basing the large inter-galactic vessels on the moon and ferrying passengers and freight thereto even more fuel could be saved and this is what happened.

For the next twelve years exploratory missions set out as soon as the ships could be built and by 2077 more than two dozen different worlds had been identified as suitable for human colonisation. At last a solution had been found to the problems caused by Earth's ever-increasing population and dwindling natural resources. An intensified programme of building ships capable of carrying large numbers of passengers swung into operation and by the end of 2078 the exodus was in full swing. By that time cryogenics had become a very exact science, so to obviate the need for large food stocks to be carried the passengers were simply frozen as soon as they boarded and restored to normal temperatures a day or two before arrival at their destination.

Although the four nations of the United Kingdom had long been politically independent of each other financial considerations made it advisable for them to have a joint approach to matters related to space travel. Thus the manufacture of ships was in the main centred on the Midlands of England and South Wales, the training of crews for the ships in Northern Ireland and the spaceport itself situated on Rannoch Moor in Scotland. As a boy growing up in nearby Aberfeldy I had been fascinated by the sight of the regular missions lifting off from the Moor and by the time I was sixteen I knew with absolute certainty that I wanted to go into space. Luckily I was able to pass the stiff entrance exam and even stiffer physical examination and was accepted for the Space College, passing out in June of 2082.

The passenger carrying ships were all of a similar design, no matter the country of origin. Each one could carry two thousand passengers plus a number of farm animals and poultry which were also cryogenically frozen. On ships going from Britain the crews consisted of a Commodore, two Captains, four First Officers, eight Second Officers and two engineers. The Commodore and the two Captains worked eight-hour watches, the engineers were simply called out when needed and the rest were on six-hour watches. Thus at any one time in the control cabin there would be the Commodore or one of the Captains, one First Officer and two Second

The Far Side of Nowhere

Officers. The latter acted mainly as pilots, though it wasn't unknown for a First Officer or Captain to take over the controls from time to time. The Commodore, Captains and engineers had their cabins adjacent to the control cabin, the remaining officers were scattered around the starboard side of the ship.

Apart from opening up the pathway to deep space the Gonzales-Mallan drive also inspired the establishment of small colonies on both the moon and on Mars. These were in the shape of mining camps, providing a valuable supply of metals and minerals which had become scarce on Earth. After leaving Space College most graduates spent two or three years on the regular runs to the moon and Mars to gain experience, after which they could apply for posts on the long haul ships. On my own third such application I was successful and was appointed as a Second Officer on the 'Caledonian Sunrise' under Commodore Morrison, due to make her maiden voyage with a full complement of crew, passengers and animals and bound for a planet called Paladia. The journey thereto would take eleven months and we lifted off from Rannoch Moor on the 23rd of September 2085.

The Sunrise was an awesome sight, nearly three-quarters of a mile in length and a quarter of a mile wide at its broadest point. When I reported for duty on my first day I felt more nervous than at any time in my previous twenty-seven years of life. But I soon settled in, helped by the rest of the friendly crew. By good fortune they were not all strangers to me. Two of my fellow Second Officers had been a year ahead of me at Space College and I'd met both of them on a number of occasions. Nicola Holt, blonde and extremely good looking, hailed from Hampshire, while David Lee, quiet and studious, was a Yorkshire man. And one of the engineers was Welshman Glyn Hutchison, with whom I'd made one trip to the moon and one to Mars on the regular freighter runs.

Everything went smoothly until two weeks before we were due to touch down on Paladia. The routine was that over the last three weeks of the voyage we would 'de-frost', the slang term we used for resuscitation, a handful of passengers each day, so that we had plenty of help on hand to ease the discharge of passengers and cargo when we arrived. It was annoying in a way to have non crew members wandering around the ship, but experience in the past had proved that it was the most efficient way of speeding up the ship's turnaround.

On the day in question I'd been on the morning watch from eight a.m. until two p.m., after which I'd gone to the canteen for a meal. I was relaxing in my cabin afterwards prior to spending an hour or so exercising in the gymnasium provided for crew members when there was a loud bang and a massive lurch in the ship's forward motion. At the same time the main lights went out, to be replaced by the emergency lighting system. The ship itself seemed to be spinning out of control to the extent that I could feel my lunch churning inside my stomach. With difficulty I climbed off my bunk and switched on the cabin's visiscreen.

My first act was to set the controls to an outside scan of the ship. What I saw horrified me. The whole of the forward section, which included the flight deck, and part of the port side had been flattened. Bits of wreckage were drifting away into space. Widening the scan I saw what had caused the damage. A huge asteroid was moving away from the ship at speed. As far as I could judge it must have been at least eighty miles in diameter. Even so our deflector screens should have made it a simple matter for the ship to avoid a collision. The inference was that at the very moment prior to impact a fault had developed in the deflectors – an unlikely scenario, but the only explanation I could think of. My reaction was that things could have been worse, but even that thought was quickly banished when I surveyed the immediate surroundings of our wrecked ship. Less than fifty thousand miles away gaped the opening to a black hole!

The ship was being sucked into the vortex and we were close enough for the inside of the hole to be visible. I could see faintly a turbulence which boded a rough passage. I quickly threw myself on my bunk and strapped myself down. I was not a moment too soon. The spinning motion of the ship increased seconds later and there was also the feeling that we were being bumped from side to side. Gravity seemed to fade away and I could feel my body becoming weightless and straining to rise from the encircling straps. The digital clock above my head had stopped and I think I lost consciousness for a while. It could have been seconds or it could have been several minutes: I had no way of telling.

When I came to the ship had stopped spinning and was travelling smoothly, though still at extreme speed. I scanned the outside once more to confirm the damage done and realised that only one course of action was open to me. That was to round up as many of the crew and resuscitated passengers as I could and abandon ship. The larger lifeships were all on the port side and had almost certainly been destroyed, but there were ten smaller craft, each capable of taking twenty passengers, on the starboard side quite close to my cabin. These should still be undamaged. Speed was of the essence, as I had no way of knowing how long the remains of the Caledonian Sunrise would stay habitable. The ship could explode or implode at any moment.

I unstrapped myself and went out into the long corridor outside my cabin. Already some of the passengers were emerging from cabins. We had resuscitated just over a hundred up to that point, mainly single people but including three families with children. Thankfully I hadn't removed my uniform, which made it easier for me to give orders and not have them questioned. As loudly as I could I shouted down the corridor: "Follow me. We have to abandon ship."

About thirty people, young and old, had joined the procession by the time I reached the bay holding the lifeships. I could see at a glance that No.

1 was out of commission. Without stopping to ascertain the reason I moved on to No.2 noting thankfully that it seemed to be in good order. Further down the bay I could see some activity around two more of the ships and caught a glimpse of Second Officer Elaine Rogerson, also in uniform. Quickly I marshalled the first twenty of my followers into the lifeship together with the three children. I told those remaining to move down the bay to one of the other ships before boarding, closing and locking the entry hatch and checking that all my passengers were seated and strapped in. Once I was satisfied I went forward to the pilot's cabin, closed the door behind me and activated the drive. My one thought now was to get clear of the mother ship as quickly as possible.

The moment we left the exit port I raised the drive lever to full power. In case of an explosion I wanted to be as far away from the Sunrise as possible. The lifeships were fitted with a modified version of the Gonzales-Mallan drive and could attain similar speeds to the larger vessels. Thus within ten minutes we were over a million miles clear and I relaxed slightly, but not for long. I and my passengers were clear of any immediate danger, but had it been a case of out of the frying pan into the fire? We had food, in the shape of vitabars, and water for approximately forty-eight days and if we hadn't found a habitable planet at the end of that time we were doomed anyway.

With considerable trepidation I switched on the long-range sensors and started scanning through three hundred and sixty degrees. The Sunrise was still discernible far behind us, but there was no sign now of the black hole through which we'd come. Through the first two hundred and ten degrees the sensors registered nothing but the blankness of deep space. Then my heart leapt. At the extreme range of the sensors I could detect solid matter! We were too far away as yet to determine exactly what it was, but I realised that it must be fairly sizeable to register on the sensors. I offered a silent prayer and set a course in the appropriate direction.

Some two hours later I was able to confirm that a primary star with a planetary system revolving round it was just about a day's journey ahead. I went into the cabin and told the passengers what was happening, then doled out water and vitabars to keep them going. I noticed that they had all remained strapped in, and I suggested they should take it in turns to use the toilets and get such exercise as they could in the confined area around the seats. I had expected questions, but everyone seemed subdued and there were more than a few frightened faces among them.

Once I'd seen to the passengers I returned to my cabin. There was nothing I could do for the next few hours, so activating the autopilot I tried to snatch a little sleep. This was easier said than done, though I did manage to doze for short periods. The clock on the control panel had registered 3.55 p.m. at the moment we jetted away from the main ship and it was just after midnight before the sensors could give me enough information to assess what lay ahead with any accuracy. My hopes were justified: ahead lay a planetary system. Though my instruments were not sophisticated enough to give me an exact calculation it appeared to me that the primary star was smaller and not quite so bright as our own sun back on Earth. There were five planets revolving round the sun. Respectively they were approximately thirty, seventy, ninety, one hundred and fifty and four hundred million miles from that sun. My first inclination was to head for the third planet because of its similar position to its sun as Earth had to our sun. Then I reasoned that if this sun was weaker it was probable that climatic conditions on the second planet could be nearer those of Earth.

I weighed the pros and cons for nearly an hour before coming to a decision. In the end the fact that the second planet was slightly nearer to our present position than the third swayed my judgement. I also took into account the fact that I had sufficient fuel and some to spare to orbit and then land on the second planet and if it was unsuitable to take off again and head for the third. A cursory check of the main cabin showed that all the passengers were asleep. Going back to my own quarters I closed the communicating door and tried to follow their example.

It was 5 p.m. the following day when I made the first orbit of the second planet. From some two thousand miles above the surface the view was promising. Though I had no way of measuring it seemed to be about the same size as Earth. Large areas of green suggested vegetation and even larger areas of blue presaged water. There were two polar caps, about equivalent in size to those on Earth. I could see no areas of blackened land or desert that would result from excessively high temperatures.

In all I made three full orbits of the planet, each at a slightly lower level, to ascertain the best place to land. I was looking for an area with a good supply of water – either a river or a lake – plus a reasonable amount of woodland and a large flat plain suitable for cultivation. I saw any number of spots that fitted these requirements, but my final decision was made because of an added attraction. This was nothing less than a range of low hills containing a number of caves at ground level or just above. I realised as soon as I saw them that these would give temporary living quarters until some form of housing could be built.

It was at six forty p.m. that I started my final descent into a valley shaped like a shallow letter V. Two low ranges of hills, not more than a thousand feet in height, met some two miles or so behind my landing ground. A number of streams flowed down from around the apex to form a river some five metres wide which flowed close to the western side of the valley. The caves I had spotted were on that side and less than a quarter of a mile away from the river. A mile to the north of the lifeship and on the same side of the river was a considerable area of woodland and another forest was visible about a mile south on that side. The rest of the area was fairly flat grassland. During the descent I'd had time to notice that the spot was around thirty or so miles from the shore of a large ocean, that most of the land to the south was flat and that a herd of animals of some kind was grazing less than a mile from where I proposed to land. At that juncture I didn't stop to consider whether they were potentially a food supply or intelligent life! It was more important to find out if conditions were suitable to support human life.

CHAPTER TWO

A muted bleep from the computer roused me from my reverie. The results of the tests were appearing on the screen. My spirits rose rapidly as my eyes ran down the data in front of them. The atmosphere was close to that of Earth, showing a marginally higher percentage of oxygen, equivalently less of nitrogen and similar trace quantities of argon, helium, carbon dioxide and hydrogen. Gravity was 99.2 percent that of earth and the water was 99.98 per cent pure, with minute traces of sodium, calcium and magnesium salts. The analysis of the soil sample proved that it was almost identical to that of Earth except that there was very little clay present. The outside temperature was sixty-five degrees Fahrenheit.

Armed with this good news I left the tiny laboratory and returned to the cabin. The passengers all looked at me expectantly, but all I said was: "With you in a moment" and went into the pilot's cabin. I had one more task to perform. Now that I knew that the planet was habitable I could activate the radio signal that would reveal my whereabouts to any other lifeship within a thirty million mile range. I knew that I had been the first away, but I had no means of knowing how long it had taken others to leave the mother ship. Once that was done I went back into the main cabin to pass on the good news.

"You'll be pleased and relieved to hear that this planet is capable of supporting human life," I told the waiting audience. "Air, water and soil are almost identical to Earth and the outside temperature is a pleasant sixty-five degrees. However, we have to be cautious in our optimism as we're by no means out of the wood yet. Although the scene outside looks peaceful there could be hidden dangers that are not immediately obvious. Please take the utmost care outside and don't wander out of sight of the ship for the moment. Also we have to find a food supply within six weeks. Although we carry a variety of seeds it will be several months before any crops that we plant come to fruition."

The Far Side of Nowhere

I paused for a moment to see if there were any questions, but none were forthcoming. "I'm going to open the door just now, but please confine yourselves to walking around the ship for exercise. There'll be plenty of time for exploring later. You can drink the water from the river, but please don't, under any circumstances, eat anything. Don't even chew a blade of grass. Now before we go out, is there any here who is proficient in the use of a standard stun gun?"

Two people put their hands up, a man and a woman both in their late twenties or early thirties. The woman spoke first. "June Mathieson. I was a police officer for eight years back home and fully trained in weaponry of all kinds." "Harry White," the man introduced himself. "Ten years in the Army, ending up as a sergeant with an infantry regiment and also fully trained in the use of guns of all kinds."

"Wait there a minute," I told them. Going through to the rear of the ship I unlocked what we called the 'Survival Room' and took out two Mark Eight stun guns, standard space service issue, plus a couple of torches. I took these back and handed them to Harry and June. "In front of you and a few hundred yards away you'll see seven or eight caves. I want you to check out each one, making sure there are no life forms in them, either animal or insect. If any of the caves look as though they go back a long way or have passages out of the main cave don't explore them fully but mark them in some way. My idea is that we'll use one or more of the caves for sleeping purposes once we know they're safe. Set the guns to stun. We don't want to butcher anything until we find out what's what. O.K.?"

They nodded and I unlocked the exit door, ran out the short step ladder attached and preceded the others into the open air, taking a deep breath as I did so. The air was fresh and untainted and felt great after the long hours in the synthesised atmosphere of the lifeship. June and Harry followed me out and set off purposefully in the direction of the caves. One by one the rest of the passengers emerged, most of them taking my advice and walking around the ship while scanning the immediate horizon. I followed a number of them to the bank of the river, which was flowing at a fair speed. Kneeling down at the edge I scooped up a little of the clear water into my hands and drank deep. The water tasted slightly sweet but was very refreshing.

Looking more closely towards the middle of the river I spotted several fish. In size they were equivalent to a large trout, but they had flatter heads than a trout and were a very pale silver in colour. Hopefully they would be a source of fresh food. Moving back I dug the toe of my boot into the ground at a point where the grass was the shortest. The soil underneath was dry, dark in colour and light in texture. It looked like a rich loam, which hopefully would make it eminently suitable for crops. The grass all around was quite short, nowhere more than four inches high and looked as though it had been grazed, probably by the herd of animals I'd seen briefly on my orbital approach.

Bernard Stocks

It was half an hour or so before Harry and June returned and the former made their report. "We've checked all eight caves. The two furthest to the right are larger than the others and have passages leading off the main area which we didn't explore. We marked these with a small heap of stones. The others are clear and the third from the left looks the best bet for sleeping quarters. It's big and roomy and will take all of us comfortably. Better still, there's a small secluded chamber at the rear with a rivulet running through it that will serve as a toilet."

"Excellent," I replied. "Now how fresh are the two of you?" They both said they'd slept well over the last few hours and felt wide awake and fit. "Good. I think it would be advisable to mount a guard during the night just to be on the safe side. I'm going to have to stay by the radio in case any of the other lifeships got away and try to make contact. Split the time between you and find a couple of volunteers to provide company. There's a couple of pick handles in the store that they can arm themselves with." Raising my voice I spoke to the rest of the group, who had gathered round. "We're going to use the third cave from the left as our dormitory for the time being. I'll dish out sleeping bags and a couple of lamps just now, then you can make your way over there and get bedded down. It will be dark within the hour, so there's nothing useful that can be done at the moment. I suggest you try and get as much sleep as possible. There's a lot of hard work ahead of us in the next few days. Susan, will you give me a hand again, please?"

Susan followed me into the ship and from the survival room I took out twenty of the twenty-one self-inflating thermal sleeping bags. These were of a relatively new design and extremely efficient. I'd had an opportunity to test them during my time at Space College. As part of our survival training we'd been taken to the far north of Canada and abandoned for three days with only the sleeping bags and a supply of vitabars and water. Apart from keeping us warm the bags were very comfortable and could be adapted for use as overcoats as well. Each bag packed down to a parcel not more than nine by eight by six inches and in that form were as light as a feather. An added bonus was that they expanded to the size of the user, which meant that the three children could each share a bag with an adult.

After we'd handed out the sleeping bags I made a short speech. "So far things are going well for us and the prospects of survival are quite bright. The ship is well stocked with seed for planting, we have three spades and tomorrow we'll make a start on preparing the ground. The sooner we get organised the sooner we'll have fresh food to eat. If there'd been two or three hours of daylight left I'd have made a start tonight in fact, but there's no point in working in the dark. So get as much sleep as you can and be ready for a few days – or weeks – of hard graft. Good night."

I waited until they'd all reached the selected cave safely, made a quick examination of the outside of the lifeship to double check that there had been no damage done and then settled myself in the pilot's cabin in front of

The Far Side of Nowhere

the radio. Truth to tell I was close to exhaustion. I doubted if I could stay awake all night but my hope was that if I did doze off the bleep that the radio would emit if a message came in would rouse me. A minute or two later I heard a sound from the main compartment. Going to investigate I found that Susan had returned.

"What are you doing here?" I asked her.

"I've come to man the radio for you," she replied. "Look at you. You're worn out and you'll be fit for nothing tomorrow if you don't get some rest. I've been sleeping for most of today, and most of last night, too. Show me what to do, then get your head down. If any messages come through I'll wake you."

For a moment I was disposed to argue, but then I realised the girl was talking sense. I gave her a quick lesson in operating the radio, thanked her and left her to it. There was just enough room at the side of the seats in the main compartment for me to lie full length. I settled myself down, zipped up my sleeping bag and was dead to the world within three minutes. I awoke briefly a couple of times in the first hour or two after dreams that were close to nightmares. In one I was on board a ship at sea which was sinking. A storm was raging, and as fast as we launched the lifeboats they were breaking away from their moorings and floating away into the night. In another I was on a strange planet with a weird looking green sky confronting a huge animal with gaping jaws and dripping fangs. I was trying to run, but my feet seemed stuck to the ground. Thankfully after that my sleep was dreamless!

I awoke to feel hands shaking me. When I opened my eyes I discovered firstly that it was daylight and secondly that Susan was desperately trying to waken me. It took me a moment to come to and understand what she was saying. "Matt, Matt, wake up. Come and look."

Struggling to my feet I followed her to the nearest porthole and looked out. My first inclination was that I was still dreaming. Two more lifeships were on the ground close by and a third was about a hundred feet up and descending slowly. Even as I watched the hatch of one of the ships opened and people began emerging. The first one out I recognised immediately as First Officer Colin Dignam, a member of the shift that preceded mine. Telling Susan to wait a moment I hurried into the tiny toilet and splashed some water on my face and arms. By the time I dried off I was fully awake and ready to greet the newcomers. My immediate thought was one of relief. Apart from outranking me Colin was a highly experienced officer with more than twelve years' service and close to promotion to Captain. He was much more fitted to bear the burden of command than I was and I wouldn't be sorry to hand the responsibility over to him.

He greeted me with a smile and a handshake. "We were more than halfway to the third planet when we picked up your radio signal," he began. "I figured that you wouldn't have activated it if the environment wasn't suitable so we changed direction and, well, here we are. Have you had much of a look round yet?"

I brought him up to date with all that had happened to us, by which time the third ship had landed and we had been joined by two other Second Officers, Elaine Rogerson and Dave Lee. Colin had pulled out a notebook and made a couple of entries therein while I'd been talking. Closing it with a snap he said: "Let's get everybody gathered round and try and bring a bit of order into the chaos. Can you get your crowd over here Matt?" Some of my passengers were already emerging from the cave and I hurried over to root out the rest of them. Harry and June assured me that they'd had a quiet night's guard duty.

At five feet nine inches tall and slimly built with dark brown hair and a rather pointed face Colin wasn't exactly an imposing figure, but he had an air of quiet authority about him. In the past I'd only spoken briefly to him as we changed watches but he had the reputation of being very fair and a good boss. Elaine was a couple of inches shorter, also slim and with short black hair. For some reason I always had the impression that she tried to make herself look as unattractive as possible. While she stopped short of being beautiful she had pleasant regular features, a warm smile which surfaced frequently and a husky speaking voice without the trace of an accent.

Dave Lee was the opposite of the other two. Like Elaine and Colin he was on the watch before mine. He stood half an inch over six feet in height, with fair hair and what I can only describe as a craggy face. Solidly built he looked exactly what he was; a former rugby player. He always seemed to have a ready grin on his face and a twinkle in his eye. Although I hadn't seen a lot of him on board due to working commitments the fact that we had met at Space College had provided a bond between us and we had chatted for as long as possible every time he handed over to me.

Once everyone was assembled around one of the lifeships Colin raised his voice and started speaking. "I'm going to put a suggestion to you all. It's obvious that if we're going to make any progress and achieve anything that we'll need organisation. That means the inevitable committee. Are you all willing to let the four of us form that committee in the short term? We have all had a measure of training in survival techniques, so we are probably the most qualified to deal with the task. At the end of, say, three months we'll have an election to form a more permanent committee. By that time we will all know each other and be able to pick the right people for the job. But we don't want to force ourselves on you, so if anyone thinks they are better fitted to run things, or if anyone has any other objections please say so now."

Colin looked round the whole group, giving anyone who wished ample time to make comments. No one spoke. "Thank you for your trust," he continued. "I promise that we won't let you down. Now we'll need the morning to draw up some plans, so I suggest that most of you can spend

The Far Side of Nowhere

the time exploring the immediate neighbourhood. But remember that we are entering unknown territory and take great care, particularly you six young ones. If you're going out of sight of the ships please go in groups of not less than three. The reason for that is that if someone does meet with an accident of some kind one can stay with the victim and one can come back for help. Secondly, do not, repeat not, eat or chew anything, not even a blade of grass. There are strict rules for testing whether unknown food is safe and we must stick to them or risk poisoning. Matt here tells me the water is safe to drink, but so far nothing else has been tested. Thirdly do not approach any animals or touch any birds or insects that you may see. Are there any questions so far? And please, if you're speaking, give your name first so that we can all get to know each other."

A small and rather plain looking woman in her early thirties put up her hand. "Eileen Wilson. I'm a fully qualified biologist. I'd like to start a study of the flora and fauna as soon as possible. Is it all right if I go ahead?"

"Indeed yes," answered Colin. "Any information you can provide will be vital. But please make sure you have at least two companions with you at all times, and be extremely careful handling any specimens you take. If you don't have some kind of protective gloves with you I can supply some. By the way, if you need laboratory space each of the lifeships has a small laboratory at the rear. Please feel free to use any of them. Any other questions?"

"Dr. Stephen Wallace," announced a florid faced heavily built man in his forties. "Is it possible for someone to catch one of those animals in the distance and a couple of fish from the river? From a medical point of view it would be desirable to get some fresh food into the diet as soon as we can. I know the testing procedures and would be happy to supervise the trials."

"Unfortunately the animals are all on the other side of the river, so we can't do anything in that line until we can find a way of crossing. If anyone fancies their hand at fishing you can maybe make a rod of some kind and see if you can grab two or three fish, though. Any other questions?" None were forthcoming. "Right. We'll dish out the day's ration of vitabars at half past one and then meet again, by which time we'll have laid our plans and be able to allocate work to everyone. Just before we break up though can I ask if there are any engineers here." Two men raised their hands. "And are there any farmers?" Again two hands were held aloft. "Could the four of you remain behind for a moment, please. The rest of you can take the morning off," he ended with a broad grin.

Once the crowd had dispersed Colin beckoned those of us that were left to follow him to a grassy bank close to the river and sat down. We grouped ourselves around him and seated ourselves in turn. His first words were to the two engineers. "There are two things we need to have

13

Bernard Stocks

as soon as possible. Most urgently we need a bridge across the river. Can that be done?"

"Paul Cooper," the younger of the two introduced himself. "It should be quite easy. Those trees to the north of us look similar to earth's pine trees and from this distance look very straight in the trunk. If we could cut down a few of those, chop them down to the right length and split them in half lengthways we can make a strong and serviceable bridge."

"Good," said Colin. "There are eight battery driven power saws between the four ships. They should be fully charged, so get hold of them, round up half a dozen strong men and get started. The second requirement is to get some sort of power supply. Any thoughts on that?"

The older of the two engineers stroked his chin. "Walter Butter. If we can get a supply of metal we should be able to rig up some kind of wind turbine and hopefully construct a simple generator," he said thoughtfully. "That would be the simplest method. Given that we can get some metal there's also a possibility of using the river to construct some sort of water driven turbine."

"There's no problem regarding generators," Colin told him. "There's one in each of the lifeships and they can easily be removed or adapted. And there'll be plenty of metal. During our meeting we'll be discussing dismantling and cannibalising two of the four ships. That should provide all you need. However, the bridge is the vital need at the moment. I'd be grateful if you get weaving on that right away."

The engineers left us and Colin turned to the two farmers. "In each of the ships there's what we call a survival room, containing seeds of every description. I'd like the two of you to take a look at them and then make plans for getting stuff planted as soon as possible. Once the bridge is in place you can get across and mark out the fields you'll need. Concentrate on potatoes, cereals, green vegetables and root vegetables. I've got other plans for dealing with salad crops and fruit."

When the farmers had left in their turn Colin turned to the three of us. "There's a couple of things to settle before we get down to some detailed planning. First off we have to decide which of the two lifeships to keep and which to cannibalise."

"We might as well scrap mine," offered Dave. "There's some damage to the rear port side that I sustained as I left the *Sunrise*. It's not serious, but if the other three are structurally perfect then mine should go."

"Probably mine would be the second choice," said Elaine. "It must have been used at some time before the crash and not refuelled. It was only just above half full when I left the *Sunrise* and now I'm down to less than twenty per cent. I presume we'll be transferring the remaining fuel from the two that we're scrapping."

"Right," said Colin. "That's decided. We'll siphon off the fuel before the end of the day and then the engineers can get busy dismantling the two we're scrapping. Now the other thing I wanted to say is this. We've got three months to prove that we're the right people to take charge of things. To do that we've not only got to plan properly, we've also got to earn the respect of the whole group. Now we're not going to do that by sitting on our backsides and talking all day long. I suggest that we take our full share of the heavy work during the day and have our meetings in the evening. Do you agree?"

Elaine, Dave and I looked at each other and nodded. I spoke for the three of us. "If you hadn't brought the subject up I was going to mention it myself," was all I said.

CHAPTER THREE

By twenty past one our plans were laid and we were ready to face the meeting. Thankfully it was a fine day, dry with a slight breeze and a temperature close to seventy Fahrenheit. Most of the assembled throng made themselves comfortable on the ground facing the four of us. Colin brought the meeting to order and began.

"There's something I want to say before we get down to brass tacks. A number of you have asked about our chances of being rescued. I'm sorry to have to say they are negligible. If I had to give odds I would say less than one in a thousand. If it hadn't been for the black hole I would have made it an even chance, but it's already been proved that black holes prohibit communications. After the Brazilian ship *Cruzeiro* and the Russian *St. Petersburg* were lost in a similar way to ourselves the Russians sent out a couple of scout ships to investigate the phenomenon of the black hole. When they eventually found one, one ship entered: the other stayed outside. The idea was that the ship inside would relay a running commentary to that outside. The moment the first ship entered the hole the commentary ceased and the ship was never heard of or from again."

"However, even if there was a reasonable chance of rescue we would have to go ahead on the assumption that we were stranded. It will be easier for all of us if we accept that we are here for the rest of our lives. Let's forget the past and look to the future. The other thing I want to make clear is that the next few months, possibly even the next few years, are going to be hard on all of us. Obviously our first target is survival, and to achieve that we will have to graft all day and every day. And we will have to face many hardships and heartbreaks. But I'd like to think that we can aim higher than mere survival. Let's decide from the outset that not only are we going to survive, but that we are going to achieve the highest possible standard of living, for ourselves, our children and our children's children. The harder we work in the next few months the more likely we are to reach that goal."

Colin smiled. "That's the sermon out of the way, you'll be pleased to hear." There was a ripple of laughter. "Now let's hear from our experts. Paul, would you like to start?"

Paul Cooper was at the edge of the group. He stood up and turned to face the crowd. "Thanks to this gentleman sitting next to me we'll have a bridge across the river by nightfall. I'll get him to tell you how we'll do it. Dan, if you will."

The man in question rose to his feet and faced the assembly in his turn. He was an impressive figure. I judged his height at six feet seven. He was broad in the chest, probably around thirty-five, with short dark brown hair, brown eyes and an open, weather-beaten face.

"Daniel Dunn," he introduced himself. "I'm a joiner to trade nowadays, but I spent five years as a lumberjack in Northern Canada. The trees in the forest to the north of here are similar to pine trees, but not only are the trunks straight, the branches are dead straight as well. That makes them easy to work with. What we've been doing is this. We've cut down four trees, all of which have trunks about nine inches in diameter. These trunks we've split in half lengthways and we will lay them across the river flat side up. This will give us a bridge some six feet wide. We'll fashion the branches into rough planks, which we'll lay crosswise on top of the trunks to make the bridge more solid. That will get us across to the other side. Later on I'll fit some sort of handrails for extra safety."

Paul took it from there. "We measured the width of the river by attaching a thin rope to a stone, throwing it across and then dragging the stone to the edge. We marked the rope on our side, then pulled the whole lot back. The river is sixteen feet, four inches wide at the point we're proposing to cross. We've cut our tree trunks to twenty-four feet, which gives us ample anchorage on each side. We're going to lay the first two sections after this meeting. If you all want to come down and watch it should be quite interesting."

"Thanks, Paul and Dan, and well done," approved Colin with a nod. "Next let's hear from the farmers."

Only one of the two stood up. "Gavin Stewart, from Devon," he announced in a broad west country burr. "We've looked over the supplies of seed in the survival rooms and we plan to start off with a minimum of six fields this year. One will be for potatoes, two for green vegetables and one for root crops. The other two we'll devote to cereals, probably one of wheat and one split between maize and barley. Each field will be about the size of a football pitch. The soil looks to be rich and light and easy to work. We think the best approach would be to strip off the top layer of turf first, then start digging the ground over. The turf can be used to form a low wall around each field, just in case the animals we've seen take a liking to the crops. Once we've planted up our first six fields we can start preparing more for next year. The planted areas may need weeding and watering and there'll be some transplanting to be done later but that shouldn't need more than two or three people."

Colin nodded approval and looked over at our biologist. "Eileen, have you been able to find out much about our surroundings."

Eileen Wilson got to her feet and looked around uncertainly. "I've only got some visual observations to make. I haven't had time to do any laboratory work as yet. In this area anyway the ecology is very simple indeed." She seemed to lose her nervousness as she warmed to her subject. "Firstly the grass is all of the one variety, similar to Earth grass, but fairly coarse. Though I searched over a wide area I couldn't find any wild flowers. There are only three species of trees. One we have already spoken of – the pine-like coniferous trees in the forest to the north. The woods to the south are home to two types of deciduous tree. One has pale green leaves with three lobes, a bit like a clover leaf in shape. The other has dark green serrated leaves slightly similar to dandelion leaves. Incidentally, by the look of the trees it is early spring here. Both types have a profusion of flower buds, but no flowers as yet."

"In addition to the trees there are two distinct types of bushes. These are mostly on the outer fringes of the wood, and particularly thick where it touches the bank of the river. I thought at first that they might be young trees, but when I looked at them more closely I don't think they are. One of the bushes has oval leaves with smooth edges, the other squarish leaves with serrated edges. Both types also have flower buds but no flowers. The ground throughout the wood seems to be a kind of leaf mould with just an occasional tuft of grass; again no sign of wild flowers."

"There is insect life here, again very simplified. There is a flying insect about the size of a bee, but shaped and marked quite like a ladybird. I managed to capture one and will be dissecting it to learn more about it. So far I've seen three distinct types of butterfly. The largest is coloured purple and yellow, the other two are green and pink and light blue and black respectively. One would suppose that if there are butterflies there must be caterpillars, but I haven't been able to find any. I've seen two types of bird, both fairly small. One is similar to a magpie with distinctive black and white markings, the other is like a very small parrot and can be red, yellow, green or black. A few have a combination of those colours. I've dug around in a few places but so far I haven't seen any signs of insects or other animal life in the ground. That doesn't mean that there isn't some, though."

"The area of the wood fringing the river is home to a species of aquatic birds. If I had to describe them I would say that they are a cross between a duck and a goose and as big or bigger than the latter. For safety's sake I didn't go too close to them, but I did notice that they make nests in the riverbank. That suggests the possibility of eggs. The river itself has two distinct types of fish – at least that's all I've seen. One is silver and very like a trout except that the head is flatter and the other is the size of a large salmon, mottled in black and grey and vaguely looks like a mackerel."

"Finally, with the aid of binoculars, I've been able take a look at the animals on the other side of the river. They're rather weird. Imagine an animal almost the size of a Shetland pony with a face like a pig and the body of a sheep, covered in what looks to be like a black wool fleece and you get the picture. Incidentally, I spent about half an hour watching them. I saw no signs of any communication between them and no indication that they have any intelligence other than that of normal animals. They spent the whole time simply grazing in the way that cows and sheep do back home. If you do manage to shoot one for food testing I'd like to have it for dissection purposes." She ended on an apologetic note. "I'm afraid that's all I've been able to find out so far."

"You've done wonderfully well in such a short time," praised Colin as Eileen sat down. "Has anyone else anything to contribute?" After a moment's silence a small, spare, elderly grey-haired man rose to his feet.

"William Haddow," he introduced himself in a faint Yorkshire accent. "I was a teacher of mathematics during my working life, but I've also been a keen amateur astronomer since my teens. I've been making a few measurements during the morning, very rough ones at the moment but they will become more accurate the longer we're here. First off, I can confirm what Eileen has said. It is indeed early spring, probably around the first week in April. By this time tomorrow, from sightings I'm taking of the sun's position, I'll be able to determine the length of the day. However it already looks fairly certain that the day here is longer than twenty-four hours. I can give you a more definite figure this time tomorrow, but early indications are that it is somewhere around thirty minutes longer. That means that, unless we can find a way of making the minutes on our watches and clocks longer, we might as well throw them away. It will take three to four weeks before I can get any idea of the length of the year and maybe as much as three months before I can be totally accurate. But I think we can be pretty sure it won't be the three hundred and sixty-five days we've been used to."

"Thanks, William, that's very useful," said Colin. "As far as adjusting watches is concerned I'll leave that to the engineers to ponder over. We'd better start some sort of calendar, I suppose, for the sake of convenience. Let's call yesterday Monday, April the first. We'll work on from there using an earth calendar until William can give us an accurate number of days in the year, then we'll make adjustments accordingly. Is everybody happy with that?"

There was a murmur of approval. Colin then asked if anyone else had any observations, but this time there were no takers. Taking some notes from the pocket of his tunic he started to outline the plans that we'd drawn up at our meeting. "Obviously our main priority has to be the food supply and ideally I would have liked to put everybody on to digging the

Bernard Stocks

fields. Unfortunately we're handicapped by having only twelve spades. So we've decided to form a number of work parties. We'll allocate twenty-four people to the farm. That means twelve digging at any one time. Initially the other twelve can carry away the turf to form the banking round the fields: once the digging starts in earnest you can take turn about so that everyone can have a decent rest between working spells."

"The second working party we'll call the engineering group. Anyone with building, plumbing, joinery or similar skills will form this group under the direction of Paul and Walter. Their main tasks will be first to provide us with some sort of electrical power and then to erect some sort of shelters – simple log cabins or the like – so that we can vacate the caves and have a more civilised way of life. This group will also look at ways to make our work easier. By this I mean the possibility of making some sort of plough and some way of grinding corn. As time goes on there will be other things that spring to mind that will improve our society."

Colin shuffled his notes. "The next group we'll christen the crofting group. Is there anyone here with experience of smallholding or of large-scale gardening?" No one spoke for a full half minute. Then a man at the back of the crowd rose reluctantly to his feet.

"Trevor Shields, from Derbyshire. I'm not sure if this qualifies me, but I was manager of a garden centre for nearly seven years."

"That should do nicely for what I have in mind," stated Colin. "I want you and your group to do a number of things. First of all we'd like you to mark off an area away from the farms – possibly this section in front of the caves. Once the six main fields are planted we'll pass on two or three of the spades so that you can prepare the ground. Your job will be to grow salad vegetables – lettuce, tomatoes, beetroot – that kind of thing. There's a fair amount of plexi-glass in the ships, so consult with the engineers about rigging up some kind of greenhouse. Secondly we'd like you to start growing fruit trees and bushes from the seeds and stones we have in the survival rooms on the ships. The aim should be to set up orchards in two or three years' time with the trees and to use any bushes, such as raspberry, gooseberry and currant bushes, as boundary hedges for the fields. And thirdly we'd like your group to be responsible for the collection and storage of seed for the future. Liase with the farmers on this one. Can you handle all that?"

"I'll give it my best shot," promised Trevor, though he still looked a bit doubtful. I made a mental note to keep a close eye on the crofting group in the next few weeks.

"The final group I want to set up just now we'll call the supply group," Colin continued. "Is there anyone who has had experience of large-scale catering?"

A buxom middle-aged lady with short fair hair stood up immediately. "Dorothy Cole, from Swansea," she stated in a pronounced Welsh accent.

"I was a cook in a large secondary school for five years and then spent four more as a school meals supervisor."

"Just what we're looking for," said Colin. "Once we get a supply of proper food I'd like you to take charge of the catering. We'll lay on some help for you. There's no point in individuals cooking for themselves; it's much more efficient to cook for the whole company. Assuming that those animals and large birds and the fish in the river prove edible two people at least will work with your group supplying fresh food each day. Anyone who has had experience of fishing and or hunting, or even poaching please apply." That earned a laugh.

"I've a few more things I want to say before we allocate everyone to one of the groups, but before I do are there any questions?""

A youngish woman rose to her feet. "Linda McWilliams, from Edinburgh. Is there any chance that any of the three ships that have disappeared into black holes could have landed here?"

Colin turned to me. "I think Matt's better qualified to answer that than I am," he said.

I thought for a moment. "It's a possibility, I suppose. I made three orbits of the planet from different angles at three hundred miles up or less and I saw no sign of any ships, wreckage or evidence of other inhabitants. That doesn't mean there aren't any. There's bound to be a large area of the surface I didn't cover."

Elaine broke in at this point. "There have been at least thirty black holes reported since space exploration and travel began. Those other ships could have gone through any of them. So the mathematical odds against them being here are at least ten to one."

"Once we've ensured our food supply and have settled into shelters outwith the caves we can do a more detailed survey of this world," Colin promised. "But it's not a priority right now. Any other questions?" None were forthcoming so Colin continued. "I've three more things to say. Firstly it would be helpful if we had some background on everyone, so Elaine is going to take a kind of census. During the rest of the day, could each of you, children included, seek her out and give her your name, age, occupation. Also tell her if you have any skills or hobbies other than your main job. This will help us to allocate the right people for tasks that may arise in the future. Incidentally, if you don't like your given name this is a perfect opportunity to change it."

"Secondly, can I urge all of you, particularly the young ones, to continue to take every possible safety precaution. Remember that there are only ninety of us, so every single person is vital to survival; we cannot afford to lose anyone. Keep going around in threes, and take the utmost care when you are near the river. The current is quite strong and if anyone falls in, even if a good swimmer, we have no way of rescuing you. As well as ensuring your own safety please watch out for others."

Bernard Stocks

"My final request is this. Over the next couple of weeks I'd like you to think about and discuss among yourselves the kind of community you would like to have. Soon we will have to take decisions on matters such as religion, marriage, education and the laws by which we will be governed. One of the advantages of having a small group like this is that we can all have our say and all play our part in shaping the future of our world. Just to give you one example of a decision that must be made. There are more women than there are men. Now it's important for survival that everyone capable of having babies and who are willing should do so. That will affect our decisions on marriage. And now let's get the various groups formed and then go down and see our first bridge being laid."

CHAPTER FOUR

It didn't take more than a quarter of an hour to allocate our working parties, by which time our watches showed half past three. With Paul Cooper and Dan Dunn leading the way we all set off towards the river. I was towards the rear of the crowd when I heard someone call my name softly. I turned round to see Susan at my back.

"Can I talk to you a moment, Matt?" she asked nervously.

"Sure. Go ahead."

She hesitated for a moment and then a deep blush spread across her face. "It's about those babies," she almost whispered. "I.. that is I'd... well I'd like to have them with you." The last few words came out in a rush.

I was too surprised to respond immediately. Though I'd liked what I'd seen of her so far I certainly had not harboured any romantic thoughts. My mind ticked over rapidly. She was an attractive lass; a bit young for me probably but in the new civilisation that we were creating that was not a great concern. I could do a great deal worse, I mused.

I took her hands in mine. "How old are you?" I asked.

"Seventeen," she replied. Then she added almost defiantly: "And you'd better know now that I'm not a virgin."

"Neither am I, and in any case that's not important. You realise I'm ten years older than you," I said.

She gave the ghost of a smile. "I find older men are more attractive," she replied impishly.

I pulled her towards me and kissed her lightly. "In that case I thank you for the compliment and I accept your proposal." She hugged me tightly and returned my kiss. I held her at arm's length and smiled as I said: "Now that's settled can we go and see the bridge, please?" She laughed and we headed off for the river bank arm in arm.

When we arrived the first of the half tree trunks was about to be dropped across the river. Two notches had been cut about four inches below the top of the trunk and a rope had been tied securely to them.

Bernard Stocks

Three men held the trunk upright while two others guided the rope itself and started to lower the trunk towards the opposite bank. The first two attempts had to be aborted as the trunk swung round at an angle. The third try was successful. The trunk dropped straight and true on the far side, with about a foot of wood resting on solid ground. By expending all their energy two of the men managed to push it another eighteen inches to ensure that it would not slide back into the river.

Paul Cooper then tied a rope under his armpits, handed the end to someone standing close by and crossed to the other side on his hands and knees. Another man followed him using the same procedure. Untying the original rope from the tree trunk he signalled for it to be drawn back across the river. The remaining three trunks were lowered in the same way as the first while the two on the opposite bank manoeuvred them into their correct positions. Hey presto! We had a bridge.

"We'll add the rest of it this evening," announced Paul when he crossed back. "Tomorrow we'll fasten the planks crossways to strengthen it." He raised his voice. "It's quite safe as it is, but for the moment make sure when you're crossing to walk in the middle of one of the trunks."

The first to cross were the two farmers. They'd armed themselves with a supply of twigs about three feet long with which they would mark out their proposed fields. Harry and June followed them. They were still armed with the stun guns I'd given them the night before and their job was to try and kill one of the sheep like animals. Two sturdy looking men went with them to carry the spoils, if any. A little further down the riverbank a man and a woman were fishing. They'd fashioned a couple of rough fishing rods. I wondered what they were using as bait, and leaving Susan I went and asked them.

"Bits of coloured cotton made up to resemble flies," the man told me. "I used to do a lot of trout fishing near my home in Northumberland and I always made up my own flies." As he was speaking the woman got a bite and a minute later she'd landed one of the silver fish. I left them to it.

As I rejoined Susan a couple of men came up to me. "There's a good bit of daylight left," he said without preamble. "If you can give us a spade each we can go across and make a start lifting some turf. One of the fields is marked off already."

"Good idea," I told him. "I think I'll join you. Come with me and I'll bring out the three from my ship." Turning to Susan I said: "Can you find Colin and let him know what we're doing, please." She went off without a murmur.

Less than ten minutes later the three of us were hard at work. We all started at the same end of the field, one at each side and one in the middle. As Gavin Stewart had said the soil was very light and the turf could be cut away without a great deal of effort. One by one more people, including three of the women, came and joined us until all twelve spades were in use. By the time daylight began to fade we had cleared almost a tenth of the field. Gavin and his fellow farmer, a Dorset man called Peter Gibson, had by that time marked off all six fields in two rows of three.

After a quick wash in the river I headed back across to the field in front of the caves. Someone had been collecting brushwood and had started a fire. I spotted Susan nearby and asked her what was happening.

"June and Harry killed one of the shigs and Mrs. Cole is cooking a piece if it on a spit over the fire," she informed me. "Then she's going to cook some of the fish."

"What in heaven's name is a shig?" I asked her in wonderment.

She laughed. "One of the children came up with the name. If it's half a sheep and half a pig then it must be a shig." She laughed again. "Let's be thankful we're not calling them peeps! Working on the same principle the large birds in the forest have been christened gecks – half geese, half ducks! No-one's caught one of them yet, though."

Hand in hand we went over to the fire, around which most of the group were gathered. Dr. Wallace was supervising operations.

"I'd like nine volunteers, please, either four men and five women or five men and four women," he called in a loud voice. A forest of hands went up and he spent several minutes in making his choice. I noticed that he selected those who looked the least healthy. I supposed that his theory was that if they had no ill effects the stronger among us would be certain to be all right. I whispered as much to Susan and she nodded agreement.

Two spits were now in place above the fire. One held a piece of meat, presumably from the 'shig', the other two whole fish. Dorothy Cole was gently turning both at the same time and a mouth-watering odour was emanating from them. I began to drool – and to wish I'd been one of the volunteers!

In about five minutes the doctor pronounced that both meat and fish were ready and asked his first three volunteers, a man and two women, to step forward. "We'll start with the meat," he decided. Lifting the spit from the fire he took out what looked to be a hunting knife and detached the meat. Cutting off a small piece, roughly a one-inch cube, he turned to the man. "Make sure it's not too hot and then put it in your mouth. Hold it there until I tell you to start chewing. Keep on chewing gently until I tell you to swallow. If it tastes unpleasant or you start feeling unwell spit it out immediately. Understood?" The man nodded and followed instructions.

Twenty seconds after putting the piece of meat in his mouth the doctor told him to start chewing. Eighty-nine pairs of eyes were riveted on him as he slowly masticated his sample. His face gave nothing away. After a full minute he was told to swallow. Anxiously we awaited his verdict.

"Very pleasant," he reported after due deliberation. "It's very tender, tender as fillet steak or young lamb in fact. The flavour is difficult to pinpoint. It's fairly strong, sweeter than beef. I'd say that the nearest thing I've had is venison that's been well cooked."

Bernard Stocks

There was a communal sigh of relief. The two women then took their samples and the same procedure was applied to the two varieties of fish. The smaller silvery fish was said to have a strong taste similar to mackerel, the larger and darker fish was compared to halibut. Not one of the nine guinea pigs seemed the worse for wear after the test.

"I want all nine of you to move into cave number two with me for tonight," ordered Dr. Wallace as he wound up the proceedings. "I'll position you all around me, so that if you have any reaction during the night I'll be right next to you. If you feel unwell, even if only very slightly, you are to wake me immediately. If none of you show any adverse effects by morning you'll all get much larger pieces. Meantime I'm taking charge of what's left. No-one is to touch it until I say the word." So saying he produced three plastic bags, obviously purloined from the supply in the lifeships' survival rooms, and scooped up the remains of the meat and fish.

Colin had an announcement to make before everyone drifted off. "There's no point in leaving the seats in the lifeships any more. If some of you will report to the ships we can unscrew them from the deck and take them into the caves for extra comfort." He turned to Dave, Elaine and myself, standing nearby. "Would you each supervise your own ship, please. I'll get them to leave four or five seats in mine that we can use for meetings."

Before going to my own ship I had a quick and private word with Susan. "As soon as the seats are cleared out bring your sleeping bag into our ship. We can maybe make a start on those babies tonight if you feel like it."

She blushed. "I do," she whispered simply.

It took nearly an hour to get all the seats removed. They'd all been bolted down securely and Dan Dunn proved to be the only one among us strong enough to loosen more than a dozen of the fittings. At last it was done and Colin called the three of us in for a meeting.

"Not a bad start," he summed up. "In just one day we've got our bridge, our working parties set up, our food testing underway and the beginnings of our first field. I've noticed, too, that the unmarried ones are beginning to pair off, including our Matt." This was said with a smile. "One thing we don't want is anyone having casual sex with more than one partner. It could prove disastrous for the next generation. In fact I'm going to ask Doc Wallace to say a few words on the subject tomorrow. Everyone seems to be in good spirits, so we'll have to try and keep the momentum going. All I want to do tonight is assess the particulars that Elaine has been taking. Have you managed to get round everybody?"

"Everyone except the four of us," she answered with a grin. "With your permission I'll do that now."

She quickly noted down our details, made a few calculations on a separate sheet of paper and then announced her findings.

"We have four married couples," she began. "Two have no children, one has three and the other two. There's also one ten year old girl with no parents. They must have been left in the ship. The other children comprise a twelve-year-old, plus two of ten, one nine and one eight. As far as I can make out there are no liaisons amongst the remaining seventy-six of us apart from Colin and I and Matt and Susan. We've a wide variety of trades, professions and skills," she continued, "many of which will be valuable to us. I won't go over all of them, but we've got teachers, builders, mechanics, computer buffs, at least one poacher and three keen anglers, two of them women. I'll have the occupations tabulated so that if we're looking for any specialists at any time I can find them quickly. Not that it's important, but you might like to know that our complement comprises nine Scots, five Welsh and four Irish. The rest are English."

"In a way I would have liked a few blacks, Asians and Chinese amongst them," said Colin thoughtfully. "It would give us some different genes to throw into the mix."

There was little else for us to discuss at that time so we broke up fairly quickly. I felt like some exercise and walked for some way down the riverbank. It was a pleasant night, not too cold, and despite the physical exertions of the late afternoon I felt as if I could walk for miles. On my way back, just before I reached the area where the ships were grounded I saw a figure silhouetted ahead of me in the moonlight. When I got closer I realised that it was Colin. He was still as a statue, his gaze fixed on the river but obviously his thoughts were far away.

"Worried, Colin?" I asked him softly when I was close.

"A little, Matt," he confessed. "I remember reading somewhere that the minimum number of people in a community needed to guarantee long term survival is five thousand. We've got ninety. That means the odds against us are over fifty to one. I'm not much of a gambler, but if I was I wouldn't be likely to take a bet at those odds. I'm beginning to wonder if we might not have been better off if we'd all perished in the *Sunrise*."

"For heaven's sake don't let anyone else hear you talking like that," I urged him. "You of all people have to be positive and optimistic. Look on the bright side. We have a place to live and it looks as though we'll have a supply of meat and fish until we can produce our own crops. Sure, the odds don't look good for the long term future, but we have to do the best we can in the here and now. Don't forget, too, that more people could be drawn into that black hole at any time."

"I suppose you're right," he admitted. "Don't worry. I'll put my cheerful face on again before I meet anyone else. And thanks."

I left him and returned to my ship. It had been something of a shock to me to find Colin in such a depressed mood. He had seemed so confident in his leadership from the moment he had arrived and I hoped that his sombre mood would dissipate overnight.

Bernard Stocks

Daylight was filtering through the cabin's portholes when I awoke in the morning. I turned lazily and looked at Susan sleeping peacefully beside me. She looked so young and vulnerable and I felt a surge of tenderness at how freely she'd given herself to me. I didn't think I was in love with her yet, but there was a sensation inside of me that love might not be too far away. I woke her with a gentle kiss and went outside to wash. Already I could see a fire burning brightly over towards the caves: Dorothy must have risen at the crack of dawn.

The first item on the agenda was the second food testing session. By the time Susan and I joined the throng around the fire both meat and fish were sizzling away on their respective spits. The nine volunteers had suffered no ill effects overnight so this morning they were to be given normal portions. Doc Wallace carved off about half a pound of meat for each of them and a similar amount of fish, which were eaten with obvious enjoyment by the guinea pigs. The rest of us watched in envy.

When they had finished the doctor gave instructions. "I want all nine of you to stay close to me for most of today. If none of you have had a reaction by three o'clock I think we can pronounce both meat and fish as fit for consumption." He turned to June and Harry, who had been appointed as our hunters. "At that time I'll let you know if we have the green light, and you can lay on another shig. One should comfortably feed the whole company. We'll try and vary the diet by having meat one day and fish the next, so you can tailor your activities accordingly. We've still to test the offal like liver, kidney and heart. That's supposing they have those organs of course. Eileen will no doubt tell us once she's dissected our first specimen. But before you do anything else could you please catch one of those wading birds. What have they been called? Gecks, isn't it? We'll test them as soon as possible. Oh, and try and get a couple of their eggs, too."

At that we broke up into our groups and prepared to start our first full day of work. I was scheduled for another session of turf cutting, while Susan had been allocated to the crofting squad. Colin proposed to put in a shift with each group during the day. Dave and Elaine were both with me in the fields and we worked close to each other. It was a pleasant day, overcast and a little on the chilly side, but ten minutes with the spade sufficed to start me sweating. Now and again I took a moment to look around me, and I was pleased to see that everyone seemed cheerful and that no one was slacking.

By lunchtime we had made significant progress. Turf had been stripped from over half of the first field and Gavin decreed that when we resumed eight of the spades would be used to continue stripping while the other four were detailed to start digging the cleared ground. Collecting my vitabar from Dorothy I walked round to see how the other groups were faring. My first port of call was the bridge. Planks had been laid crosswise across the full length and Dan had made a start on putting simple railings along the side. As I turned away Dave's lifeship caught my eye and I noticed that two six foot square chunks of metal had been cut out of the side.

The crofting group had made a good start too. A fair-sized area just south of the caves had been marked off. Trevor Shields was still at the scene and showed me what had been done.

"We could have done with a few spades," he said, "but we found a trowel in each of the survival rooms and we've been working with those. It takes much longer but at least it means we can plant some things right away." He indicated two freshly dug patches about four feet by three. "We'll be putting some lettuce in there this afternoon. I plan to have about eight plots the same size; the others we'll use for beetroot, celery and more lettuce. Now over here you'll see that we've cut out and dug over some circular areas about the size of large flower pots. The ones in this area will all be used for tomatoes. Once we've finished planting them we'll fence off another area close by, dig out similar flower pot sized holes and make a start on the fruit trees and bushes. The engineers are busy at the moment, but once they've some time to spare they're going to build us a greenhouse of some kind. That will let us force things along a lot quicker."

He seemed to have lost the nervousness he'd shown the previous day. He spoke with real enthusiasm and there was an alertness about him that hadn't been there previously. My earlier worries about him were obviously unfounded. He had more to tell me. "This afternoon three of the group are going to make a full exploration of the two bigger caves at the far end. If there's nothing unpleasant lurking there we can use them for storage. We might even be able to grow a few things in them as well. I saw some mushroom spawn amongst the seeds in the survival rooms and mushrooms should do well at the back of a cave."

By this time everyone was drifting back to work. I had a quick word with Susan in passing. She had a message to pass on from Colin. "There'll be a meeting of everyone after the evening meal," she informed me, " so don't go wandering off."

Then it was back to the field. For variety, or so he said, Gavin gave everyone a spell of digging during the afternoon. Despite the shortage of spades the work progressed quickly and proved not too tiring. We worked in twenty-minute shifts. One shift was spent turf cutting, one stacking the turf, one digging and one resting. From somewhere Gavin had unearthed a whistle, which he blew to signal each changeover. It proved an ideal formula. Men and women alike were still going strong when five o'clock came and I heard no complaints of tiredness. I suspected that there might be some stiff limbs by the following morning though – mine among them!

To everyone's joy the nine volunteers were still hale and hearty. A full-grown shig was roasting on the spit over an open fire. The odours emanating from it were tantalising. A few yards away another fire was roasting the carcass of a geck and two large eggs were boiling in a makeshift pan. Moving closer I detected a far less pleasant smell. It wasn't strong, but it reminded me of an occasion when I had walked over a manhole cover leading to an open sewer. The flesh of the geck itself was a dull greyish colour. Doctor Wallace, Elaine and Colin were standing nearby and I heard the doctor saying: "I've a feeling we can write off the poultry from the menu. That smell is a good indication the meat isn't fit to eat. I'm not even going to ask for volunteers. I'll taste a tiny piece myself. Those eggs should be done. Let's have them out and have a look at them."

Elaine produced a large spoon and carefully lifted out one of the two eggs, placing it in a metal mess tin that was standard space service issue. The doctor took out a knife and a piece of cloth from his pocket. Holding the egg carefully he sawed away at the shell. There was a sharp crack and the most ghastly smell assailed our nostrils. If you can imagine putting your nose an inch away from a heavily chlorinated pail of sewage you'll get a good idea of the stench. We all stepped back involuntarily. Doc Wallace looked at us with a wry grin and said: "Eggs are definitely off, folks." Cutting off a tiny piece of the roasting bird he put it carefully into his mouth and chewed twice before spitting it out into the fire. "Revolting," was his only observation.

By this time a queue had formed at the other fire and we lined up at the back. Everyone in turn was given a chunk of the shig meat about half a pound in weight. There were no knives, forks or plates of course; we all ate from our hands like savages. When I had been served I wandered off and joined Susan, who was sitting with a couple of other girls some distance from the fire. We ate in silence. I don't know about the others, but after five days of living on a diet of vitabars that slice of meat was the best meal I could ever remember. As the volunteers had remarked the previous day it was very tender and did indeed taste quite like venison.

CHAPTER FIVE

Just before seven o'clock Colin ushered us all into one of the unoccupied caves. Two or three hurricane lanterns provided an eerie light. A shelf of rock at the side of the cave made a perfect seat for the other three committee members and myself. Once everybody had settled down on the floor Colin rose to his feet.

"I propose to have a meeting at this time every night for the first few weeks," he began. "We'll take a report from the heads of each of the working groups every night. That way we can all keep up to date with what's happening. Also if anyone wants to make suggestions or comments they will have the opportunity to do so. Can we start with the farming section, please."

Gavin Stewart stood up and ambled round to face his audience. "Thanks to the hard work of the whole group we've done well today. The first field has been stripped of turf and a start has been made digging it over. With the turf we've constructed a wall about three feet high all round the field, which should keep out any prowling shigs or other as yet unknown animals. Tomorrow we'll split the work force in half. One half will continue digging, the other will begin stripping field number two. We're proposing to use the first field for potatoes, so with any luck we'll have some if not all planted by the end of the week."

Paul Cooper spoke next for the engineering group. "Dan and his helpers have finished the bridge and may I say they've made a first class job of it. In case a second bridge should be desirable we've identified three or four places both up and down the river where one can be placed. Walter and I have spent most of the day designing a wind turbine which we can link up to one of the ship's generators to give us electrical power. We'll start putting it together tomorrow. Dan has some ideas regarding the building of huts. He'll be cutting the necessary timber to put one together and see how it looks."

Bernard Stocks

Trevor Shields gave his report in very much the terms he'd spoken to me at lunchtime. During the afternoon his group had dug out more of the flower pot holes and had planted some three dozen tomatoes therein. With the approval of the engineers he'd taken some of the plexi-glass from Dave's ship and was using it to cover the tomatoes during their germination period. "It's not the same as having a greenhouse," he opined, "but it doesn't look as though frost will be a problem on this world and the signs are that the climate will be slightly warmer than that of Britain. With luck the tomatoes should ripen eventually even though they're outdoors."

Speaking for the catering side, Dorothy told us that we had sufficient fish for breakfast for all of us next morning and more would be caught during the day. She had spoken to Colin and they had agreed to discontinue the issue of vitabars. This made sense. We had about forty days' supply of the bars admittedly, but any number of things could happen to cause a food shortage and it was comforting to have an emergency ration available.

Eileen Wilson had spent the day in the laboratory of Colin's ship dissecting the various specimens she had been given. "The shigs are very interesting," she reported. "They're mammalian in structure, but they have two livers and two stomachs instead of one of each. There are also two kidneys, two lungs and a heart in the exact centre of the thorax. The digestive system appears to be normal, but so far I haven't worked out how their food, all vegetable in nature, selects which stomach to enter. Both appear to be in regular use. The specimen I had was a female and the reproductive organs are the same as those of a sheep back on Earth. I've one disappointing piece of news. There was a small quantity of milk in the mammary glands. I probably shouldn't have, but I tasted it. It was foul. I can't describe it exactly, but it was sour and chemical tasting. So I'm afraid any thoughts of using the shigs for milk is out of the question."

"The three birds are all similar internally to Earth birds. The smaller birds live on leaves, according to the contents of their stomachs. I found no trace of any kind of insects that they might have eaten. The gecks, as I believe they've been christened, eat some small fish, which they swallow whole and digest later. Their main diet, though is grass and leaves from the bushes. Both varieties of fish are indistinguishable from Earth fish. Incidentally, from a food point of view the roe should be edible as well as the flesh of the fish. The same goes for the offal from the shigs. The livers, heart and kidneys have no harmful chemicals in them. They should be tested in the same way as the meat, though, just to be on the safe side. The fish appear to use as food a kind of weed that grows underwater on the banks of the river. I still haven't found any trace of insects in the river or on land."

She turned towards Colin. "Tomorrow, if it's all right with you, I'd like to roam further afield and see whether there's anything different a few miles away."

"I've no objection," said Colin. "But I must insist on the usual proviso. Take two people with you, one of them armed. If you want to travel a distance we'll break out the altabs. For those who don't know of them they're small tricycles, battery powered with a range of about a hundred miles between charges. Altab is an acronym, by the way. It stands for Advanced Land Travel Auto Bike and there's one in each survival room. They're easy to control and can achieve speeds of up to thirty miles an hour. They also have large panniers attached. We'll make sure they're all put on charge tonight." His eyes swept the gathering until he picked out our amateur astronomer. "William, are you any further forward in calculating the length of the day?"

William Haddow stood up. "I'll double check over the next few days, but I can say with some certainty that it's twenty-seven minutes longer than an Earth day. We can adjust watches and clocks accordingly. Bert McComb, here," he indicated an elderly grey-haired man next to him, "is an experienced watch and clock repairer, and he tells me he can make the necessary adjustments without any trouble. I suggest that everyone with a watch or clock should make arrangements with him to have it done."

"Thanks, William," Colin took over again. "I've just a couple of things to say before we close the meeting. First of all I think everyone should give themselves a pat on the back. We've made tremendous progress today; far more than I expected. Please keep up the good work. Secondly, there's something I should have said before this. Please do not throw anything away, no matter what. Remember that we don't as yet have a source of new metal, paper, glass and other raw materials. We'll have to recycle everything we need for a long time to come. We'll set aside one of the unused caves for everyone to dump their rubbish in. Are there any questions or any comments that anyone would like to make?"

I thought there might have been a few, but nobody spoke and gradually people began to drift off to their own caves. I suspected that most were tired after the hard physical work of the day and wanted to retire early. The four of us stayed behind for twenty minutes or so, then Colin suggested we retrieved the altabs from our survival rooms and checked that they were fully charged. "Then we can all get some well-deserved rest," he smiled.

Unfortunately our progress wasn't maintained the following day. We awoke to a grey morning of low cloud and driving rain. Though the sleeping bags could be adapted to serve as waterproof clothing it was almost impossible to work in them and Colin quickly decreed that outdoor activity was out of the question. Dorothy and her group had risen early and kindled a fire in the cave we'd used for the previous night's meeting. We breakfasted off fish and water, a couple of brave souls having made trips to the river to ensure an adequate supply. Harry and June insisted that they would go fishing, the former jokingly telling us that wet weather meant that the fish were easier to catch. Everyone else lounged around in the cave, making frequent trips to the entrance to view the unremitting rain. It had turned quite chilly as well and we were glad of the warmth of the fire.

After breakfast Colin called Dave, Elaine and myself over. "This is just what we didn't need. We built up a good momentum yesterday and spirits were high. If we get much of this weather it's going to affect morale. However, while we've got some spare time I'd like to explore the two larger caves," he suggested. "Bring torches with you and we'll make a start."

We'd numbered the caves from the southern end. Number one was unoccupied and the smallest of the lot. Two, three, four and five provided sleeping quarters for the survivors. Six was the one we were currently using as a canteen and meeting place; seven and eight were the two that had subsidiary caves in addition to the main one. Trevor Shields and his crofting group were planning to use number seven for storage purposes and that was the one that we looked at first. The main cave branched into two about twenty yards from the entrance. The left-hand fork led to a large chamber about thirty yards square with a roof some twenty-five feet above the floor. It was dry as a bone and I could see the logic behind Trevor's plan to use it for a store. Retracing our steps we traversed the right-hand arm. After fifteen yards this further sub-divided into three narrower passages. The first one we tried became narrower and narrower as we went along until it became little more than a cleft in the rock. We shone all four torches into the opening, but we could see little except that the passage continued to shrink.

"Hm," Colin said thoughtfully. "It looks as though it just peters out, but to be on the safe side I'll get Trevor to block this off, just in case it's home to any small nasty looking creatures. Let's have a look at the other two."

These were almost identical in length and each finished in a medium sized chamber. One thing I did notice was that it was very warm once one left the main cave. I mentioned Trevor's idea of growing mushrooms to the others.

Dave nodded. "I was just thinking that. And there's another thing. If the engineers can give us unlimited power we could rig up some sort of lighting system in here and use the warmth and light to force plants on."

Cave eight was far more complex and at Elaine's suggestion we each made a rough map as we went along. In all there were some sixteen passages, some of which had connecting tunnels. Two of the passages had clefts in them that were over fifty feet deep, and we spent an hour building up barriers of loose rock to effectively block them off. Five passages ended in chambers of various sizes. Like those in cave seven they were bone dry, but unlike seven there was a distinct chill in the air. We all agreed that eight should be used for food storage – when we had any food to store!

It was after one o'clock before we'd completed our exploration and returned to cave six. Most of the group were sitting around simply killing time but some had found work to do. Dr. Wallace informed us that the engineers had taken a small party into Elaine's ship and were busy putting together the working parts of the wind turbines. Dan Dunn was sitting in one corner of the cave studying some sheets of paper spread out in front of him. He looked up when we approached.

"I've been trying to work out the best way of providing housing," he told us cheerfully. "It'll have to be very basic, I'm afraid, but at least it will provide shelter and privacy." He showed us the sketches he'd made. "It's just a simple one-roomed cabin," he explained, "not much more than a garden hut, really. It'll be wooden, of course, including floor and roof, and about fifteen feet square. Easy to build, but there are two foreseeable problems, one short term one long term. The most urgent is windows. Even if we only provide one small window in each cabin there'll only be enough plexi-glass for about twenty-five. That's unless Trevor gives up his plan for a greenhouse."

"What's the long term problem?" asked Colin.

"Nails and screws," Dan replied. "There's a good supply in the survival rooms, so thankfully it probably won't occur in our lifetimes, but as the population increases, or we decide to make bigger and better cabins there'll come a time when there are none left. Mind you, I could put a cabin together without using screws or nails, but it would take a lot longer."

"Will the cabins be waterproof?" Elaine wanted to know.

"I can't absolutely guarantee it," said Dan, " but I noticed that there is a lot of yellowish mud on the bank of the river where the forest to the south touches it. It looks like a kind of clay and if it is it should harden once it's dry. Once this rain goes off I'm going to collect some and try a few experiments. If they work we'll be able to spread the mud over the roof and walls and if we're really lucky it will harden like plaster or cement. Incidentally, I should be ready to start on the first one in three or four days' time, so it would be a help if you can tell me where you want me to put it."

Colin asked for suggestions. "As far as I can see we've got three options," said Elaine. "There's the other side of the river, north of where we're planning the fields to farm. Or we can use this side of the river, either north or south of where the ships are sitting."

"The other side of the river is out," I pointed out. "Trevor's planning to use that area eventually for an extension to his kitchen garden, as he calls it. I would plump for this side and to the north. With the hills closing in the site would be less exposed to the wind."

"I'd go along with that providing there's enough space," Colin said. "We'll need about forty-two cabins and I'd like each one to have enough room for a fair-sized garden. Food is going to be our number one priority for many years to come and it would be helpful to supplement the main supply by having individuals growing some of their own."

Bernard Stocks

While he was talking Dan was busy making some calculations on a scrap of paper. "There should be enough space and more," he pronounced. "It's about a mile from here to the pine forest yonder. I make that about thirty five yards between each house if we build them in a line. If you want more we can build two rows. There's enough space between the river and the hillside to do that."

We eventually settled on one row, to be built about fifty yards from the riverbank. As Elaine pointed out we didn't want living quarters too close to the river. There was always the possibility of localised flooding and the danger of younger children falling in.

"What about heating?" Dave wanted to know.

"That depends upon how much power the engineers can give us and how much piping we can salvage from the ships," said Dan. "If there's plenty of power available it shouldn't be too difficult to make a boiler and pipe the heat through all the houses. I doubt if we'd be able to make any kind of radiator but you'd be surprised at how much heat a single length of pipe can generate. There'll be no difficulty in running pipes through the cabins after they're built."

CHAPTER SIX

The rain started to slacken off just after half past two and by three o'clock it had ceased and a watery sun was peeping through the clouds. The air of depression which had pervaded the day began to lift as everyone trooped outside and began work. Dave and I headed for the fields where Gavin allocated the jobs in the same way as the previous day. By the time the light began to fade we'd made a fair amount of progress, though not as much as we'd hoped. Nearly half the first field had been turned over and turf had been stripped from roughly a quarter of the second one.

Supper was a much more cheerful meal than breakfast had been, particularly when William, our tame astronomer, announced that the following day would be dry and sunny. Seemingly he considered himself an expert forecaster. I just hoped he was more accurate than the bulk of the professionals back on Earth. Our meeting after we had eaten was shorter, but despite the curtailment of activities caused by the rain there was progress to report. The engineers had put together two experimental wind turbines which they proposed to test the following day. They'd also designed a water turbine. Their idea was to dig a narrow semi-circular channel about three feet wide and five feet deep at a point in the riverbank where the current flowed the fastest. In this they would place the turbine, which would be linked up to a generator in one of the lifeships,

"I can't absolutely guarantee that it will work first time," said Walter Butter, "but even if it doesn't we can modify it and keep plugging away until it does work. The theory is sound at any rate."

Eileen had postponed her trip into the unknown until the following day and had nothing further to report. Trevor simply stated that his group had continued where they left off the previous day. Dorothy announced that the menu for the next day, Friday, would be meat, the hunters having brought in another couple of shigs. "I'm afraid it will be roast again," she apologised. "I did consider making a stew instead, but without plates and cutlery it would be too messy to eat."

Colin told the assembly of Dan's cabin design and our decision on the location of the ensuing settlement. He also had a request to make. "As you've heard Dan's discovered mud that looks as though it could be clay in the river bank where it touches the forest. If anyone has any spare time over the next day or two we'd like you to bring some back and see if it's of any use for making pottery. I can't see any way of making knives and forks at present, but if we had bowls to eat out of it would be a big step forward. For one thing we could have that stew that Dorothy promised us."

Someone asked if we couldn't use the metal from the cannibalised ships to make bowls.

"We really need all the metal that we can get for other things," was Colin's reply. "Though if all else fails that might be an option."

Having spent a large part of the day in discussion we decided not to hold a committee meeting that evening. I was quite pleased, as it gave me a chance to have a proper talk with Susan. Up to now our conversation had been confined to the present and the future: we knew nothing of each other's past life before we'd landed on the planet. I asked her how she had come to be on the *Sunrise*.

"I was going to Paladia to join my parents and older brother," she told me. "They wanted me to finish my education on Earth first." Suddenly her eyes filled with tears. "I suppose I'll never see them again," she sobbed. "And they'll think I'm dead."

I put my arms around her and held her close. There were no words I could use that would take away the pain. For one so young she'd held in her grief courageously so far and I thought it would do her good to let it all out in tears. After three or four minutes she sniffed and pulled away from me.

"I'm sorry," she apologised. "I'm being selfish. You must have family you've lost too."

"My mother, father, sister and brother back on Earth. They'll grieve, of course, but they knew the risks when I joined the Space Service. Hopefully they'll accept it eventually. At least they'll always believe that I died doing what I really wanted to do."

For a while we talked about our families, then I changed the subject and asked her about the people she was working with in the crofting section. She seemed to like them and had made one or two friends of her own age. Next I asked her what the general feeling was amongst the group on how our committee of four was organising things.

"Everyone seems happy enough with the way you've started," she said. "But there's one thing I think you should know. A lot of the chatter I've heard holds the view that it's a one-man show – that Colin's running things and the rest of you are just going along with him because of his rank."

"To an extent that's true," I admitted. "But we're going along with him not because of his rank but because he's making the right decisions. They're exactly the same decisions I would have made if we'd be the only ship to survive and I'd been put in charge. You can tell people not to worry and that there's no chance of him becoming a dictator. If we disagree with him over anything we'll make our voices heard."

Thankfully our would-be weather forecaster was spot on and the following day, Friday, dawned dry and warm. I had a quick word with Colin over breakfast and reported what Susan had told me. He looked thoughtful.

"I suppose it must look that way," he said eventually. "Somehow we'll have to change that impression."

"How about rotating the four of us in addressing the evening get-togethers," I suggested. "That might just do the trick."

"Good idea," Colin replied. "I'll have a word with Elaine and Dave."

The good weather remained through Friday and the following day and every section made good progress. By Saturday night the first field had been fully planted with potatoes, the second stripped and turned over and about half the third stripped. The wind turbines were working without a hitch and the water turbine was almost finished. One of the spades had been diverted from the fields to dig the channel in which it would be placed. That would be done on the following Monday. Trevor reported that most of the fruit stones and seeds had been planted to a total of one hundred and sixty trees and around the same number of bushes. His group's next task would be to plant more salad items. Dan Dunn's group had been cutting timber prior to making a start on the first of the cabins; that too was planned for Monday.

It was a cheerful throng that gathered for the Saturday night meeting. The others had accepted my suggestion to rotate the chairman. Elaine had taken Friday's meeting and Dave was leading on Saturday. After taking all the usual progress reports and answering the inevitable questions that followed he called on Eileen to tell us about her explorations. She'd had to postpone her tour of exploration on Friday when we discovered that the altabs were not fully charged. Accompanied by June and Harry she'd set off immediately after breakfast that day and had only returned a few minutes before the evening meal.

"We've covered a fair amount of ground today," she reported. "First we crossed the river and headed due south. About twelve miles from here we came to a broad river, at least four times as wide as this one, flowing westwards. By climbing a nearby hill and using our binoculars we were able to see that it flows into the sea in the far distance. The best estimate we can give is that the sea is around thirty miles from here, give or take a few miles. Sticking to the riverbank we travelled some twenty-five miles east until we came to a range of hills about five or six hundred feet high."

"The slope was quite gentle and we had no difficulty in riding the altabs up to the top. On the other side there was a vast plain stretching as far as the eye can see. We picked out several forests, all of them much larger that the ones nearby, so there's no shortage of available timber or of agricultural land. Neither is there any shortage of meat. We saw literally thousands of shigs wherever we went. And we did make one really interesting discovery. In the far distance from the top of those hills we saw a herd of much larger animals. They were about the size of elephants, a lightish brown in colour, with small triangular heads and rather fearsome looking horns. As far as we could see they had no tails. Had they been nearer we'd have tried to capture or stun one for a closer look, but we were concerned that we might not have enough power in the batteries to get us back here. One thing I should mention, though. They were moving in this direction, albeit very very slowly. We should keep an eye open in case they come close. At that size they could do an awful lot of damage just by walking through the camp."

"Other than that I found no new species of either plants, insects, animals or fish. Of the half dozen clusters of trees we passed four were deciduous and two coniferous. Each wood was about half as big again as the two we can see from here."

Colin had a question to ask. "One of the things we lack is salt. Is there any possibility of making it in the laboratory?"

"If you can give me unlimited quantities of metallic sodium and hydrochloric acid I'll make you as much salt as you want," replied Eileen with a laugh. "Otherwise no."

"In that case the distance from the sea could be important," was Colin's comment. "One more item on the list of things to do. When we get time we'll have to explore the possibility of evaporating seawater to get a supply of salt."

Once Eileen had finished Dave had a couple more points to make, ones we'd already discussed in committee.

"Firstly the four of us think that unless there's any emergencies Sunday should be treated as a day of rest. Does anybody disagree?"

There was a murmur from the audience, then one youngish man stood up. "I don't much fancy sitting around all day getting bored, nor do I fancy going for a walk in the countryside. If it's dry I'd rather carry on working." A number of people were nodding and a few were heard to say "Me too." Dave asked for a show of hands from which we gathered that just over half of those present agreed with the protestor.

"Let's put it this way, then," said Dave decisively. "All those who want to do some work can do as much or as little as they please. But there should be no stigma attached to anyone who chooses to be idle. Is that acceptable to everybody?" Nods all round proved that it was.

"The second point I wanted to make about tomorrow is this. Until we decide our attitude to religion we think there should be a short service every Sunday morning for those who wish it. Unfortunately none of the four of us have any church connections, so I'm asking now if anyone feels able to conduct a makeshift service, even if it's only a short prayer or two and a reading from the bible. Does anyone have a bible with them?"

The Far Side of Nowhere

It appeared that one middle-aged lady, Joyce Haggart by name, had a pocket bible. It took a little persuasion, but eventually she agreed to provide a service on the morrow. No sooner had that been settled than a somewhat younger lady rose to her feet.

"Bridget Lamont from County Derry," she announced in a broad Irish brogue. "Can I ask how many present are Catholics?" About twenty hands went up. "Right. I have a Missal with me and I'd be happy to conduct Mass every Sunday for those who wish it."

Susan and I, along with Colin and Dave, attended Joyce Haggart's service at nine o'clock the following morning. It was very simple, opening and closing with a prayer and with two shortish readings from the bible in between. Elaine, who was a Catholic, went to Mass, which was held some distance away. It was a dull, grey morning with heavy cloud overhead. There was no rain, but a strong hint that some was on the way. About forty people had elected to work and I decided to join them. Dave came along with me and Susan went off to her group. Those who weren't working mostly went off to explore the surrounding areas, both north and south. I noticed that Dan and all his crew were among those working. Their self-allotted task was to bring all the timber down from the northern wood to the site where the first cabin would be built.

During the midday break I went to look for Colin. Unable to find him, I tracked down Elaine and asked her if she knew where he was.

"Haven't a clue," she said. "After the service he and the two engineers broke out three of the altabs, crossed the river and headed south. He didn't bother to tell me where they were going, so your guess is as good as mine."

Those of us who were working carried on until just before three. After half an hour of light drizzle the rain began in earnest and we reluctantly abandoned the fields for the day. Colin and the engineers returned shortly after five soaked to the skin. When I asked him where they'd been he said abruptly that he'd tell us later. Once again the sight of rain had dampened everyone's spirits and the evening meal was a sombre affair.

We held our committee meetings in Colin's ship. Dave's and Elaine's were gradually being torn apart and usually had one or both of the engineers working in them and Susan was living in mine. When we foregathered that Sunday evening we finally learned what Colin had been up to that day.

"Sorry if I've caused some sort of a mystery," he started by apologising. "I've been following up a thought I've had, one that I want us to discuss tonight. It's something that's been on my mind since the first day and I'd like to hear your views on the matter. To put it briefly I'm worried about the fact that we're all together in one place. If there's any sort of disaster, like a flash flood, an earthquake or something similar it's on the cards that the whole colony could be wiped out at one go. I'm wondering if it might be a good idea to split up into two or three groups a few miles apart. For that reason we've been surveying the surrounding countryside today."

"We started by going due south to the bank of the broad river that Eileen told us about last night. From there we went twenty-five miles east and fifteen miles west. I'd like to have gone a bit further west to try and gauge the distance to the sea, but there's no way of crossing our river where it meets the larger one. In passing I'd say Eileen wasn't far out and that we're about thirty miles to the sea from here. Anyway, the upshot of our travels is that there are five or six suitable sites along the riverbank where colonies could be set up and thrive. Each site has ample timber supplies near at hand, plenty of land for cultivating and herds of the inevitable shigs for food. Like our river that one is teeming with fish, too. There are only two drawbacks that I can see. There aren't any caves for shelter, which means that we'd have to build cabins before anyone could move there. And the river is too wide to put a bridge across, not that that's of vital importance in the near future. The only way we're ever likely to cross is by lifeship or by making a causeway and to do the latter we'd need to ferry rock down from here. There's very little close to the river."

"What sort of time scale are you thinking of?" I queried. "I don't disagree with your reasoning, but surely our first priority is to get the food supply guaranteed here?"

"Agreed," replied Colin. "I haven't had time to think it through properly, but off the top of my head I'd suggest that, if we do go down this road, once Dan's built the first fifteen cabins here he should start on the chosen site or sites. Similarly, once the first twelve or fifteen fields here are dug we should start preparing the additional settlements. I don't envisage anyone moving away permanently until next spring at the earliest."

Dave didn't seem too convinced. "Isn't there a danger of the communities growing apart?" he wanted to know. "With only four altabs and twelve miles between each township there's not going to be much commuting back and forth. The last thing we want is individual groups bringing in their own laws and policies."

"A lot depends on whether we get re-elected when we hold the vote in three months' time," Colin replied. "If we do then my idea is that at least one of us will be with each group to ensure continuity of policy. We can use the altabs to meet somewhere equidistant from each. It would mean, too, that each area would have its representative on the committee and would only vote on its own member and not for all of the committee."

"What about the generators?" asked Elaine.

"No problem," said Colin. "We'll move one of the two remaining ships to a point halfway between the two new sites. There's enough in the way of cables to supply up to a distance of six or seven miles."

We talked around the matter for nearly an hour. Elaine and I were broadly in agreement with the general principle but Dave could not be talked round. In the end we decided to sound out the views of the whole group.

"You're taking tomorrow night's session, Matt," Colin said to me. "Tell everyone what we're suggesting, ask them to think it over during the week and we'll discuss it in detail next Sunday."

And that's how we left it. On my own initiative I added a rider to my closing remarks on the Monday night. "We'll have a general meeting next Sunday afternoon at, say, two o'clock and hear your views then," I told the meeting. "At the same time we'd like to make a start on discussing the other major issues to be resolved. We'll talk about religion, though I get the feeling that most of you are satisfied with the provisions we made yesterday. We'd like to get your views on marriage and also on what laws we should bring into operation. Things to consider are how we deal with such things as theft, violence and deliberate malingering. Hopefully none of these will become a problem, but we need to have measures in place just in case. Once we know what you all think we'll draft a constitution for approval."

Doctor Wallace was working in the laboratory of Colin's ship, and before we separated for the night we went to have a word with him. We were all concerned with the lack of variety in the diet and wanted his professional opinion.

"You don't need me to tell you that it's not very satisfactory," he commented. "We're getting plenty of protein and ample fat, but there's a deficiency of carbohydrate and essential vitamins. Without milk and eggs there's a shortage of calcium, too, which could have a harmful effect on our teeth in the years to come. I'm particularly concerned about the children. They desperately need fresh fruit and vegetables if they're to remain healthy."

"We should have a supply of vegetables in about three months," remarked Colin. "But unless any of the indigenous trees and bushes produce edible fruit it's going to be a good five years or more before we're growing any appreciable quantity of our own apart from tomatoes and possibly rhubarb."

"Have we got rhubarb?" asked the doctor.

"I checked with Trevor a couple of days ago," Elaine broke in. "There was a packet of rhubarb seed in each survival room apparently. He's planted all of it, but unfortunately he can't tell us how long it will take to mature. His most optimistic estimate was that we would have some by this time next year."

"Let's hope he's right," commented Doctor Wallace. "Plenty of rhubarb in the diet would go a long way towards making up the general deficiency of fruit. Though it probably won't be popular with either the children or the adults," he added with a wan smile.

CHAPTER SEVEN

During that second week we only lost one full day and a quarter of another to bad weather. By Saturday night four fields had been prepared and a start made on stripping a fifth. Two fields had been sown with cereal crops to add to the one devoted to potatoes. A small part of number four had been used for the initial planting of brassicas and root crops. These would be thinned out and transplanted at the appropriate time. The water turbine was finally working after having been adjusted and refined four or five times and between that and the wind turbines we now had ample power. The engineers had run cable from the generator in my ship to all the caves in use and plundered every available light fitting from the two ships being dismantled. Each cave now had three sources of light. Though they were quite dim they represented a significant advance and gave everyone's morale a boost.

Perhaps our biggest step forward that week came with the discovery that the mud on the riverbank could be moulded and dried to form bowls suitable for eating. We had no way of glazing them, of course, and they were on the fragile side, but at least they were usable. Another benefit was that it gave the six children something to do. Though they had willingly worked alongside their parents most of the jobs were too heavy for them and they tended to get in the way. By Friday evening everyone had two bowls and Dorothy was able to vary the menu slightly with meat and fish stews. It was quite a sight to see the stews being made. The engineers had removed the fuel tank from Dave's ship and modified it to make a large metal cooking pot.

Trevor's group were also using the mud to make flower pots. By the middle of the week his crofting group had used up all the land allotted to them and were taking over the largest of the caves. We had reserved that for eventual food storage but there was ample room for both uses. I wasn't sure how well things would grow in the cave with little or no sunlight, but Trevor's idea was to start off from seed inside and then transplant outdoors

The Far Side of Nowhere

once the plants were big enough. For this he planned to use the gardens of the cabins once they were built as well as any extra space he could find across the river.

Dan and his team had nearly finished the first cabin by Saturday night. The design was simple: four square posts driven into the ground to form the corners, then planks nailed across for the walls and the roof. The planks themselves were rough to the touch as unfortunately the tools in the survival rooms did not include planes or chisels. Because of the shortage of plexi-glass each cabin would have only one small window about two feet square. Thankfully hinges had been supplied in the survival rooms, so there was no problem in fitting a door. All Dan had left to do was to complete the wooden floor and cover roof and walls with mud. The latter he intended to delegate to one of his team and he himself would start on the second cabin over the weekend.

At our Wednesday night committee meeting Paul and Walter, the two engineers, asked to speak to us.

"We've gone about as far as we can with the power supply, and Dan doesn't need any help from us with his building programme," opened Paul. "The troops are making two or three more wind turbines as a standby and Walter's working on a design for an electric oven. Other than that we've nothing in hand. What would you like us to look at next?"

As it happened we had talked briefly on the subject the previous evening. "There are a few things that we should start thinking about," said Colin. "In about four months or so we're going to need some method of milling corn to make flour. That's probably the number one priority. Secondly, if it's at all possible, some improvement in toilet facilities would be a big step forward. Thirdly I'm hoping to take a trip down to the sea in the next day or two. If as I suspect it's salt water we'll need some method of evaporating it to give us a supply of salt. I'm thinking in terms of a kind of large shallow heated tray or trays that we can fill and leave to evaporate. Obviously we can't transport water here in sufficient quantities and we have no power to use for boilers nearer the sea. However, if you can come up with anything more efficient that would be a bonus. And finally for the present we'll need a way of extracting sugar from the sugar beet that the farmers are planting. Again my own thoughts are some kind of large vat which can be heated. There should be more than enough metal to make one." He paused for a moment or two and then added with a grin: "That should keep you busy for a while. If we get any other ideas we'll let you know."

"The oven will certainly be of benefit," chipped in Elaine. "At the moment we're wasting a lot of time and effort gathering wood for the fires. It should make a midday meal possible as well. I've heard several complaints about there only being two meals a day."

I got a surprise the following morning. Colin came to see me before breakfast with a suggestion. "You've been working without a break since you landed. I think you should take the day off and make the trip down to the sea instead of me. Take Eileen with you and take Harry and his stun gun as well in case of emergencies."

Thus it was that just before nine o'clock the three of us set off. This was my first time on a altab. I found it easy to steer and manoeuvre, but the saddle wasn't too comfortable after the first twenty minutes or so. We headed in a south-westerly direction, skirting the range of hills in which the caves were situated. After about seven miles the hills petered out into a gently undulating plain. Small copses of trees were dotted here and there and we passed one fair-sized forest some fifteen miles from base. Herds of shigs were everywhere. There was certainly not going to be a shortage of meat for years to come.

After travelling for an hour and a quarter we came to another low range of hills which I estimated to be about three hundred feet in height. The slopes were gentle and the altabs took them easily. When we reached the summit we could see the ocean in front of us, some three miles away. By the time we reached the shore the trip meter was registering thirty-eight miles. As we'd come by a slightly roundabout route I estimated that the direct distance from the camp would be about thirty-five miles.

We'd arrived at a wide bay, with a foreshore mainly of pebbles and small rocks. The beach, if one could call it that, was about twenty metres wide and the tide looked to be coming in. The waves broke gently in the slight breeze. In the distance the water was a greyish shade of blue, not unlike the Atlantic Ocean as seen from the west coast of Ireland. Small pools dotted the area of beach that we could see and almost as one we each selected a pool, dipped a finger into the water therein and touched it to our tongues.

"No doubt about it being salty," commented Harry. "In fact I'd say the salt content was pretty high."

Elaine unfastened her anorak and from somewhere within pulled out a number of plastic bags and bottles. Taking one of the latter she went carefully down to the water's edge and scooped up a sample. Then she turned back to us. "While we're moving around the beach, keep your eyes open for any kind of life. I'm thinking particularly of things like jellyfish, shellfish, small marine insects and the like. If you find anything give me a shout and I'll try and capture it for dissection and study."

For the next twenty minutes or so we each prowled around on our own, but I certainly didn't see anything that remotely resembled a living creature. One or two of the larger pools had strands of a kind of seaweed; not the common fronded type, but of long silky strands like a tassel. When we came together again I confirmed that Eileen had taken a sample, also that there did not appear to be any other variety of the weed around. Harry had made an interesting discovery. In a shallow declivity some distance from the incoming tide he'd come across a white deposit on the landward slope. He'd tasted it carefully and guessed that it was salt. Eileen gave him a plastic bag and asked him to collect as much as he could.

"I'll test this when we get back. If it is salt I can purify it and we'll have a little for cooking purposes. It will also confirm that we have a supply if and when we find ways of processing the seawater. Meantime, Matt, would you come with me. I want to go out on to that headland over there and get a look at some deeper water."

The headland she was referring to was about a third of a mile from where we were standing. It consisted of a spur of rock jutting almost a hundred metres into the sea. Thankfully when we reached it we found it was several metres wide and fairly level on the top. Scrambling over jagged rocks has ever been a chancy business and I was reluctant to risk an accident so far from base. We had walked along some two thirds of the length, one on each side with eyes scanning the water; then Eileen gave a whistle.

"Come and look at this, Matt," she said quietly. I moved to her side, looked down and nearly overbalanced in my amazement. Floating peacefully about three feet below the surface was the largest flat fish I had ever seen. At it's widest point it must have been at least a metre and a quarter across and about the same from top to tail. Head and tail were grey, the rest of the body was a dazzling white. It was lying at a slight angle and as far as I could judge it was about twelve to fifteen centimetres thick.

"That would make a meal for a few people on it's own," Eileen remarked with a light laugh. "Pity we've no way of catching it."

We carried on to the extreme end of the headland and then came back down the opposite side. It was there that we saw our second species of fish, a kind of giant cod that must have weighed all of ten kilos. But there were still no signs of shellfish or jellyfish, nor of insects of any kind. At a number of points seaweed, the same variety as in the beach pools, was evident below the surface. Just before we reached the start of the headland we spotted a school of smaller fish similar to sardines, but bright blue in colour. Like the giant cod they were feeding off the seaweed. Eileen commented that, like all the other living creatures on this world, the fish appeared to have a purely vegetarian diet.

Before we left the headland we walked back to the seaward end and I studied the surrounding area through binoculars. Another large headland half a mile to the north restricted my view in that direction, but I could see several miles down the coast to the south. There seemed to be little variation in the seashore all the way down. Finally I pointed the glasses out to sea and scanned the horizon through one hundred and eighty degrees.

"Looking for ships?" asked Eileen sarcastically.

"Hardly," I replied. "I wanted to see if there were any islands in view. If we should ever get attacked by large and unspecified animals it might be as well to have an island refuge picked out. However, there are none, so that kills that idea." I was only half joking. So far we'd seen only a fraction of the planet's surface: there could be any number of as yet unseen dangers lurking.

We'd brought some cold meat and water with us, so we decided to break for half an hour for a meal and a rest. While we were eating Eileen had a confession to make. "The ecology of this world has me totally confused. In normal circumstances the various life forms prey on each other, thus maintaining a natural balance. But here that doesn't happen, yet although there are plenty of each species none seems to have overrun the planet. I would have expected more variation in the life forms, too. It's usual for new or changed types to appear every so often due to corruption of the genes. There must be a complete absence of any kind of radiation here, but even without that there should have been some changes."

When we resumed our journey we headed south along the coastline for about ten miles until we came to the junction of the broad river with the sea. Then we turned eastwards and followed the river for some twenty miles or more until we came to its junction with the river that flowed through our camp. We had no way of crossing this, of course, so we prepared to head northwards.

I looked across our river and turned to the others. "I would guess that the other side is one of the places Colin has earmarked for future settlement." In truth it looked the ideal spot. From the junction of the rivers the ground was level for about a hundred metres, then sloped gently upwards to form a plateau about a mile and a half square. About half a mile along our river was a fair-sized deciduous forest, while a similar distance along the broad river stood another large forest of the straight-branched conifers. Heading diagonally inland the ground was flat with only the occasional tree; space and to spare for extensive cultivation. As with everywhere we'd journeyed so far herds of shigs decorated the landscape in all directions.

We spent some twenty minutes at the site before turning our altabs northwards and homewards. Apart from one or two undulating slopes the countryside was unchanged, with deciduous forests here and there, mostly about the same size as the one nearest to our camp. As far as possible we rode along the riverbank, though several times we had to detour to avoid woodland that grew down to the water's edge. At a point where we estimated we were some four miles from camp we were just about to veer round a smallish copse when Harry, who was in the lead by some fifty metres, gave a shout, leapt off his machine and raced to the water's edge. He quickly turned and shouted to us to come to him. We did so and saw to our horror a small form clinging to a bush growing over the bank.

"It's young Wayne Beaton," exclaimed Eileen. "Is he still alive?"

"I'm not sure," replied Harry. "I can't quite reach him. His eyes are closed and I can't tell from this angle if he's breathing or not."

I pulled Harry back from the bank. "I'm lighter than you," I told him. "You hang on to my legs and I'll go over the side and try and get to him."

It wasn't an inviting prospect. The lip of the bank was made of wet, crumbling mud, with the surface of the water about a metre and a half below ground level. The current was racing and even a strong swimmer, which I am not, would have struggled to keep pace swimming against it. Because of the bush it wasn't possible to get to the youngster from directly above. Waiting until Harry had a firm grip on my ankles I slithered over the edge and tried to twist my body round through an angle of ninety degrees, all the time scrabbling to get some sort of handhold on the mud at the side. At my furthest round I was still almost an arms' length away from Wayne.

"Get Eileen to hold one leg and lower me right over the side," I shouted back to Harry. The noise of the rushing water drowned out his reply but he must have heard me because within seconds two hands were gripping each leg and I felt a gentle push forward. This gave me the space I needed and I was able to get my left hand under Wayne's arm and drag him far enough towards me to get both hands firmly locked around his chest. It wasn't a moment too soon. Despite the warmth of the day the water was ice cold and already my fingers were numb. I shouted to be hauled back up, but before the words were out of my mouth I felt myself being dragged to safety.

As soon as I was back on terra firma Eileen took Wayne from me and immediately started pumping his chest and giving him the kiss of life. He looked in a bad way. His eyes were closed and his face and hands were tinged with blue. My hands were still frozen so I told Harry to try for a pulse.

"There's a very faint one, but it's very erratic," he reported after a few seconds.

I thought quickly. "You two stay here with him and carry on with the artificial respiration. Keep him as warm as possible." I ordered. "I'll get back to camp as quickly as I can and get Doc Wallace. It's too much of a risk to try and take Wayne back to camp immediately."

They both nodded and I wasted no more time. Keeping the altab at its highest possible speed I raced back to base. Thankfully the doctor was in his small surgery on Dave's old ship. I acquainted him with the situation as quickly as I could. While I was still speaking he crammed some instruments into his bag and literally within seconds he was on my altab and speeding away southwards.

CHAPTER EIGHT

I'd expected to see some signs of panic in the camp, so I was surprised to find that everything was normal. From this I deduced that Wayne, who was the youngest of the three Beaton children, had not yet been missed. Only Elaine of the committee was in view, watering plants outside one of the caves, so I went over and told her what had happened. Her first thought was for the parents. Mrs. Beaton was one of the catering group; her husband was in the fields. I volunteered to fetch the latter and to try and track down the two older Beaton offspring. By the time I returned with Joe Beaton the children were already with Elaine and their mother. We questioned the two of them closely, but neither could shed any light on the mystery.

"Wayne went off by himself after breakfast," was all Gary, his older brother, could tell us. "We haven't seen him since."

"You two should have kept him with you," his mother scolded. "Damn it, he's only eight years old. He needs someone to keep an eye on him.

Gary was inclined to argue the point. "We can't watch him every second of the day," he protested. "You know very well he doesn't take a blind bit of notice of me or Emma."

I slipped away back to my ship to shed my wet and muddy clothes. Making sure that no one was watching I went naked down to the river and had a quick dip to shed the surplus mud attached to most of my body. Back in the ship I dried off. None of us had much in the way of spare clothing, but I managed to find a pair of dungarees and put those on. Word must have got round the camp quickly because by the time I got back to Elaine and the Beatons most of the group were assembled.

It was almost an hour before the three altabs came into view. We all moved forward as Dr. Wallace carried the still unconscious boy into his surgery. Eileen held up her hand for silence. "Thankfully Wayne's still alive and breathing," she announced. "But he hasn't yet come round and his condition is still serious though not critical. The doctor wants time to do a full examination, so would Mr. and Mrs. Beaton please wait for twenty minutes before going in to see Wayne."

I could see that the Beatons were none too pleased with the delay, so I took them aside. "It could mean the difference between life and death," I told them. "The doctor needs to give all his attention to Wayne and with the best will in the world he can't do that if the two of you are fussing around and getting in his way." They saw my point, though they didn't look any happier about the delay.

Colin and Dave were on hand by this time and demanded a full report of the day's events, including our findings on the seashore. I called Harry and Eileen over, and between us we covered all that we had done. Then Eileen excused herself, saying that she wanted to start analysing the samples that she'd taken while there was still some daylight left. Though it was only five o'clock nobody seemed disposed to return to work and most stood around outside the surgery waiting for news.

It was just after six, as we were all lining up for our evening meal, when Dr. Wallace emerged. "Wayne has recovered consciousness, I'm pleased to say," he told us. "He's still very weak and will need round the clock nursing for a couple of days, but there doesn't seem to be any serious damage and he should be right as rain and back to making mischief within the week. For the moment he should have no visitors apart from his parents until after lunch tomorrow."

A cheer greeted the doctor's announcement and we ate our meal with lightened hearts. Colin was scheduled to take the evening meeting and in his opening remarks emphasised once more the need to be careful in everything we did. "That applies particularly to you young ones," he said sternly, turning towards the small group. "Please do not ever go off anywhere on your own. Stick together at all times and watch out for each other. And stay away from the river. I'm sorry to sound brutal, but if it hadn't been for Matt, Harry and Eileen we'd either be burying Wayne right now or left forever mystified by his disappearance. It must not happen again." He gave heavy emphasis to his last sentence.

Dan completed the first cabin the following day and at six o'clock we had an opening ceremony. Elaine unearthed some ribbon from somewhere and tied it across the front door. Our committee had decided even before Wayne's mishap that the Beaton family should be given the accommodation and this proved a popular choice. To his embarrassment Dan was chosen to perform the ribbon cutting and to usher in the new occupants. The interior was, of course, just as bare as the caves, but at least it gave the family some privacy. Hardly had they crossed the threshold when their day was completed by the appearance of Wayne, looking pale but otherwise unhurt.

"Once we've got all the cabins up we'll get around to making some furniture," Dan promised. "In the meantime, if you want to brighten things up, I suggest you make some flower pots and get Trevor to give you some seed to grow indoors. That will give you a splash of colour and an extra ration of lettuce and other things."

"Once the pressure of other work wears off we can get around to shearing the wool off some of the shigs," was Colin's contribution. "I don't see any way of dyeing it for the moment, but the engineers may be able to make some kind of spinning wheel so that we can make curtains and drapes. But that's some way into the future, I'm afraid."

It was Sunday afternoon before we got the full story of Wayne's mishap. Earlier in the week he'd watched as one of the men caught a fish with his bare hands. Desirous of emulating the feat, but not wishing to risk the laughter of the other children, he picked a spot on the farthest outskirts of the wood from the camp. The inevitable happened. He managed to get his hands close to a fish but needed a few more inches. In gaining these he fell in and was swept away on the current. Luckily he was able to swim, but the water was flowing too strongly for him to turn around. It was all he could do to keep himself afloat until he grabbed hold of the providential bush under which we'd found him.

At least some good came of the episode. Wayne himself had had such a shock that he stayed well clear of the river from that moment on. The other children became ultra careful anywhere near the banks and stopped playing there altogether. Even the two older boys abandoned their own rod and line fishing. But it could all have ended so easily in tragedy.

Our Sunday night meeting was the least harmonious to date. Elaine was in the chair, and once the reports had been taken opened up the discussion on the long-term issues. There was no hassle regarding religion. Everyone seemed happy with the provisions laid on, and as one man succinctly put it: "We can start thinking about building churches once everyone has a home with furniture and fittings."

It was when the subjects of marriage and the suggestion of splitting up into two or more communities came up that there was a sharp difference of opinion. On both issues it seemed that our group was split right down the middle and the exchanges became heated and at times acrimonious. Half wanted to have formal marriages. I noticed that the existing married couples among us were with that faction. Half wanted merely a verbal agreement. There still seemed to be some belief among the latter that sooner or later we would be rescued, much as all four of us on the committee insisted this was next to impossible. Many expressed the opinion that being tied down to marriage would lead to problems if indeed we were to return to the normal world. In vain did Elaine point out the ease of divorce in the modern society.

It was the same story when we finally abandoned that subject and considered Colin's suggestion of splitting the group into two or three. Once more the exchanges became heated and once more there were roughly equal numbers for and against. Eventually I lost patience with the whole thing. At the end of a particularly heated argument between four or five of those present I took advantage of a sudden lull in the volume and made my little speech.

"It's obvious from what's been said that we're never going to agree on either of these two issues. Before we come to blows may I suggest that we leave the both matters open until the election of a new committee in three months' time. That will give us more time to think things over. If we're still divided then it will be up to the new committee to make the decisions one way or the other. Those in favour please signify."

Thankfully the majority raised their hands. Elaine flung me a grateful look and jumped in hurriedly. "I was hoping to discuss possible laws tonight as well, but in view of the time I think we'll leave that open for another day. Thank you and goodnight." At that she turned and walked out of the cave, quickly followed by Colin, Dave and myself. We retired immediately to Colin's ship to hold a post mortem on the night's events.

"Unfortunate," was Colin's summing up of the whole matter. "Everyone's been united and totally behind us up to now. I expected there'd be dissension somewhere along the line, but I hoped it wouldn't come this soon." He turned to me. "That was a good idea of yours to bring things to a close, Matt. At least it postpones a final decision on both matters. Only problem is that we're likely to be re-elected once the vote is taken, so we'll be landed with making rules that will only get the support of half the colony."

"You seem confident that we will be re-elected," Dave commented.

"It looks probable," replied Colin. "With all due modesty I think we've done a pretty good job so far and the comments I've heard have all been complimentary. I've been keeping my eyes open, too, and I don't see anyone coming forward as a potential leader, with the possible exception of Doc Wallace. But he wouldn't be willing to take command. I spoke to him a couple of days ago to see if he wanted to join us on the committee, but he turned the offer down very firmly. His view is that people coming to consult him expect full confidentiality and he couldn't promise them that if he was also involved in decision making." And that's where we left things.

We were blessed with fine weather over the next seven days, losing only one hour to a short sharp rainstorm. Our progress was there for all to see. Our first six fields were now planted, except for the transplanting that would need to be done later. Work was now proceeding to clear at least another six in readiness for the following year. The first of the crofting section's plants were showing through the soil and Dan's second cabin was finished and ready for occupancy. By now he had trained three of his assistants to the point where they could work unsupervised, and he expected to complete at least one cabin a week. With progress in the farming section exceeding expectations we deployed extra hands to the cutting and shaping of timber to cope with the increased demand. Dorothy was now the proud possessor of a large electrically powered oven and had been promised by the engineers that within days she would have an electrically heated boiler. The engineers were planning a similar boiler, but much larger, for the processing of sugar beet later in the year. To cope with the extra power needed they had installed another four wind turbines, though at present the existing two plus the water turbine were providing us with electricity and to spare.

William Haddow, our amateur astronomer and weather expert, had some interesting facts for us at our Sunday night meeting. "I still can't give you an accurate forecast of the length of the year," he commenced. "I can, however, state with some certainty that it is between three hundred and forty-five and three hundred and sixty days. I've also made a detailed study of the weather conditions since we arrived here. Again there is margin for error but I'm fairly certain that the climate of this region of the planet is close to that of southern Spain. That means temperatures in the eighties and nineties during the summer, plus little or no frost, snow and ice in the winter."

"Though it may take us two or three years to get used to the heat it gives us a definite advantage when it comes to agriculture. Not only will things grow more quickly than they did back in Britain, but we'll be able to grow a much wider range of fruit. Oranges, lemons, grapes and grapefruit should all thrive here. I checked with Trevor, and he's confirmed that we have seed for all these. In fact he has already planted most of it. Oh, and one other thing. The lack of frost will give us a much longer growing season. We'll need to experiment, but there may even be the possibility of growing two crops of certain items in one year."

I was chairing the meeting and deliberately kept away from the divisive subjects of the previous Sunday. The mood in the camp had been good all week and I didn't want to upset the harmony. Early on in the week we'd suggested that as our main objectives had been attained more quickly than we'd expected everyone could ease off, but it was noticeable that no one took advantage and continued to work hard. There were one or two, of course, who tried to 'swing the lead' by pleading illness or fatigue. We had instituted a rule right from the start that absence from work could only be approved by the doctor, and once he identified the persistent offenders in this respect he became ruthless in separating the genuine from the spurious.

Our next potential crisis arose the following Tuesday. It was the warmest day of the year so far and Dave and I were sweating in the fields, spades in hand and some twenty metres apart, when he called out to me.

"Look over there," he yelled, pointing vaguely in a north-easterly direction. I did so, and saw immediately what had attracted his attention. About a mile from us a herd of the large wild animals that Eileen had spotted distantly on her first southern trip were moving slowly towards us.

Even at that distance they looked huge. Handing my spade to a woman who had been resting nearby I went across to join Dave.

"I'm going back to camp for binoculars and a stun gun," I told him. "I'll also bring Eileen back with me if she's around. In the meantime keep an eye on them. If they speed up and come too close get everybody back to the camp."

It took just a couple of minutes to get back to my ship, collect my binoculars and to alert Elaine. Colin was away with the two engineers to explore the junction of the two ranges of hills to the north. There had been some discussion as to the possibility of using one of the waterfalls as a power supply and they wanted to survey the terrain. Eileen was in her makeshift laboratory. June Mathieson was with the crofting section nearby and I told her to grab her stun gun and come with us.

The three girls and I went quickly back to the fields. Dave reported that the herd had only moved about twenty yards during the time I'd been away but was definitely heading in our direction. "We'll need to divert them," he said. "If they continue on their present course they'll cause all sorts of damage to the fields and flatten the whole camp."

I thought rapidly and made a speedy decision. "Right. Dave, Eileen and June, come with me. Elaine, keep watching and if necessary give the word to evacuate the fields. Get back to camp and get everybody into the caves. We'll try and turn them."

"Will do," replied Elaine crisply. "And for God's sake be careful."

"We will," I promised.

Before setting off I took a couple of minutes studying the beasts through my glasses. Having had a good look myself I handed the binoculars to Eileen. "I can't see any indication of communication between them, so I assume they can't be classed as an intelligent species under the Space College rules. Would you agree?"

She took her time, but after at least four minutes she simply said: "Agreed."

As we walked towards the herd I gave my instructions. "As soon we're close enough for you to get a clear shot, June, we want one killed. Eileen will want to dissect and study it and we can test it for its potential as a source of food. Once you've made your kill set the gun back to stun, about quarter strength at first and see if you can turn them. If that doesn't work increase the strength gradually. If they look like charging us, scatter and get the hell out of here as quickly as possible."

At about a hundred metres June called to us to halt. By this time we'd had ample opportunity to study the beasts, of which there were over a hundred. They were just as Eileen had described them to us, though possibly they were even bigger than elephants. They had a somewhat incongruous look about them, their heads seeming far too small not only for their bodies, but also for the horns surmounting them. Despite their size they didn't seem to hold any terrors for the shigs, who continued to graze peacefully among their giant brethren. The latter were also cropping grass in absurdly small mouthfuls.

A line of five animals led the pack. Taking careful aim at the one in the middle June fired, aiming between the close-set eyes. At first it seemed as if the shot had had no effect. Then slowly the animal sank to its knees, making no sound. June let loose a second shot and the massive body quivered slightly and then was still.

"Good shooting, June, " I said quietly. "Now for phase two."

She adjusted the controls on the stock of the gun and gave each of the four remaining a short burst. They gave what I can only describe as a wail and turned sideways but made no attempt to retreat. Increasing the power June gave them a second shot on the rump. This time they did move away a couple of yards, bumping into the next line of some ten animals. Again increasing the power June systematically fired bursts at random at every beast within range. Panic ensued and the whole herd started milling around. June continued to fire. After what seemed to me to be an eternity but was probably only a few seconds the herd started moving back whence they had come at a smart pace, almost a trot. Further treatment from the stun gun didn't generate any greater speed, but made sure that the retreat continued.

We waited until they were at least half a mile away before we moved forward to examine our specimen. Even lying down it was taller by half than myself and I estimated the length at a good eight metres. To ease the tension that was still apparent I turned to the girls and joked: "Right. Which of you is going to carry our prize back to base?" That drew a laugh, but transporting the carcass anywhere was going to be a problem. I could only guess at the creature's weight but it was pretty obvious that even ten strong men would struggle to carry it. Then I remembered the wheeled pallets that Dan Dunn had made to transport timber from the forest to his building site. That solved the problem of movement: all we had to do was find a way of lifting the body on to a pallet.

I passed on my thoughts to the other two and after some reflection Eileen came up with the answer. "Send out a couple of people with one of the power saws. They can cut up the body under my direction and we can take it back to base in pieces. Meantime I'll stay here and make a preliminary examination."

"That's a good idea," I said with some relief. "June will stay here with you, just in case the herd returns to do battle. And I repeat. Don't take the remotest chance. The least sign of danger and you get yourselves away out of it as fast as you can."

They both nodded and Dave and I headed back to bring Elaine up to date and to make the necessary arrangements. Warning the workers in the fields to keep a close watch on the horizon and be ready to evacuate at a moment's notice I set off for the northern forest to collect a pallet and two experts with the power saws. On the way back I brought Dan up to date and apologised for taking two of his staff. He was philosophical about their loss. "We've enough timber here on site for the next couple of days, so it shouldn't hold us up. If it does I'll know who to blame," he added with a grin.

It was close to nightfall before the cutting up of the 'big thing', as the children christened it, was complete and the pieces brought back to camp. Eileen took various internal organs into her laboratory for further examination, then handed over what was left to Dorothy for cooking and edibility tests. These would take place the following day. Colin and the engineers had returned earlier and I'd given them a rundown of the day's events.

Unfortunately our hopes that the big thing would provide some variation to our shig and fish diet proved in vain. Half a dozen volunteers were requested for the tasting process, but though Dorothy tried three or four ways of cooking a portion of the shoulder, loin and belly all were too tough to chew. Even the thinnest strips of meat defied our human teeth. The only edible part of the animal was the liver, though even that took a lot of chewing. It was obvious there was no justification in killing purely for the sake of one small portion of the beast so with regret we abandoned all hopes of having found a new source of food.

Eileen later reported that the big thing was a normal, earth-like mammal, with one liver, two kidneys and one heart. The hooves were similar to those of horses and the horns made of bone. Once she'd finished all her tests we burned the flesh, but kept the hide, horns and hooves. Though we could not think of an immediate use for them there was every possibility that they could serve us in some way in the future. Both Dave and I had at times during the day taken an altab a few miles out in the direction that the herd had been travelling in retreat. Through binoculars they were visible in the distance. On my last trip around half past five I estimated that they were some four miles distant and still moving away from us at a slow pace. At that evening's meeting we warned everyone to keep their eyes open when working in case the herd returned.

With all the excitement it was close to nine o'clock before we managed to hold our committee meeting. It was then that we finally got to hear what Colin had been doing during the day.

"I've been wanting for some time to take a look at the point where the hills meet to the north of us," he reported. "There was the off chance that there might be something useful there, but mainly I wanted to try and locate the source of our river. It's always seemed to me that the flow was too constant for it to be down to rainwater running off the hills, and I was proved right. There are three smallish openings at different points some way apart and between fifty and a hundred metres above ground level. Water is gushing from each constantly, forming three small rivers which come together in a large pool or small lake, call it what you will, just north of the coniferous wood. There are obviously underground springs feeding the three small rivers. We discussed the possibility of piping the water down to the camp here to give us a constant supply of fresh running water, but the distance is too great. We don't have anywhere near the amount of pipe that we'd need. Other than that we made no sensational discoveries. We examined the rock face closely up to a height of about two hundred metres, but there's no sign that there are any metal deposits."

CHAPTER NINE

Our fifth week on the planet started off badly. We awoke on the Monday morning to persistent rain, which lasted for two whole days. There was no wind and it was very warm, but the rain was unrelenting. Once again the mood in the camp was sombre, and became even more so as two potential crises reared their heads. The first was the more serious. Though the bed of our river was of rock the sides were earthen, and before long the water became discoloured and then turned dark brown. It was obviously unsuitable for drinking, washing or cooking and we were reluctant to use Dorothy's equipment to boil it for fear of silting up the attached pipework. I for one was thankful that right from the start Colin had insisted that all water containers should be refilled the moment they were empty.

The second concern was that the river would burst its banks. Normally the surface was a metre or more below most of the bank, but by Tuesday lunchtime one or other of us was braving the elements at regular intervals to check the level. Thankfully only two small areas where the banks were lower caused some localised flooding, though large pools of water were evident on the fields that we had planted.

It was amusing to see the reaction to the ban on using the river for washing. Because of the overall temperature the rain was quite warm. The children were the first to realise the possibilities. Shortly after eleven o'clock sounds of merriment drew us to the mouth of the cave we were all in to see the six of them, mother naked, disporting themselves in the rain while pretending to be taking a shower. Half an hour or so later two or three brave souls among the adults had followed their example and by late afternoon nearly all the company had appeared to do likewise, including myself and Susan, Colin, Elaine and Dave and his partner Fiona. We felt a bit self-conscious to start with, but our inhibitions soon faded and I for one thoroughly enjoyed the experience.

Bernard Stocks

Our committee meeting on that Monday afternoon was a long one and for the first time there was a certain amount of dissension. The session started off quietly enough with a decision to make each month thirty days long until such time as Walter could give us an accurate length for the year. "After all," Elaine pointed out, "It's only an arbitrary thing anyway."

Next Colin brought up his suggestion of splitting the colony. We spent nearly an hour weighing up the pros and cons, at the end of which time Elaine had gone round to Dave's point of view and was against the whole idea and even I was beginning to have doubts.

"Look at it this way," said Dave. "There's a fifty-fifty split amongst the troops on this issue. Now it's a major decision, perhaps the most important one we've had to consider up until now. I for one wouldn't be happy to go ahead unless there was a large majority in favour. I don't say that I'll always oppose it: but now is definitely not the right time."

Elaine agreed with Dave, I sat on the fence and in the end Colin agreed reluctantly to put the matter on the back burner.

There was more argument when we moved on to the next topic – education of the children. "We'll have to make some decisions on that soon," insisted Colin. "In fact we should have done it before this. I don't mean just the six we have here now. I'm thinking of those as yet unborn. What are we going to teach them, and how are we going to teach them? Should we do it in conventional schools, or on a one to one basis with their parents?"

Elaine was scathing. "As usual, Colin, you're looking much too far ahead. It'll be five years before we need to start worrying about that. As far as the present lot are concerned, what can we teach them? They presumably know how to read and write and do simple arithmetic. We can probably give them some instruction in the sciences and some more advanced maths, but that's about all. There's absolutely no point in teaching them languages and the geography and history of Earth have no meaning any more. As for the unborn, we can worry about that nearer the time – if we're still in charge of things, which is by no means certain."

As soon as she'd finished speaking I jumped in. "Sorry to disagree with you Elaine, but I think Colin's right to be looking that far ahead. The trouble is he's looking in the wrong direction. It's all very well to talk glibly about teaching children to read and write, but tell me this. How do you teach them to read when there aren't any books? How do you teach them to write when there's no paper and no writing implements? I know there are two or three hundred sheets of paper and an assortment of ballpoints and pencils lying around the lifeships, but how far are they going to go among the even the first thirty or so children? Let's get the engineers and anyone else with an inventive turn of mind on to finding a way of making a substitute for paper and some sort of writing materials. Then we'll consider the curriculum."

"Which doesn't solve the problem of our current six young hopefuls," remarked Elaine.

Colin made to speak, but Dave interrupted. "I've been giving some thought to that over the past few days. As you know, my partner Fiona is or was a teacher in a secondary school before signing up to go to Paladia. She and I have been talking about it and between us we've come up with a suggestion. I've looked at Elaine's card index and I see that apart from William Haddow we have both a primary and a secondary school teacher in the company in addition to Fiona. Let them put their heads together and devise a programme of education. Lessons should be for three hours in the mornings. Meantime we find out what the kids are good at and what they'd like to do as they get older. In the afternoons they can work with whoever comes nearest to their particular desires, as a sort of apprenticeship. For instance, if someone wants to be a doctor they can be assigned to Doc Wallace, a joiner to Dan and so on. That way they'll not only be learning but also preparing for the future."

It didn't take long for the four of us to reach agreement on Dave's proposals. We decided to talk to the six children, one at a time, the following day if the rain persisted. Dave thought that the kids might be overawed at facing the whole committee, but as Elaine pointed out they knew all of us well by now. "As long as we handle them gently and with the occasional touch of humour," this with a sidelong glance at Colin, "I'm sure they'll enter into the spirit of the thing. Apart from Wayne's little exploit they've all shown themselves to be sensible."

That seemed to satisfy all of us, so we moved on to the next topic, raised by Dave. "I've noticed a general slackening off over the last week or so. Morale is still reasonably high, but most people aren't putting so much effort into their work as they did earlier. Is there anything we can do to improve matters?"

"I think it's only natural," said Colin. "Everyone started off at a very high tempo, perhaps because we pushed them a little too hard. All along I've been expecting some kind of backlash and I don't think it's too serious. We've accomplished our main targets faster than I expected, so it won't do any harm to take things more easily for a spell. The first shoots are appearing among the stuff that we've planted and that should provide a boost."

"There's another factor which I think plays a small part," I opined. "Despite all our warnings there are still a sizeable number among us who think it's only a matter of time before someone comes along and rescues us. The thought has kept them going and kept their spirits up. But as the days go past and nothing happens they're at last beginning to accept what we told them. In some perverse manner they're now thinking we've got all the time in the world and they're losing their sense of urgency."

"The monotony of the diet's an even bigger cause in my opinion," stated Elaine. "I'm beginning to dread mealtimes and facing the same old things day after day and I'm sure I'm not the only one."

"I don't disagree," I said. "But there's nothing much we can do about that for the present." I sighed. "I never thought the day would come when I'd give my right arm for a simple plate of cabbage and mashed potato. Even some salt or spice in the food would help."

"We may eventually solve the salt problem, but you can forget about spices," Colin told us. "Dorothy has been experimenting with just about everything in sight, in collaboration with Doc Wallace of course. She's tried the leaves of all the trees and flowers, the seaweed Matt and Eileen brought back, even the grass. She's even tried grinding up the bones of the shigs, but everything is completely flavourless. We'll just have to wait until our crops mature. In the meantime we'll keep an eye on the overall mood and if necessary give everyone a reminder that we're not out of the wood by a long way."

It was Elaine who brought up the final matter of the meeting. "I don't know about everyone else, but I'm getting tired of referring to the 'new world', 'the colony', 'the big things' and 'the river'. Isn't it about time we gave names to everything?"

"I haven't given it any thought up to now," said Colin. "I suppose it might make people feel more at home. Any suggestions?"

We had quite a lot of fun bandying names about. Provisionally we decided the most appropriate name for the world would be New Britain, and for the settlement itself Landfall. The two rivers would simply be referred to as Narrow River and Broad River, and the big things became the mammoths. These names were approved at the evening mass meeting by a large majority.

We'd just about finished when Eileen put her head round the door and asked if we had a few minutes to spare.

"All the time in the world while this rain lasts," Colin said with a laugh. "What's on your mind?"

"A couple of things that might interest you," she replied. "You know I've been puzzled by the life forms on this world. Because they don't prey on each other, apart from the gecks eating small fish, I couldn't understand why the planet wasn't overrun. Well, I think I've solved the problem. I suppose I should have realised that Mother Nature always provides a balance, and the answer here is quite simple. Births are limited. I've been studying the shigs closely and I notice that there are very few babies in the flock. As far as I can estimate there are about three hundred animals in the one nearest us and only a couple of dozen or so offspring. It looks as though just sufficient babies are born to replace those that die of old age. If I'm right that means that the life span of a shig is not less than twelve and not more than fifteen years."

"You probably are right," mused Colin. "And if that's the case we're creating a problem by killing them for food. I don't want to look too far ahead," this was said with a wry sidelong glance at Elaine, "but it's something we should bear in mind as the years go by. At the moment we're killing around ten shigs a week, but that will increase in years to come as the population grows. Does your theory apply to the other wild life?"

"It seems to. I've found plenty of geck nests but very few eggs or young gecklings. Similarly with the birds and insects; there are hardly any young birds, larvae or caterpillars to be found. The other thing I wanted to tell you, if you haven't already noticed, is that the trees and bushes are in full flower now. I've given them provisional names, though not very imaginative I'm afraid. The clover-leafed tree I've simply called the clover tree and similarly the one with dandelion shaped leaves. The bushes I've also called after their leaves: oval bush and square bush. Respectively the clover trees have bright yellow flowers, the dandelion trees white, the oval bush a deep maroon and the square bush light blue. Interestingly all the flowers are shaped like their respective leaves."

After Eileen had gone I thought Colin would have wanted to discuss the implications of a falling shig population, but he merely remarked that we had plenty to discuss at our next meeting.

The rain eventually ceased late on Tuesday evening and sunshine greeted us when we arose on Wednesday. A quick tour round the site assured us that the effects of the previous two days' downpour had been minimal. There was still flooding at the two points where the riverbank was lowest, but even that was receding rapidly. The pools of water on the fields had disappeared and by lunchtime the water in Narrow River was running clear again. After checking that sufficient containerised water was still available we told everyone that for safety's sake no one should use river water for drinking or cooking until the following morning. Eileen was asked to run tests just before nightfall to ensure that the water was pure again. I'm not sure whether it was self-delusion or not but all the plants that were showing through appeared to have grown in the previous forty-eight hours. The potato and cereal fields in particular were looking more green than brown now.

We had duly talked to the teachers and the six children on the Tuesday. By common consent formal schooling would start the following Monday morning and in the afternoon the apprenticeships would begin. I suppose we were lucky that the children all wanted to specialise in different things. Emma Beaton wanted to be a nurse or a doctor so she became Doc Wallace's pupil. Brother Gary fancied engineering so Paul Cooper took him under his wing. Wayne wanted to be a farmer and the remaining three opted for cooking, crofting and hunting respectively. We all agreed that it wasn't ideal, but it was the best we could do in the circumstances. The morning lessons would cover mathematics and science, plus as much English as could be taught without books. Eileen had been persuaded to give one lesson a week on the biology and ecology of the planet plus some more general related topics.

As if to compensate for the previous downpour we had day after day of sunshine, with temperatures rising to the low eighties. All our crops thrived in the fine weather and more than one person swore they could actually see them growing as they watched! Accepting William Haddow's prognosis of a frost-free winter we planted two additional fields to the original six that had been planned, one of which we devoted to sugar beet, of which we'd previously only allowed for a small quantity. After two weeks of unremitting heat a new problem arose – drought! The engineers were quickly relieved of all other duties and given the task of creating a pumping system by which we could water the fields and Trevor's 'market garden' as he liked to call it. After a little trial and error we set up an efficient system, though in doing so we used up just about all of our supply of pipes. Bang goes the central heating for the cabins, I thought.

With eight fields planted and four more prepared for the following year we gradually scaled down the farm workforce and assigned the people concerned to other activities. Once again we increased the size of Dan's group, which was already completing two cabins a week. Three women and one man were given the task of finding ways to make clothes and shoes from the raw materials that were on hand. These consisted mainly of the shig pelts and the items we had retained from the dead mammoth. This group also had the unenviable job of repairing existing clothing. We had some needles and a quantity of thread in the lifeships' survival rooms, but Colin was specific in his instructions to what became known as the textile group.

"It won't be all that long before the thread runs out, and eventually the needles will break. Use both for the moment, but devote some of your time to finding ways to make clothes without either. If you find that the mammoth hide or horns will be useful let us know and we'll get Harry and June to provide more. But your main source of raw material is the shig skin, and there's plenty of them. In time I hope the engineers can come up with some sort of spinning wheel so that we can make wool."

In fact the shig skins bade fair to provide excellent garments. The fleece was thick and strong and the inside was soft and velvety to the touch. It wasn't long before the group produced the first prototypes of jackets and trousers. At this early stage they had to be sewn of course and were loose fitting, but they were very comfortable to wear and easy on the skin. The only problem was that they were too hot to wear when working under the summer sun. A heartfelt request was made for shorts for both men and women and a kind of brief halter for the latter. Nearly every man was already working bare to the waist.

The hot and dry weather persisted throughout the month of June and our crops grew apace. All the time we were keeping a close eye on the native trees and bushes. By the end of the month many of the flowers had died away and the first fruits had begun to form. We nearly missed those on the clover tree as they closely resembled the leaves, but as they grew they changed to a yellowish green. By the last day in June the lobes were each some two or more inches in diameter and the most advanced were beginning to turn yellow. The dandelion tree had produced tiny triangular nuts and the oval bush had green fruits about the size of a blackcurrant. The latter, however, were still growing. There certainly seemed to be food possibilities in all three, but it looked as though the square bush would prove a disappointment. So far it had only borne tiny winged seeds. One heartening note was that all the trees and bushes were heavily laden. If any should prove edible there would be an abundant supply of fruit for the autumn.

On the first day of July, exactly three months after our arrival, we held the promised election for a new council. At least, we tried to. Dave had chaired the evening meeting and once the normal business had been concluded handed over to Colin.

"As you know," the latter began, "we said we would elect a new committee after three months and the time is now. I've just a couple of things to say before we get down to voting. Firstly I think we should agree beforehand that the new committee serves for six months only before the next election. After that they can be held annually. Secondly Doctor Wallace has asked me to tell you that he does not wish to be considered as membership of the committee could conflict with his medical responsibilities. Thirdly, if you approve, I think the best way to conduct the vote is for everyone, children included, to write down four names on a piece of paper, fold it and put it somewhere centrally. Three people can then be selected at random to count the votes and announce the result. I've prepared enough pieces of paper and there are a couple of dozen ballpoints to share. Are there any objections to that method?"

Nobody spoke for a good half minute and Colin was just about to resume when Dan Dunn stood up.

"Why go to all that bother?" he asked. "You four have done a pretty good job up to now and I don't see any point in changing things. I vote that we elect the four of you en bloc. Who agrees with me?"

A veritable forest of hands rose aloft. Colin looked taken aback for a moment but rallied to say: "Is there anybody against the motion, or anyone who feels they should be on the committee?" Not a single hand was raised. "All I can say is thank you on behalf of the four of us for your confidence. I can promise you that we will continue to do our very best for everyone."

CHAPTER TEN

The events of the third week in July will forever be imprinted on my memory. After three months of routine labouring to establish ourselves on New Britain we had all, I think, become a little complacent. We seemed to have forgotten that time does not stand still and the last thing we expected was a surprise of any kind.

The first small hint that the week was going to be somewhat special came on the Monday evening and it was a personal one. I had just returned to the lifeship from a day's work in the fields. Susan looked a bit preoccupied, but waited until I'd washed my face and hands before speaking.

"I've something to tell you, Matt," she began and then hesitated. Then it came out with a rush. "I've missed my last two periods and I've been feeling sick these last few mornings."

It took a moment for her words to sink in. When they did I took her in my arms and kissed her. "That's great," was all I could think of to say, inadequate though it was. "Tell you what. Let's go and see Doc Wallace right now and get it confirmed."

We did just that, only to find Dave pacing nervously around the small waiting room. "Fiona?" I asked, and he nodded. After a couple of minutes Fiona emerged from the surgery. She was a very plain, almost mousy looking girl whose major attribute was the most marvellous speaking voice I have ever heard. But at that moment she looked absolutely radiant. "Two and a half months," she announced proudly. We just had time to congratulate her when Susan was called into the doctor's room. Dave and Fiona wished me good luck as they left.

A scant few minutes later Susan came out to tell me that she too was 'two and a half months gone' as she put it. We were a happy couple as we headed off for the evening meal, where we were showered with congratulations. It turned out that Susan and Fiona were not the first.

Three other women had been confirmed in the previous week, but had for some reason kept the news to themselves.

Susan and I had settled down comfortably to co-habitation. I think we both knew that our relationship was based more on friendship and necessity than on love, but we had developed a mutual respect for each other and were easy and happy in each other's company.

Tuesday's surprise came at evening mealtime. When we lined up for our sustenance, fish that evening, there was a pile of small fresh green cos lettuce waiting for us, one for each person. Most opted to have it with their main course, but Susan and I decided to have it as a starter. It was a taste of heaven. Our mood was heightened still further at the evening meeting when the farmers told us that they proposed to lift the first supply of potatoes the following Monday and that there would also be some green cabbage to go with it. That news raised a huge cheer, which prompted Gavin Stewart to warn us that initially we could only expect such fare every third day. To round off the evening William Haddow announced that his calculations were complete and that the year on New Britain was 354 days long. It took just a few minutes for the assembly to follow his suggestion that we make alternate months thirty and twenty-nine days respectively, starting with January having thirty days.

But if the previous two days had provided new talking points, Wednesday eclipsed all that had gone before. Colin, Dave and I were all working in the fields that day. Just before eleven o'clock I heard a loud shout of "look up there" from behind me. I was facing south at the time and though I looked up as requested I could see nothing out of the ordinary. Then someone close shouted: "Behind you, you fool". I turned round. Everyone had stopped working and all were gazing open-mouthed at the sky.

At first I thought I was seeing things. In fact I muttered to myself: "It can't be real. It's a hallucination." But it was all too real. Floating slowly, stern first, over the junction of the hills to the north was the wreckage of the *Caledonia Sunrise*. It was unbelievable. I knew incontrovertibly that there was no way the ship could be flown from the stern. Yet there it was, in plain view and coming slowly towards us. Then I spotted the tiny shape at the front and realised that the remains of the ship were being towed by a lifeship and as it came closer I could see clearly the chains that connected the two.

Colin and Dave had by this time moved closer to me and it was the former who spoke first. "I estimate they'll land about six miles south of here. Come with me. We'll collect Elaine, break out the altabs and go and meet them."

We suited the action to the words and some ten minutes later we were riding at full speed in the wake of the descending ship. Colin's estimate was pretty accurate; we'd covered six miles and topped a gently sloping ridge when the ship came into view about half a mile ahead of us. It had landed, but the shattered bow was facing us and we could see no signs of life. The lifeship was hidden from view. We all stopped instinctively and I heard Elaine muttering to herself. "There must be someone alive. There must have been someone to pilot the lifeship."

"No point in sitting here," I said. "Let's go on down and see for ourselves."

Barely had we started up again when people began to emerge from behind the ship. Two were some yards in front of the rest and even at that distance I recognised them immediately and waved. I was delighted to see that the one on the right was Nicola Holt, the girl from Colin's watch that I'd known briefly at Space College. I was equally delighted to see the one on the left. George Rutherford had been the First Officer on my own watch and as far as I was concerned had been the perfect boss. Though firm and somewhat strict, he was a quietly spoken man with an understanding of human foibles – particularly those of inexperienced Second Officers. He'd had to admonish me a couple of times in our first few days on the *Sunrise* but it was done quietly in private and in a way that made it seem like practical advice rather than a ticking off. His forbears had come to Britain from the West Indies in the 1980's. After brief sojourns in London and Manchester they finally set down roots in Bolton, where his grandfather and father became highly respected lawyers, founding a family firm. George had other ideas, however. From an early age he'd hankered to go into space. He left the legal profession to his two brothers and joined the Space College, from whence he graduated as the best cadet of his year. Still only twenty-six, he had had a glittering future in front of him until the accident to the *Sunrise*.

As we got closer I noticed that Nicola had her left arm in a sling. Closer still and I could see that she was very pale and drawn. Her blonde hair had grown considerably in the three months since I had last seen her and now hung down limply well past her shoulders. Then we had reached them. Jumping down from the altab I went straight to Nicola and gave her a careful hug and a kiss on the cheek. I didn't speak. Then it was a handshake for George and at last I found my tongue. "It's so good to see you both again," was the only greeting that I could think of.

George laughed. "That's exactly what the others said. And by the way, it's mutual. But come into the ship and have some coffee while we swap stories."

"Did you say coffee?" asked Elaine unbelievingly.

"I did indeed," replied George with another laugh. "There are still some of the ship's supplies left, although they're getting thin on the ground now."

He led us round to the rear and up a ladder into the hold. From there we made our way to what had been the crew's canteen. On the way I got a closer look at the lifeship. It seemed a bit more battered than our four had been. Once we were settled round a table George busied himself in the kitchen and we asked Nicola how she'd managed to hurt her arm.

"I was in the corridor when the collision occurred," she told us. "I got flung about twenty yards and crashed into an open door. I think I must have fainted, but as soon as I came to I realised my arm was broken. Luckily George came along at that moment and did some emergency first aid with some rough splints and bandages."

"You'd better come back with us and get our doctor to have a look at it," remarked Colin. "I take it you've got altabs on the lifeship." She nodded.

While we revelled in the taste of real coffee George gave us a summary of events leading up to their arrival on New Britain.

"I was relaxing in my cabin when the collision happened. Once I'd assessed the damage on the visiscreen I realised that the only sensible course was to abandon ship. I headed for the launching bay, but I'd only gone a few yards when I saw Nicola lying in a heap on the ground. It took me about twenty minutes to make some running repairs, so by the time we got to the lifeships you must all have left. I did notice that some of the ships were missing. On the way we came across ten of the resuscitated passengers, so we herded them along as well. By this time the wreckage had passed through the black hole, but once we were away from the ship I picked up the traces of this planetary system and set course accordingly. Unfortunately I made a bad mistake. I headed for the third planet thinking that it would be the most likely to support life. Even more unfortunately our radio wasn't functioning. If it had been I would have picked up your signal and changed direction."

"Don't ever be tempted to visit the third planet. It's a wilderness of ice and rock. I made four or five different orbits looking in vain for some sign of greenery or even a glimpse of water. Nothing! Of course I'd no idea at the time what the surface temperature was. Then I had to make another four orbits to find a place that was level enough to land safely. By the time we were down I realised that we had insufficient fuel to take off, orbit another planet and set down safely. Once down I was horrified to discover that the air temperature was minus twenty-five degrees – and that was in the middle of the day! At night it dropped to minus fifty. Worse still, there was no atmosphere. I put on the space suit and went outside a few times to see if there was any hope of finding food, but of course there was nothing. Each time I was out I brought back a large chunk of ice to supplement our water supplies and we had enough vitabars to last us for three months. The future looked non-existent, believe me."

"After a month I realised the position was hopeless. I didn't discuss it with anyone, not even Nicola, but I'd made my mind up that within the next week I'd simply open the hatches and end it all quickly. There just didn't seem any point in prolonging the agony. In fact I was just two days away from doing it when the miracle happened."

"It was one of the passengers who noticed it first. The *Sunrise*, or what was left of it, was in orbit above us. I did some quick calculations that proved we had just enough fuel to take off and get back on board. I didn't know what conditions would be like on the ship, but I reasoned that we couldn't be any worse off. We went back in through the same exit we'd come out of. Glory be, the emergency power was still on. A quick test showed me that the air supply was a hundred per cent pure as well. I put on the space suit and got out and closed all the exit doors in the bay, then got the twelve of us out into what was left of the ship. The first thing I did was to go to the radio room. The radio was still working and I picked up your signal immediately."

"I still couldn't see a way to eventual salvation, but at least we would have heat, food and water for a considerable period. It was only when I checked the fuel tanks that I realised that there was enough and to spare to refuel our lifeship and make it to the second planet. At first I was simply intending to load as many of the supplies as I could on to the lifeship, but then the idea came to me that it might be possible to tow the whole of the wreckage. Obviously I didn't know what conditions were like here, but even if they'd been good the contents of what's left of the *Sunrise* were likely to be invaluable. I knew there was a risk in the operation, but I talked it over with Nicola and the ten passengers and they agreed that we should make the attempt. I won't bore you with the details of how we finally got the chains fixed; suffice to say it took me over a week and about a dozen space walks before I was confident enough to try moving the whole shooting match. Thankfully the chains held. The main problem was that our speed was severely restricted and a journey that should have taken less than twenty-four hours turned into a three-month marathon. There were many moments during that time that I was tempted to jettison the chains and just bring the lifeship on. To be honest I was dreading the landing, but that turned out to be the easiest part."

"Despite having only one useful arm Nicola was able to take over the piloting from me, so I left her with the ten passengers for company. Donning the space suit again I went back into the wreckage and did a thorough check on the freezing compartments. All the ones on the lower level of the ship had been destroyed. The impact must have broken the electrical circuits and also fractured a large part of the ship's underbelly. Some of the circuits on the top level had failed also, but around two hundred compartments seemed undamaged. After checking that there was enough food to get us here I activated the resuscitation switches. Unfortunately not everyone came back to life, but in the end just under a hundred survived. I gathered them all together, explained what had happened. They took the news much more calmly than I expected. The first thing we did was jettison the dead, a task I hope I'll never have to do again. I would have brought the bodies here for burial, but I was terrified of disease breaking out amongst the living."

The Far Side of Nowhere

"A couple of the men that survived had been army officers back on Earth. I put them in charge, told them to allocate cabins to everyone and organise catering arrangements and then went back and took over the lifeship. And not a moment too soon. Nicola was out on her feet. The rest of the trip was uneventful. We had radio contact with the survivors and I spoke to one or another of the leaders twice a day to make sure there were no problems. Luckily everyone accepted the situation. I think most of them were thankful just to be alive."

There was silence for a couple of minutes while we digested his story. Then the questions flowed.

I got in first, just ahead of Colin. "How many people are in your group then?"

"Ninety-six adults and twelve children, including myself and Nicola," responded George. "By children I mean anyone under sixteen, though in fact the oldest is fourteen and the youngest nine. Of the adults there are forty men and forty-six women. They range from sixteen to just over sixty, though that's only a guess. I haven't asked anyone their age."

"If I remember rightly," Colin was determined not to miss a second opportunity, "a fair number of farm animals are cryogenically frozen in one of the cargo bays. I seem to remember them being listed on the ship's manifest. Have you checked on them?"

George clapped his hand to his head. "I'd forgotten all about them. You're right, of course. They're in the rear lower hold, the last one on the port side of the stern."

Elaine looked round at the rest of us. "There'll be an ample supply of crockery and cutlery on board. Can we take some back with us? It'll be a treat to be able to eat in a civilised fashion once again."

"Leave that for the present," replied Colin. "It won't do us any harm to soldier on for a few more days. In any case we'd better wait and find out just how much there is. There may not be enough to go round, so we'll have to ration them out. One plate or bowl and either a knife a fork or a spoon per person."

"How much have you got left in the way of food supplies?" I asked George.

"Not a lot, I'm afraid. Three days ago I spent another few hours in the ship itself and they were running pretty low then. We maybe have enough for another four or five days at most. But surely there are food sources here. You all look healthy enough."

"I'll fill you in on that shortly," said Colin. "Meantime I think Elaine, Dave, Matt and Nicola should head back to Landfall and let everyone know what's happening. I'll stay here for a while and take a look at the frozen animals. While we're doing that I'll bring George up to date on events here. Once this lot is organised as far as food is concerned George can come back with me and we'll start to make some plans. I take it there's no shortage of water on board?"

"Absolutely none," George replied. "The recycling equipment is working perfectly. Can I make one addition to your proposed course of action. I think it would be a good idea if you made a short speech to all the survivors telling them briefly what's happened since you arrived. It will lift their spirits greatly once they know that we can make a go of things on this world."

"No problem," said Colin. "As soon as we've done that I'd like you to organise three small groups of, say, three people each. One group can make an inventory of all the supplies and cargo on the *Sunrise* and the lifeship. The second group can make out a complete list of the survivors – name, age, occupation, special skills and hobbies. We'll need that when it comes to organising work parties. The third group can kill off two or three shigs for your supper tonight." He turned to me. "We should be back in Landfall by four o'clock. Arrange our public meeting for half past five, before the evening meal. There's a lot of planning to be done in a short time, so we'll want as long as possible for our committee meeting. It goes without saying that we'll co-opt George and Nicola on to the committee."

Nicola jumped in quickly. "If it's all the same to you, Colin, I'd rather you left me out of things." We all looked at her. She hesitated for a moment and then burst out: "You'd have found out sooner or later anyway. I decided early on in this trip that the Space Service wasn't for me and I was intending to resign anyway when we got back to Earth. I don't quite know why I feel this way. Heaven knows I was keen enough going through College and on my early trips. But more and more I've felt the responsibility weighing on me and making me depressed. So if it's all the same to you I'd rather be one of the foot soldiers from now on. I'm sure you'll be able to find a job for me, even if I do have only one good arm at the moment."

"If that's the way you want it Nicola, then that's the way it will be," Colin said gently. "But if you should change your mind at any time in the future the door is always open for you."

"Thanks, Colin, but I don't think that will happen." She turned to me. "Matt, can you help me break out an altab. It's not too easy with one hand."

After a brief word with George and Colin Elaine and Dave came with us. Like myself, both wanted to see the conditions inside the lifeship. Simple curiosity I suppose, because this one was the same as all the others. While we were looking round Elaine said with a grin: "It looks as though Colin's going to get his way after all." Dave asked her what she meant.

"There's no way we can accommodate all this crowd at Landfall. We're going to have to set up at least two extra sites. That should make him happy."

Dave looked at her searchingly. "Are you saying that he's unhappy? I haven't seen any signs of it."

Elaine pondered. "Unhappy is probably the wrong word. Moody would perhaps be a better description. Living with him as I have for the past three months I've seen the side of him that the public never sees. Putting it bluntly, he's a worrier and a perfectionist. It's not megalomania: he doesn't give a damn about his personal standing. His one desire, that's with him from the moment he wakes until the moment he goes to sleep again, is to make this colony succeed. He thinks of nothing else. Even when we're alone he's bouncing ideas off me, asking me what I think of this or think of that. I'm hoping that now that George is here he'll lighten up just a bit."

We took the journey back to Landfall at a slow pace. Although she didn't complain it was obvious that Nicola was finding it uncomfortable steering the altab with one hand and by the drawn look on her face I surmised that she was in some pain. On the way we took turns at bringing her up to date with all that had happened to us since the collision and providing thumbnail sketches of some of the leading lights of our community. It was just after half past one when we got back to camp and while Elaine took Nicola off to see the Dr. Wallace Dave and I called everyone together and gave them an outline of the day's events so far. I expected that there might be a few complaints at the bringing forward of the evening get together, so to forestall them I promised that George would give them a fuller account of his adventures. One of the women asked me what George was like.

"He's black, he's handsome, he's about twenty-six, he was my boss and a damn good one. He's also a strict disciplinarian, so there'll be no swinging of the lead when he's around," I informed her with a laugh. After Dave brought the meeting to a close we went to the surgery, but Nicola was still closeted with the doctor. Dave and I decided there was no point in hanging around and went back to the fields to resume work there.

CHAPTER ELEVEN

Colin and George appeared just before five. They'd arrived some fifteen minutes earlier and Colin had spent the time showing George round the site and introducing him to as many people as possible. Before the meeting I managed to have a few words with Nicola. She told me that the doctor had re-set her arm as the fracture had not healed properly. It was, however, a clean break with no complications and she would be as good as new in a couple of months.

George didn't seem unhappy about the promise I'd made on his behalf and repeated substantially the story that he'd told to us earlier in the day. Colin was chairing the meeting and after taking the usual reports from the section heads he told the assembly that as we had a lot to discuss in committee he proposed to end the session without the usual contributions from the floor. There were no objections, though whether this was because everyone understood and sympathised or because they were simply hungry and desperate for their evening meal was unclear, to me at any rate.

We got down to business just before seven. Colin opened the proceedings by saying that he and George had not had the chance to formulate any plans beforehand, other than that they'd like to hear our suggestions first. He then handed each of us copies of the two lists they'd compiled earlier. "I'd suggest we spend a few minutes studying these first as they'll have a bearing on everything we decide. List one is of the equipment, cargo and supplies on the *Sunrise*; we didn't have time to check the lifeships, but their contents will be the same as our own. List two is of the survivors and their trades and professions."

I had barely started scanning down list one when Dave gave a whoop. "Look at this, a plough. Just what we needed. That'll speed up the work no end. Hey, and underneath that there are two lorries." Then a thought struck him and he turned to George. "How are they powered?"

"Rechargeable batteries. If you remember, they've discovered very little oil on Paladia up till now, so all the gear that's going out to them has to be electrically operated."

"Here's something else that'll prove invaluable," I put in. "Five flying belts. I'd forgotten they were on board. A vote of thanks for modern science." Flying belts had been around since the end of the twentieth century of course, but the recent boom in space travel had seen new technology applied since the first crude models. Though we called them belts they were in fact small seats, also battery powered. The modern ones had a range of over a hundred miles before recharging and could fly at speeds of up to eighty miles an hour.

"Here's another welcome sight," said Elaine in her turn. "A consignment of garden tools. Three dozen spades, hoes, rakes, shears, pickaxes, even pruning knives."

"I don't see any seeds in the list," remarked Colin. "That's a bit of a blow."

"Not really," Dave commented. "Remember there's the survival rooms in George's lifeship and the four lifeships that are left in the *Sunrise*. And Trevor told me a couple of days ago that we've only used about two-thirds of our own supply so far. He's even got a store of fruit seeds and stones that he kept back in case the first sowings failed."

"There's a couple of standard fittings that will prove invaluable," reflected Elaine. "The medical room on the *Sunrise* will boost Doc Wallace's supplies and equipment, and the ship's library is going to solve at least one of our teaching problems."

The list of personnel unfortunately didn't look so rewarding. I'd hoped for at least one more doctor and more engineers and skilled tradesmen. We did have three teachers, one farmer and two joiners among the complement, but the rest comprised accountants, computer technicians and clerical workers plus a fair few unskilled or hitherto unemployed in the ranks. A second look at the list revealed one that I'd missed, namely a second year medical student. It looked as though Dr. Wallace was going to get a second apprentice.

I looked at George. "I take it these three Patels are of Asian origin." He nodded and I turned to Colin. "That answers one of your prayers – some diversity for the gene pool."

"You'll have a bit more diversity," George put in. "Apart from myself, two of the women who survived are black. One is of Nigerian origin, the other's forbears hailed from South Africa."

Once we'd studied the list in detail Colin rapped on the table for silence. "George and I have been pretty busy and haven't really had much time to discuss the situation. Hopefully you three have been giving matters some thought during the afternoon, so we'd like to hear your views and conclusions, if any. Would you like to start, Matt?"

Bernard Stocks

I looked at Dave and he gave me a nod of encouragement. "Dave and I have been discussing things on and off during the afternoon, and we're pretty much in agreement," I began. "My first inclination was to leave the new arrivals in the main part of the ship, cultivate the land around it and eventually build up a settlement there. But as Dave pointed out to me, there are two main objections to that. Firstly, though recycled water may sustain life it is much preferable to have the real thing. Secondly, sooner or later we'll need to cannibalise the ship for the raw materials we'll need. So it looks as though Colin's earlier plan for two new settlements is the solution."

"We thought one at the junction of Narrow River and Broad River and one about ten miles east of that," Dave added. "It'll mean that Landfall is still the biggest, but we might get some of the people here to move on and thereby even up the numbers between the three locations. But I don't think we should force anyone to move. If we can get volunteers, fair enough, but if not we should leave things as they are."

"You might find that some of the folk here have friends amongst the newcomers," Elaine pointed out. "They might be very willing to move. Tell you what, let's pin up these personnel lists that we've got here in one or two prominent places so that everyone will know who has joined us. Who knows, we might be flooded with transfer requests. On another tack, I take it that we'll be splitting up, one or two of us to the two new camps."

Colin looked at George. "Any comments?"

"Nothing to add," our new committee member confirmed. "I'm pretty much in agreement with all that's been said. Incidentally, I've had some experience working with radio. It'll be a simple matter for me to fix up radio links between all the sites once they're up and running. In fact tomorrow I'll put in a connection between here and the wreck. I'd like to discuss what we're going to do with the frozen live animals once we've dealt with this issue."

"Right," said Colin. "Let's get down to it. I agree with all that's been said so far, but I'd like to take the split one stage further. You all know that one of our major problems has been the lack of salt. I took particular note when I was looking round the *Sunrise* to check on the supplies there. I'd say there's enough to last us for a couple of months, no more. So my suggestion is that we add a small settlement on the shore of the ocean, probably for a community of about twenty. They would grow most of their own food in time, of course, but their main function would be to ensure a supply of salt to all communities. You've been there, Matt. Is it possible?"

I closed my eyes and tried to visualise the site. "Yes, I think so. There's a level stretch on the bank of the river about a quarter of a mile inland. At a guess it would accommodate a couple of dozen cabins, there's certainly an ample supply of timber for building them and there's enough open land to provide at least a dozen fields. My only objection is that it will be a long distance away from the other sites. Even the one at the river junction is a

The Far Side of Nowhere

good twenty miles or more. Getting as few as twenty there means a long hike for some."

"We'll have the use of the lorries, don't forget," Colin pointed out. "Salt we must have, and I can't think of any other way of getting it in sufficient quantities."

Neither could the rest of us. Once we'd talked round the matter we soon agreed to the proposal. Dave suggested that we name the proposed new villages, as he called them and that set us all thinking. Various names were suggested and argued over until Elaine spoke out. "We're never going to agree at this rate. Let's be totally unimaginative and for the time being call them Riverside, Junction and Seashore. Once the new inhabitants are settled they can get their heads together and change the names if they want to." Her motion was carried unanimously.

"Now that's settled we need to decide how to split ourselves between the camps," said Colin. "As Matt was the first arrival I think he should stay at Landfall. If Elaine's agreeable I suggest that she and I take Seashore, George goes to Junction and Dave to Riverside. We may need to hold committee meetings less frequently once the nights draw in, but we've got a good supply of altabs now so it shouldn't be too onerous having to travel. Our meetings will be in the *Sunrise* for the moment as that's the most central point."

"I'd be quite happy to take on Seashore if you and Colin would rather stay here," I told Elaine.

"That's good of you, Matt," she replied," but I'm happy enough to go. In any case, you were the first to arrive in Landfall, so it's only right and proper that you should be the one to stay and mastermind it's future. Who knows, they might decide to re-name it Mattstown!"

"Thanks all the same but no thanks," I grinned. "I'm no glory hunter. Landfall's a good enough name for me. But if you and Colin are going to Seashore I think you should have two of the flying belts. They'll get you to meetings much more quickly than the altabs. I suggest we give the doctor control of two of the other three, so that he and an assistant can respond quickly to any medical emergency. The fifth can be left in the *Sunrise* in case of any other emergency."

This proposal was agreed immediately and the necessary dispositions for making a start on the new arrangements were quickly agreed. Dan, Trevor, the two engineers and Gavin Stewart, the younger of the two farmers, would have a roving assignment between the three new sites, using the wreck as their base. Two of Dan's assistants would be transferred as well. Peter Gibson, the older farmer, would remain at Landfall. Colin, Elaine and Dave would relocate to the *Sunrise* from the next day and Dr. Wallace would be given the choice of following suit if he so wished. If not, he could move from Elaine's old ship to Colin's. With Dave moving out as well we could forge ahead with dismantling the two vacant ships. Once plans had been finalised for the new areas some workers from

Landfall would be taken daily by lorry to one or other of them to add to the workforces there.

"I should know but remind me. What's the situation as regards the fields here?" asked Colin.

"We've got eight planted, six more dug ready for next year and we've just started stripping a fifteenth," I told him.

"It's your decision now, Matt," he looked at me quizzically. "But can I suggest you leave just two people stripping turf from now on. As each new field is stripped we can send the plough across to turn it over. We'll leave you with three spades and commandeer the rest to supplement what we have available elsewhere."

"That's fine by me," I stated. "We're well ahead in our preparations for next year, so it's only fair that the bulk of the effort and equipment should to the new areas."

"Thanks. Now there's one other thing. With the communities we're proposing it's vital that we have another bridge over Narrow River, as near as possible to its junction with Broad River. If you're all in agreement I'd like to get the engineers and Dan on to that even before they start looking to set up wind and water turbines at the new sites. I'd also like them to do a survey to see if it's possible to get a bridge across Broad River. It's not vital, but sooner or later we'll want to cross it." He looked round and we all nodded. "Good. As soon as we've finished here I'll go round and notify all those who'll be moving on. Oh, I take it we agree that if they want to come back and settle in Landfall when their work in other places is completed there'll be no objections?" Once again, we all nodded. "O.K. George, tell us about the animals."

"It's merely a matter of when to revive them," said George. "The poultry will need to be penned as soon as they're defrosted, and I suspect the pigs should be, too. I'll check that with the farmers. And that raises two problems. Firstly the pens should be sited at the new settlements, and if we build pens for them and none of them revive we'll have wasted time and effort. Secondly, we don't want to leave it too long to revive them. I'm no expert, but I suspect that the longer they're in deep freeze the less is their chance of survival. I think we should resuscitate at least some of the cows tomorrow or Friday. The children in particular could use the milk. It won't be too difficult to herd them to pastures new when the time comes. The same probably applies to the sheep."

Suddenly I had an idea. "Surely if we clear out one of the cargo holds, and remove the plexiglass from the human cryogenic chambers we can create enough space on the wreck to house them. That way we'll find out exactly how many survive and can plan the necessary final homes for them. If I'm not mistaken the cargo includes a fairly large supply of poultry food and now that our potatoes and other vegetables are coming on stream we should be able to generate enough swill to feed the pigs. It'd mean diverting a small working group to look after them all, but it would be an ideal job for anyone who doesn't feel strong enough for more manual work."

The others liked the idea and George added another note to the growing list in front of him.

"Anything else?" Colin asked. When no reply was forthcoming he formally brought the meeting to a close. "Eight o'clock tomorrow evening at the *Sunrise*, then."

Colin went off to notify those who would be moving home next day, but I insisted on seeing Dr. Wallace myself. I told him what had been decided and asked whether he wanted to stay or go to the *Sunrise*.

"If it's all the same to you I'd rather stay here," was his decision. "If I'm getting one of the flying belts I can respond to an emergency just as quickly from here as from anywhere else. It won't take long to transfer the equipment and supplies from the ship's medical room to here if lorries are coming on a regular basis. I can put up two or three partitions in Colin's ship to make a surgery, waiting area and sleeping quarters for myself." The doctor was one of half a dozen of the community who had not taken a partner. I was pleased that he'd decided to stay and told him so.

Straight after the morning meal Colin, Elaine, Dave and Fiona packed up their meagre belongings, commandeered the four altabs and set off for their new abode along with George. The plan was that the lorries would be charged up during the day. One of them would then come on Friday morning, returning the altabs and taking the rest of those who were moving, with their partners, to Central, which was the name we'd given to the area in which the *Sunrise* had come down. I reflected that the changes meant our population in Landfall would fall to seventy-five. If we were to provide equal numbers for the two larger new communities very few volunteers would be needed. Allowing twenty for Seashore that would leave fifty-eight as the target figure for Riverside, Junction and Landfall.

I spent most of the day working in the fields as usual and fending off the many questions I was asked. To all of these I replied that I'd make a full statement at the evening meeting. Peter Gibson already knew that his colleague Gavin would be leaving, so I was a little more forthcoming to him. We agreed to carry on turf cutting with the full squad until work started at the new sites but would suspend any further digging once the fields were stripped. I think we were both thankful that a plough would soon be on hand to relieve us of the necessity for digging. The other decision I had to make on that, my first day as the overlord of Landfall, was who should replace Trevor as head of the crofting section. Luckily it was an easy choice. By far the most able of Trevor's group was Cassie Grant, a small spare lady in her mid forties. She'd been a frequent prize-winner at agricultural shows around the village in Dorset from whence she hailed. True, her prowess then had been entirely with flowers, but she had quickly adapted to the growing of fruit and vegetables and I knew she would do a good job. An added benefit was that she was well liked by those she

Bernard Stocks

was working with. Trevor approved my choice when I spoke to him, but I made no mention of the change to Cassie herself, planning to spring it on her during the evening meeting.

Round about three o'clock I was surprised to see a lorry arrive at the caves. Handing my spade over to one of the standby crew I hurried back to investigate. Dave was standing by the lorry when I got there. "We suddenly realised this morning that you'd have no transport to get to the committee meeting tonight, so I volunteered to bring the altabs back. I thought about taking some of those due to move back with me, but we haven't had time to put benches in the back of the lorry. It's a bit too bumpy to try and carry anyone standing up. Otherwise it's great to drive."

Dave set off again a few minutes later, just as it started to rain. I could see in the distance the working party getting ready to abandon the fields, so I didn't bother going back. Instead I opted for half an hour in my ship making some rough notes for the evening meeting. There would be a lot to get through.

CHAPTER TWELVE

Before going for our evening meal I told Susan that I might have to stay at Central overnight. "I don't know how long the meeting will go on for and I don't fancy trying to get back here in the dark. Will you be O.K.?"

"Don't worry, I'll be fine," she said. "If you get the chance could you do something for me while you're there. I noticed that one of the names on the list of the new arrivals was a Michael Lytwyn. There was a boy of that name at school with me and I've been wondering if it's the same one. I didn't really know him, as he was two years above me, but if it is him I'd like to meet and talk. It would be a link with the past, and we're bound to have things in common and people we both know. If you get to speak with him ask him if he went to Reading High School."

"Will do," I told her. "It's an unusual name so it's odds on it will be the same guy. And if it is you'll get to see him soon anyway. Unless I'm mistaken he's the medical student on the list, in which case he'll be coming here to study under Doc Wallace. And now let's go and eat. I'm starving."

For the first time since we'd arrived on New Britain I felt nervous going in to the evening meeting. It had been easy enough chairing meetings when the other three committee members had been beside me for support, but on this night and those to come I was entirely alone. I started off by detailing the changes that had been agreed the night before and the regrouping of the committee itself and some of the key personnel. I mentioned the fact that we would be asking for volunteers to move to another settlement. There were one or two rumblings among the audience from time to time as I spoke, denoting that not everyone was happy with what we proposed. I decided a pep talk wouldn't be amiss, so once I'd gone over all the new measures I put my notes aside.

"I know these moves aren't going to be popular," I began. "But if you think about them you'll realise that they're necessary for the good of all of us on this world. It's easy to feel aggrieved at the newcomers and blame them for the fact that our hitherto well-ordered routine is being upset. But like us they didn't ask for the *Sunrise* to be wrecked and to have to adjust to a new life and a new environment. We're in a very strong position here at Landfall, thanks entirely to the hard graft that you've all put in since we arrived. By the end of the summer we'll have at least sixteen fields ready for cultivation next spring. We have ample power, plentiful supplies of food, monotonous though it is, good cooking facilities and more than half our cabins are built. The aim now must be to bring the other three communities up to our level even though it means some sacrifices. But we will also be acquiring some benefits. As soon as a full inventory of the contents of the *Sunrise* is completed we'll be getting a share of the furniture and fittings. That means tables and chairs, bunk beds, cutlery and crockery among other things."

"All this means that there'll be one other change. With the committee scattered we'll no longer be able to discuss important matters and make decisions on the spot. Instead we'll be back to something like the form of government that you were familiar with back on Earth. We'll talk things over at these meetings, take a vote if necessary and then I'll take your views back to the committee to compare with those of the other camps. Which brings me to my final point. Do you want to continue with these nightly meetings or would you rather have them less frequently?"

"What do you think yourself?" someone asked.

"Personally I'd like to carry on as we are for the time being," I replied. "Although obviously there won't be as much progress to report there are still a lot of decisions to be made as regards religion, marriage and law and order. No doubt there'll be other matters that will arise. Can I have a show of hands, please."

A large majority were in favour of continuing nightly meetings, with only seven or eight voting against. I took a couple of questions and then formally closed the meeting at twenty to eight. Bidding a brief farewell to Susan I jumped on the altab and headed for Central.

I arrived just as most of the people were finishing off their evening meal. Colin had already eaten and met me at the entry port, taking me immediately to the lifeship where the others were waiting.

Once we were seated it was Colin himself who spoke first, looking directly at me. "We'll make this a short meeting so that you can get back in daylight, Matt. We've been giving some thought to matters, and with your approval we think that from now on we should only hold committee meetings weekly, on a Sunday. We'll all be in your position very soon as even before we move permanently we'll be spending all the hours of daylight at our respective camps. The nights are beginning to draw in and we don't want anyone travelling across country in the dark."

"I'm all in favour of that," I said with some fervour. "I'd resigned myself to spending most nights here and going back first thing in the morning and I didn't fancy the notion. It would have been a strain on me and it wouldn't have been fair to Susan."

"By Sunday at the latest we'll all be in permanent radio contact," announced George. "I'm planning a multi-directional link up between the four sites and the ship here, plus direct contact from all points to Doctor Wallace, who I gather is staying at Landfall. If anything urgent should arise during the week we can discuss it via the radio rather than calling a meeting."

"We've made a fair amount of progress today," Elaine reported. "We've split the personnel here into groups for each location and then further split each group into working parties along the lines we used in Landfall. The lorries will both be fully charged by morning. One will come to you to collect Dan and the others, the second lorry will take people to Riverside and Junction to start turf stripping. George and Dave will go with them. They've already been to the sites and laid their plans. The flying belts are also on charge and Colin and I will go to Seashore to look the place over and start planning the layout there."

"On Monday morning we'll send the two joiners from here together with another representative from each of the three building groups to you at Landfall." Colin had taken up the narrative. "They can shadow operations there for a couple of days to see how things are done, then come back and start here. Keep Dan's three assistants with you until Wednesday morning, then send two of them back here with the returning group. Happy with that?"

"I can't see any problems," I replied. "Going off at a tangent, there are two things I want to ask. Firstly, what's the position here with regard to vegetables, tinned, frozen, dried or otherwise?"

Dave spoke for the first time. "We've a dozen or so cans of baked beans left, a kilogram bag of dried peas and eight packets of a mix for vegetable soup. That's the lot, though we do have about five dozen cans of fruit, mainly peaches. In other words one day's supply."

I clapped him on the shoulder. "Then this is your lucky day, or at least next Tuesday will be. As you know, we're planning to harvest the first of the potatoes and cabbage. I'll check with Peter and we'll send you down an equal ration per person to what we're keeping. Which leads me to my second question. How soon can we get our share of the fittings, crockery and cutlery from the *Sunrise*?"

"We haven't had time today to divide it all up," said George. "I'll send enough plates, bowls, forks and spoons up with the lorry in the morning so that everyone there will have one dish and one implement. I've got a couple of people working on the fittings; as soon as they've finished we'll start sending stuff up to you on a daily basis until you've got your share. One other thing. We've packed up all the supplies in the medical centre apart from a few everyday things we're holding back for first aid. They'll reach you tomorrow as well. The cupboards and fittings from there will be with you a day or two later."

"That seems to be about it for the moment," said Colin. "Once things get settled here we'll start talking to our respective groups about laws, religion and marriage. We really should get these matters sorted out before the end of the year. Next meeting here on Sunday at one o'clock if that's acceptable to everyone."

As we broke up I asked George about Michael Lytwyn.

"I'm glad you reminded me. I should have said sooner. If you and Dr. Wallace are agreeable I'll send him to you next Monday morning. If he's understudying the doctor it means he'll be staying with you permanently, of course. Come on and I'll take you to meet him."

I said farewell to the other three and followed George into the main ship. We eventually ran our quarry to earth in the ship's library, where he had collected a small pile of medical text books. Michael turned out to be a stocky six-footer with short sandy hair and a round, freckled and open face. I liked him on sight. George made the introductions and left us together.

"I've to ask you if you went to Reading High School and if so does the name Susan Forrest ring any bells," I said.

His face lit up. "Yes and yes. Susan was a couple of years below me, but I knew who she was. One of my pals tried to date her a couple of times, unsuccessfully I should add." He seemed pleased when I told him that he'd be meeting Susan when he arrived on Monday.

I just managed to get back to Landfall as darkness began to fall. It was as well that the meeting hadn't been too long as the sky was overcast and there wouldn't have been any moonlight to ease the journey home. Susan was delighted that I hadn't had to stay over at Central and excited at the prospect of meeting her former schoolmate. Before retiring for the night I sought out Dan's two assistants to let them know that they wouldn't now be leaving us until the following week. Barely had I left them when two couples approached me with the information that they wished to volunteer to go to Seashore on a permanent basis. Both had been friendly with Colin and Elaine and made it clear that this was their only reason for wanting to go. I told them I understood and would let Colin know as soon as possible.

It was a stranger driving the lorry the following morning. Over breakfast I'd told Dr. Wallace to stand by for a delivery and instructed everyone else to wait for the lorry before going off to work. I didn't tell them why. The driver handed me a couple of large cardboard boxes and offloaded the medical supplies while farewells were being said and Dan and the others climbed aboard the lorry. As soon as it was out of sight I asked everyone to line up and opened the two boxes. As each person filed past me I handed them either a large plate or bowl and a spoon or fork. I felt like Santa Claus at Christmastime. This really was a big step forward. Our crudely made mud receptacles had served us well, but they were unsightly and brittle. These plates and bowls were of plastic and unbreakable. Once we had some tables and chairs as well eating would become a civilised activity once more and not a representation of feeding time at the zoo.

I took a little time out on that Friday morning to talk to Cassie, the new head of the crofting section. All the stuff that Trevor and the group had planted was doing well. There was enough lettuce now for a weekly ration of two per person. Many of the tomatoes were just beginning to ripen and the first supplies were expected in just over a fortnight. Most of the fruit trees and bushes were over a foot high and looking healthy. I asked Cassie when she proposed to transplant them.

"Trevor was talking about putting some out next month, but I think that's too soon," she opined. "If you agree I'd like to leave it until next March when the sap starts rising. That will give them a much better chance of surviving. Even then I might hold about a quarter back for transplanting later next year or even the following year, depending how the first ones do."

"You're the expert" I told her. "I'll leave it to your good judgement. Now there's one other thing I'd like you to be thinking about. Dan is planning to make some furniture and to add a second room to all the cabins once everyone has one. By the time he's done all that we'll have used up most of the conifers in the forest to the north. We shouldn't delay in regenerating it, so could you experiment and find a way of planting new trees, please."

I set off for Central shortly after the morning meal on Sunday. I thought it might be a good idea to spend some time meeting some of the newcomers and getting their views. As I covered the last half a mile to the wreck I blinked. But my eyes were not deceiving me. Close to the left-hand side half a dozen cows were grazing peacefully. A short distance away a flock of sheep was doing likewise. Shigs were close by in abundance but neither they nor the animals from Earth were taking the slightest interest in each other.

I called in at the lifeship first, to find Elaine poring over several sheets of paper covered with drawings and figures. She looked up thankfully as I greeted her. "The others are all away to their areas of influence, as Dave has christened them. They'll be back in time for the meeting though." I told her I wanted to meet a few of the newcomers.

"It'll be a very few," she said with a laugh. "Nearly everyone has volunteered to work, so there's not many left here. But come in to the dear old *Sunrise*. We've made quite a lot of progress since you were here last."

She took me on a tour of inspection, starting with the hastily prepared animal and poultry pens. In one of the former cargo holds a number of pigs were sleeping or rooting for food in the dried grass that had been laid down for them. Other areas held chickens and turkeys.

"We've left the ducks and geese for the moment," she informed me. "Gavin decreed that they shouldn't be revived until we could situate them close to water. For safety's sake we've also left the three bullocks frozen until we can stable them."

"Have all the animals come through?" I asked her.

"Unfortunately no," she replied. "If I can remember correctly our tally is sixteen cows out of twenty-four, three bulls, fifty-five chickens out of sixty, four of which are cockerels, and fifteen turkeys out of twenty-two. Two of them are males as well. There are twenty out of twenty-eight ducks. We've saved most of the sheep; forty-four out of fifty. All eighteen of the pigs made it. The most depressing news of all is that not one of the ten horses has survived. They would have been invaluable as an alternative means of transport. But we're already reaping some benefits. There'll be a couple of churns of fresh milk for you when the lorry arrives tomorrow morning. We've had a few eggs to date, and George will be rationing them out to make sure your parishioners get their fair share. More good news is that we've made some interesting discoveries amongst the canteen supplies. There's half a kilogram of dried yeast, which means that when we start to harvest the wheat we can have real bread. Plus there are four coffee grinders."

"What use are coffee grinders if we've got no coffee to grind?" I asked, feeling puzzled.

"Think about it, dummy," Elaine laughed. "We've got wheat and maize to grind, haven't we? The engineers haven't come up with anything in the way of a milling device yet, so we can use the coffee grinders. It'll be slow going, and the flour will be coarser than we're used to, but it's an improvement on trying to pound grain with a makeshift pestle and mortar."

"I never thought of that. Remind me at the meeting if I forget. I'll take the yeast back with me and some sugar if there is any. Eileen should be able to set up some kind of fermenting device to grow the yeast and give us a constant supply."

After meeting and speaking to those few of the new arrivals who were around I went outside again and round to the bow to inspect the damage done by the collision. I hadn't had the opportunity to take a close look at it before and was curious. Viewed from ten metres away it looked even worse than it had when I saw it through the visiscreen immediately after the impact. About an eighth of the ship's length had simply been flattened, leaving a crumpled but solid mass of metal. Here and there one or two pipes and wires were hanging loose. The one consolation was that those who had been in the forepart of the ship had not suffered; death would have been instantaneous.

I still had some time to kill before the meeting, so I went back inside the ship and prowled around the old familiar scenes, including my old cabin. Someone was obviously using it, but they'd been thoughtful enough to pack all my belongings into a cupboard. Not that I had all that much: we travelled light on these long distance space flights. There were, however, a couple of changes of clothing and shoes plus my 'Sunday best' uniform. Most welcome of all was the twenty or so photographs of the family that I'd brought with me. Stealing a couple of pillowcases from the store down the corridor I packed everything into them and took them out to stow in the saddlebags of the altab.

Dave appeared back at about half past twelve, followed shortly thereafter by George and then Colin, the latter enthusing about the flying belts. Elaine made coffee, the last of the supply she informed us, and we settled down to a long discussion. My contribution was taken first. I told them all that had happened in the two days since they relocated and added: "As you know, Peter was planning to lift the first of the crops tomorrow, weather permitting. He'll put aside equal quantities for you and send them with the lorry when it returns with our workers in the evening. He's had a look at one root of potatoes and tells me the average size is about that of a large plum. He's allocating two per person, plus two large cabbage leaves. For the first three weeks he suggests we only repeat that once a week to give the potatoes time to swell: after that we'll start lifting on a daily basis. Later on this week he plans to thin out the carrots, so you can expect some small ones on Thursday or Friday. We'll also send you some lettuce."

Colin followed me and sketched his plans for Seashore, which would be a community for two dozen people. "We've cut the timber needed for the bridge at Junction and Dan and the engineers are going to build it tomorrow. Not so good news on crossing Broad River, I'm afraid. We estimate that it's just over thirty metres wide at Riverside and probably another ten metres wide once you get past Junction. Although there are conifers tall enough to span that distance, Paul reckons that the structure would be too weak. With no means of preserving or weatherproofing wood it would start to rot fairly soon anyway. The only suggestion that he could come up with is to cut a metal plate out of the wreck. Trouble is, it would be a major operation to get a plate that size and weight from here to the river and then get it across. The only way we can think of doing it is to get a lifeship to drag it. I'm reluctant to risk that, as it could damage the lifeship. It looks as though we'll have to put the idea on to the back burner for a while and consider it at a later date."

The reports from George and Dave were almost identical. The layouts of their respective sites had been planned and cabin building would begin when the personnel designated to that task returned from their two-day visit to Landfall. Work had already begun on stripping fields ready for ploughing. As soon as the first cabins were occupied the ducks and geese would be resuscitated and taken to their new homes; the ducks to Riverside, the geese to Junction. At the same time the cows, chickens and sheep would be divided between the four centres. The pigs would go to Riverside and the turkeys to Junction. The only difficulty would be with the bulls, as there were only three between four sites. Obviously one bull would have to be alternated between two and we decided that Riverside and Junction should share. I was thankful it wasn't Landfall. Shepherding a full-grown bull on to a lorry and taking it twelve miles every once in a while didn't appeal to me!

We spent some time discussing dividing up the furniture and fittings on the *Sunrise*.

"There are ninety-two single bunk beds in the ship's cabins that are left," George reported. "As and when they're freed up by people moving into their huts we'll allocate them. If my arithmetic is correct that's just about enough for one between two. Dan can make any extra ones we need once he's finished his building programme. I did consider the shelves in the refrigeration units, but they're not really suitable. Between the seats in the lifeships and the chairs in the wreck they'll be more than two per person. You've got twenty-five cabins built already, Matt, so we'll send you up more chairs and your allocation of tables over the next couple of weeks. As you know, each of the ship's cabins had a small table in it, so between those and the ones from the recreational areas there'll be enough for each cabin, plus a few over for canteens. We'll also split up the blankets and pillows and send them out in due course, together with towels, bedding and kitchen equipment."

By four o'clock we'd covered everything we could think of and Colin brought the meeting to a close. "George will have the radio links working between here and Landfall by tonight, so we can contact each other if there's anything urgent before next Sunday. As soon as the first cabins are up in the three new locations we'll complete the links to those. Come on, Matt. We'll get you loaded up for your return trip."

I felt like a beast of burden on the way back with two large bags on my back. In addition to the two lots of my personal belongings I was carrying yeast, sugar and more plastic bowls and cutlery. Long before I reached Landfall I was wishing I'd left them to come by lorry. But the welcome I got when I distributed them just before the evening meal made up for my sore and bruised shoulders.

CHAPTER THIRTEEN

What we soon came to refer to as the daily pony express arrived just after the morning meal next day. Apart from the four men who were to shadow Dan's building group the lorry carried Michael Lytwyn plus some chairs and tables. There were also three containers of milk, a welcome sight, together with a box full of plastic beakers. I'd warned Susan to stand by and took Michael to meet her first before depositing him into the capable hands of Dr. Wallace. I thought Emma looked a bit put out at his arrival and resolved to have a quiet word with her that evening. I also took delivery of the two flying belts, which I stored for the moment in my ship. Later on in the day I would pass them to the doctor and give him and his assistants a lesson in how to use them.

The four of us who were the remnants of the farming section enjoyed our work that Monday. Under a burning sun and Peter Gibson's direction we started by lifting the potatoes. As we lifted each root we passed them to Peter, who carefully separated out the smaller ones and counted the rest into a sack. As soon as we'd enough for the Landfall contingent he prepared another sack for those at Central. Those below average size he proposed to pass on to Cassie to be stored and used as seed for the following year.

"With the warm climate here and the good soil we don't need to worry about the size of those we use for seed," he told me. "Just to be on the safe side I'll put some bigger ones aside later on, but it shouldn't be necessary."

After we'd finished work on the potatoes we moved on to the field where the cabbage was growing. Armed now with knives we repeated the performance, carefully cutting two large outside leaves off each plant, with Peter counting them into sacks. I noticed that at the far end of the field he'd put sticks beside two or three rows with bits of coloured cloth attached to them. "They're the ones that we'll let go to seed for next year," he explained.

Back in camp for a midday break I was accosted by Eileen, who looked excited. At her invitation I followed her into the small laboratory that she had set up in Dave's old ship.

"I may be wrong," she began, "but I think the fruit on the clover tree is just starting to reach maturity. Look."

She selected one of the fruits from a pile of a dozen or so. Bright yellow in colour, it consisted of three lobes in the shape of a clover leaf, each lobe being some two and a half inches in diameter and about half an inch thick. In the centre of each lobe was a tiny black spot beneath the skin.

"That spot wasn't apparent when I looked at some of the fruit on Saturday," she said. "I'm fairly certain that once that appears it denotes the fruit is ripe. Apart from the appearance of the black spot it's soft, whereas those without the spot are still hard. I did an analysis on one earlier and all I could find is water, citric acid and glucose, plus cellulose in the skin and traces of retinol, thiamine and ascorbic acid. That's vitamins A, B and C in case you don't know."

"Thanks for the lecture. As it happened I didn't know. We'll soon find out if they're ready," I assured her. "Come on and we'll rout out the good doctor to organise one of his food testing sessions."

The doctor had moved into Colin's old ship over the weekend. He'd fitted the survival room up as a small, very small, consulting room. As soon as someone could be spared to undertake the work he intended to subdivide the main cabin to make a bedroom for himself and a makeshift operating theatre. We found him in the consulting room. He and his two assistants were poring over some sheets of paper covered in his spidery handwriting. We showed him the fruit and explained our errand. After a good look at the samples Eileen showed him he went outside to round up a few volunteers, having already accepted Eileen and myself. Though they begged him to he wouldn't take Michael or Emma, joking that if the fruit was indeed poisonous he couldn't afford to lose two assistants. When I asked if losing a committee member and a biologist ranked as unimportant he merely smiled.

In all six of us were selected to take the test. We were each given one lobe of the fruit, with the usual instructions to take a very small bite at first and spit it out immediately if it tasted unpleasant. Looking braver than I felt I took a very small amount. The skin was soft and easy to bite through. I let it lie on my tongue for a few seconds before gingerly starting to chew. The flavour seemed faintly familiar, though I couldn't quite place it. It was very sweet and tasted heavenly, which wasn't surprising after not having tasted fruit of any kind for nearly four months. It needed a second and larger bite before I could pin down what the taste reminded me of. Then I realised.

"Passion fruit," I exclaimed.

One of the other volunteers nodded. "You're right," she said. "Passion fruit with just a hint of pomegranate."

The three or four spectators were looking on enviously, but the doctor refused to let them partake. "I'll give each of the six of you a whole fruit after the evening meal. If none of you show any reaction by morning I'll pass it for general consumption but no-one is to touch them before that."

As we walked away I asked Eileen if she'd been able to assess how many ripe specimens there were.

"All the dozen or so that I got came from one tree only and there were plenty other fruits close to ripeness. At a guess I'd say that there are sixty or seventy clover trees in the forest near us. I reckon there's enough to let everyone have as many as they want."

"We won't have to supply the other lot with any, either, as they'll have their own supplies," I reflected. "If the doc gives the okay tomorrow I'll detail a couple of full time pickers to keep us supplied. What about the dandelion tree and the oval and square bushes?"

"Make sure your pickers are young and athletic," Eileen warned me. "They'll need to climb the trees to get at the fruit. Most of it is out of reach from the ground. As for the rest, the oval bush has fruit of a deep maroon colour. They're round, about the size of a damson and have a stone in the middle. The one I cut open was still very hard, so I don't think they're ripe yet. Nuts are forming on the dandelion tree, but it's too early to say what size they'll be. At the moment they're like small acorns. The square bush doesn't look as though it will be any use to us. It has winged seeds like a sycamore, which don't look remotely edible."

Before heading back to the fields I did a quick tour of inspection, starting off with the cave we were using as a kitchen and dining hall. The smell emanating told me that it was fish that night. Dorothy and her crew were busy washing potatoes and cabbage.

"Do you remember how to cook them after all this time?" I asked her with as straight a face as I could muster.

She gave me an old-fashioned look and with an equally straight face she replied: "Oh, do you have to cook them?"

I laughed, and she went on: "There's just one problem. Normally I would shred the cabbage, but as we're rationed to two leaves per person I'm going to have to cook it whole, though it's not so nice that way."

"I shouldn't worry," I told her. "We'll all be so thrilled at getting vegetables again that no-one's likely to complain."

Next I went to see Cassie and the crofting section. She showed me round proudly and told me that she would be supplying lettuces on Wednesday, one per person both for Landfall and Central. Another week would see the first tomatoes on the menu. A fair number were now reddening or yellowing. Finally I checked on the building group. I was pleased to see that the visitors were not just observing, but had already started felling trees and shaping the wood under the supervision of our existing workforce.

Bernard Stocks

Before the evening meal I took young Emma Beaton aside. She was a bright youngster, medium height, plump with fair curly hair. She had also begun to show a maturity beyond her years, so I had no qualms about coming directly to the point.

"You didn't look too pleased to see Michael this morning," I began. "I know it means that Dr. Wallace can't give you quite so much attention now, but you must realise that Michael has already got a year or more of study behind him and it's important for him to work with you both to gain the extra knowledge that he'll need. I'm sure the doctor will see that you're not neglected."

She had the grace to hang her head. "I can't help how I feel," she objected. "But I promise I won't let it get to me. And Michael is very nice. But I'm worried I'll just be treated as a nurse and nothing more from now on."

"I'll have a word with the doctor," I promised. "But I'm sure nothing is further from his thoughts. We'll soon have four separate communities. As they grow we'll need a doctor in each one and you will be one of them."

It was a festive meal that evening. It started on the right note, with each person being handed a beaker with about a third of a pint of fresh milk. Even the children, who might have been expected to turn up their noses at cabbage and potatoes, tucked in with relish. Susan and I were sitting with Dr. Wallace and Michael and I could see the former looking round approvingly at intervals. "This will do everybody good, particularly the children," he remarked when he realised that I was watching him. "If that clover fruit pans out as expected I'll be reasonably happy with our diet from now on". After the meal I and the other five volunteers were given a whole clover fruit each, to the envy of everyone around. So far we had had no ill effects.

During the day I'd realised that I had a number of important decisions to make in the coming few weeks. After the evening meeting I made out a list of all that had to be done. Suddenly I felt a weight of responsibility on my shoulders. There would be no more consulting with the other members of the committee and reaching a joint agreement. These were decisions I would have to make off my own bat – and stand by the consequences. I tried talking one or two of the matters over with Susan, but she wasn't a great deal of help.

"You'll know what's the right thing to do," she told me. "Everyone likes you and they'll go along with you whatever you decide."

I went in search of Nicola. She'd attached herself to the catering group on the grounds that it was the only place she could find things to do while she only had the use of one arm. But she was even less help than Susan.

"I meant it when I said I don't want any responsibility," she emphasised. "You can count on my full support, though, whatever you decide on."

The first item on my list was education. The arrangements we'd made were working reasonably well, but with another fifteen children and more teachers they could now be put on a more formal basis. I got on the radio to George and we arranged for all the teachers to meet at Central on the Wednesday. We had six in all: three at Landfall plus Dave's partner Fiona and two others among the new arrivals. Then I sought out our three, William Haddow, a middle-aged man who'd been deputy headmaster at a large secondary school in Lancashire and a woman in her late twenties from Portsmouth who'd had experience in teaching both primary and special needs children. They were enthusiastic, even when I pointed out to them that they'd have to walk the six miles or so to the wreck.

The following morning I tackled the second item on my list. The three people that we'd allocated to making clothing had been working wonders. Already they'd produced a dozen or so of what they jokingly called 'this year's fashion model'. It was simply a one piece round-necked garment made out of shig skin, resembling a dress without a belt. They'd made two varieties, one without sleeves for summer wear and one with sleeves for the winter. They'd also made half a dozen pairs of shoes, similar to moccasins. The soles were made from the hide of the mammoth, laboriously cut and shaped by hand with a knife. For the rest of the shoe it was back to the shig skin. One or two people, particularly those of the men who were getting thin on top, had been complaining about the heat of the sun, so our intrepid threesome had produced a kind of skull cap. Now I had a new task for them.

"I don't want you to abandon what you're doing altogether," I instructed them. "But I'd like you to make a start on baby clothes. I know there's another five months or so before we'll need them, but it won't do any harm to have a supply ready before then. As you no doubt realise, we're going to need quite a lot." If anything that was an understatement. Nineteen pregnancies had been confirmed so far at Landfall alone. With nappies unavailable it was almost certain that the babies would need to be changed several times a day. At a conservative estimate that meant each one would need five changes of clothing. "Try and design something that needs as little sewing as possible. We're going to have a problem with thread in the short term."

The engineers had designed a prototype spinning wheel, but so far had not got round to building and testing it. Since the arrival of the *Sunrise* we'd had one bonus in the shape of three large sacks of cotton seed. That meant that once we could spin we'd have a source of both wool and cotton, but in the meantime stocks were running low.

The teachers' meeting lasted most of the day, but at the end of it they'd come up with an agreed curriculum and timetable to be applied in all four communities. All children under fifteen would attend lessons for three hours each morning, Monday to Friday, starting in the following week. In the afternoons they would move on to their chosen apprenticeships. The main subjects would be English, Maths and computing, suitable books having been identified and shared out from the ship's library. Once we'd had time to survey the planet in more detail we'd add geography and some elementary geology to the list. Eileen had been persuaded to give a lesson in biology to each group once a week, mainly centring on the flora and fauna of New Britain, but making the occasional mention of the variety of species on Earth. The engineers were to be approached with a view to including an occasional lecture on basic physics and electronics. In contrary to the opinions we'd expressed in our committee the teachers had unanimously decided to teach some of Earth's history.

"All the children here are old enough to remember Earth and its teeming millions," the former deputy headmaster explained. "It's only fair to give them some background and explain how they've come to live on this god-forsaken world on the far side of nowhere."

On Thursday, the trainees having returned to their own sites, I suspended work on the cabin building to enable the group time to construct a pen for the chickens we were due to receive. This was not an easy task. The walls had to be high enough to prevent the birds escaping, but the structure had to be light enough to be moved every so often as the chickens consumed the grass within. After some discussion we decided on two separate pens. Each one was about three metres square, with a door. In each of the two opposite walls we cut a small opening large enough for a bird to get through, with a sliding shutter. In this way we could move one pen at a time to back on to the other. All four walls were detachable for ease of movement. Into each pen we put a small covered hut for shelter. Once we started harvesting the wheat we would put straw down inside the huts. The job was completed by the following Tuesday and we took delivery of twelve hens and a cockerel, plus some poultry feed the day after. I put Nicola in charge of the flock: it was a job she could manage easily with one hand.

The day after we took delivery of the chickens our four cows and our bull arrived. Gavin Stewart and another man had herded them, on foot, all the way from the wreck. Peter Gibson was the only one among us who knew how to milk a cow, but two of the women volunteered to learn. They were soon proficient and took turns at the morning milking. From that time on we had milk with all our meals. Dorothy, ever on the lookout for new things to try, attempted to make both butter and cheese, but with little success. I added another item to the list I was preparing for the engineers, a churn, power driven if possible.

On average our hens began to produce eight or nine eggs a day. The five children were given one every day and we had a rota for the remainder. That meant we each got a boiled egg about once every two and a half weeks!

Sunday's committee meeting brought reports of progress on all fronts. The first cabins were nearing completion on the three new sites. Stripping of fields had begun and the bridge at Junction completed. The two engineers had already set up wind turbines at Riverside and Junction and were ready to connect them to the main generator in the *Sunrise*. Once the link up was complete water turbines would be added. Seashore presented a problem. It was too far away for a connection to be made to the *Sunrise*. Eventually it was George who propounded the solution. We would move one of the remaining lifeships down to Seashore at the earliest possible opportunity to enable a supply to be provided through its generator. Colin and Elaine were enthusiastic about the idea, as it meant they could relocate immediately. They would live in the lifeship until all the cabins were ready.

"It means we can be on hand all the time to superintend operations," Colin stated. "These flying belts are all very well at the moment, but they won't be so pleasant to use in cold or wet weather."

It was at that meeting also that we finally issued a statement on the question of marriage. It simply ruled that those who wished to get married could do so. A form of marriage ceremony would be agreed with the two ladies who provided our Sunday services. The remainder of the couples would simply continue as they were. Divorce or separation would be permissible if both parties were in agreement. Children would remain with the mother in all but the most exceptional circumstances. Finally, no objection would be made to any man taking two partners, providing all three parties were agreeable to the arrangement. This last proposal didn't meet with universal approval, but with more women than men it was necessary to give every woman of childbearing age a chance to have a family

CHAPTER FOURTEEN

The next couple of weeks saw a sustained improvement in our diet. From the middle of August we had at least one vegetable with our evening meal, often supplemented by lettuce or tomatoes. Doctor Wallace had a short spell of extra activity caused by two of the children and two adults partaking too freely of the clover fruit. Happily all that resulted was a bout of vomiting and a temporary loss of appetite. The first fruits on the oval bush had ripened and been tested with no ill effects. Again I was accepted as a volunteer. This time the taste was easier to define, less sweet than the clover fruit and with a distinct flavour of grapefruit.

By now less than a dozen couples and three singles, Nicola among them, were sleeping in the caves; the rest had cabins of their own. Susan and I were still in the lifeship and Doctor Wallace in his. With only one builder operating it was taking about ten days to complete a cabin but I wasn't too worried as it was obvious they'd all be ready before the worst of the winter. The biggest problem I had to face around that time was the deployment of the workforce. With over a dozen less bodies to play with and an increasing amount of harvesting to be done I had to work out a rota almost on a daily basis. My solution was to reduce the crofting and catering sections to the barest minimum.

It was the cereal crops that posed the worst headache. The wheat and oats were now ready for harvesting. Everything had to be done by hand; the cutting, the threshing and the winnowing. There was a shortage of sacks, so every spare container had to be brought into use. I could only spare two people to grind the crops when they were brought back to camp. At first I put them into the now nearly empty survival room in my lifeship, but the amount of dust generated soon made working conditions impossible for the two women, even though we fashioned masks for them to wear. Thankfully the coffee grinders were powered by rechargeable batteries, so the two of them moved outside where the slightest breeze blew the dust away.

The Far Side of Nowhere

On the first of September, when we gathered for the evening meal, a tantalising smell was emanating from the catering cave. It took me a moment or two to realise what it was, then it came to me. Baking bread! Dorothy had made a stew for the meal, shig meat of course, and baked enough bread for one loaf between four people. It was a sheer delight to have bread that was not only consumed during the meal but used to sop up the gravy afterwards! True the flour generated by the coffee grinders, and hence the bread itself, was much coarser than that which had been properly milled, but that didn't worry us in the slightest. After that we had bread at least twice a week and porridge for the morning meal with the same frequency.

An unpleasant task awaited our committee on the first Sunday of that month. At Central, the evening before, two young men in their early twenties, both surviving passengers, had abducted a young girl of thirteen, taken her into a nearby forest and attempted to rape her. Thankfully she'd managed to get free long enough to scream twice. Two or three men walking nearby effected a rescue, by which time she had been half strangled. The perpetrators had run off, but a posse was quickly formed and they were run to earth just before midnight. They were now locked in a small storage room on the *Sunrise*. We had a quick discussion, agreed that Colin should act as judge, and then had them brought before us, handcuffed and with an escort.

They were a surly looking pair. The girl who had been attacked was not well enough to attend, but Elaine read out a statement the victim had made. This recorded that she had been at the edge of the forest alone, picking fruit, when the accused had grabbed her and carried her deeper into the wood. George then stated the charges against the two men and asked if they had anything to say in their defence.

They looked at each other, then the taller of the two said with a touch of bravado: "We didn't do anything wrong. She was asking for it."

"Is that why you tried to strangle her as well?" I asked him. "Or was she asking for that, too." He made no reply.

We called one other witness, a middle-aged man. He testified that the day before the incident he'd seen both the men pestering the girl and had warned them off. We then dismissed the witness and had the escort take the prisoners outside while we debated our verdict. It didn't take long, as it was an open and shut case. Then the prisoners were called back in.

Colin looked at the two men sternly. "We find you guilty on all counts," he told them. "If the girl had died I would have had no hesitation in taking you out and hanging you from the nearest tree. Luckily for you she survived, so we have to devise some other method of punishment. We do not have a jail, and in any case we cannot spare anyone to act as warders. There is no room in the society we are building here for men like you, so it is the verdict of this court that you are taken to a place as far away from here as possible and left to survive as best you can." Turning to the escort he added: "Put them in the lifeship, keep them handcuffed and stand guard over them till we're ready to ship them out."

When they'd gone, Colin turned to George. "Will you and Matt do the necessary? I suggest you take them west over the ocean. If there are any islands a suitable distance away leave them there; if not carry on till you come to land again. Leave them one knife each. Take a stun gun with you and knock them out before you take off the handcuffs – don't take the risk that they'll turn on you."

Five minutes later we were airborne. We'd locked the prisoners in the storeroom as they'd started whining the minute we'd dismissed the escort. Just over a thousand miles out across the ocean we spotted a fair-sized island, about ten miles long by six miles wide. Circling over it we noted that it was well served with vegetation similar to that of our own region and that there were herds of shigs scattered across the whole area. A small lake in the southern half of the island guaranteed a supply of fresh water.

"This looks the perfect place," said George. "While I'm putting her down would you go and render our guests unconscious."

I did just that, giving them no time to talk before shooting them. They would be out for about an hour, giving them a couple of hours of daylight to find food and shelter. George landed the ship in a small clearing. We carried the two of them out, took off their handcuffs, put the knives beside them and lifted off, all in the space of five minutes.

Halfway home I voiced a thought that had been in my mind. "Do you think they might be able to build a boat or a raft and sail back?"

"Doubt it," George said after a few moments' contemplation. "None of the trees I saw are big enough to hollow out for a canoe. As for a raft, they'd have nothing to tie the components together. There are no creeping plants or vines from which they could make some sort of rope. In any case, they couldn't see the direction we took, so even if they did put something together they wouldn't know which way to sail. I'm ninety-nine point nine percent certain we've seen the last of them."

Paul Cooper and Walter Butter, the two engineers, returned to Landfall in mid September.

"We've done most of what's needed at the other places," Paul informed me. "The only major job left is to set up the machinery for getting salt from the sea and provide some kind of piping system to make the job easier. But we can't progress on that until there are enough people permanently in Seashore. As we both feel more at home here we decided to come back. George has given us the use of a couple of altabs, so if we are needed elsewhere we can get there quickly enough. Now I gather you've got a few projects lined up for us."

I gave them the list I'd made out. "I'll leave it you to decide what order you want to tackle them in, though it would be handy to have the churns as

The Far Side of Nowhere

soon as possible. There isn't exactly a surplus of milk, but there's enough now to be thinking of making a small amount of butter and cheese."

The two of them went off quite happily to start work. Truth to tell, my mind was only half on what I was doing around that time. A pressing personal problem was occupying more than half of my attention. It arose from an incident a couple of days previously. As had become my habit, I was walking round the camp last thing at night checking that all was well. A slight noise from the direction of the southern wood took me to the fringes to investigate. A short distance from me I saw a vague shape. I called out and moved towards it. To my surprise, in the dim moonlight I discovered it was Nicola, standing still and gazing sightlessly into the forest.

"What on earth are you doing here at this time?" I asked her

She turned to face me. "I often come here at night. It's so peaceful and I have a problem getting to sleep with this arm." She held it out towards me. She had dispensed with the sling, but still had a plaster cast from wrist to elbow.

I don't quite know how it happened or who made the first move, but suddenly she was in my arms and we were kissing passionately. Every last thought fled from my mind: all I could think of was her body pressing against mine, the taste of her lips and her hair brushing against my cheek. What followed was as inevitable as night following day.

Sometime later, as we lay in each other's arms, Nicola stirred and whispered: "What happens now?"

"I don't know," I sighed. "This is a complication we could have done without and one that I never expected. I know now that I want to be with you, but I just can't walk out on Susan. She's stood by me since the day we arrived, and there's the baby to consider."

We lay silent for several minutes, then I stood up and pulled Nicola to her feet. "We'd better get back or they'll be sending out search parties," I remarked.

"Tell me we can see each other from time to time," she begged. "You maybe never realised, but I had a crush on you even as far back as when we were in Space College. I kept waiting for you to make a move, but you never did."

"I was tempted," I admitted. "But I was so desperate to pass out that I made a vow to myself when I started at the college that I wouldn't let anything, not even girls, distract me." I sighed once more. "If only you'd been with us on the first day we landed. Things could have been so different. As for seeing each other, I'll have to think about it. Whatever we do we'll have to be ultra careful. In an environment like this everyone is under the microscope and it's so, so difficult to keep anything hidden for long."

We returned to the main camp without anyone seeing us, risking a kiss goodnight as I left her at the mouth of the cave she was sleeping

Bernard Stocks

in. Luckily Susan was dead to the world when I got back to the lifeship. Had she seen me I'm sure my demeanour must have given her cause for suspicion at the very least.

My dilemma was still much in my thoughts when I attended the committee meeting the following Sunday, and I still hadn't found an acceptable solution. Perhaps it was as well that Colin and George had come up with a new project to occupy my mind.

"We need to get rid of the fuel from the three remaining lifeships in the hold so that we can start breaking them up," Colin began. "Also the engineers have asked us if we can empty one of the main tanks from the *Sunrise*. They want to use it to make boilers to extract salt from the seawater. So I suggest we use both the ships and the fuel to do some exploration."

George took up the narrative. "What we propose is this. Sometime during the week we'll take one of the lifeships up above the atmosphere and make three or four orbits, taking photographs as we go. From these we should be able to make a rough map of the whole planet. This we'll study next Sunday and decide then which areas we want to explore in more detail."

"Are you thinking of moving away from here, then?" I asked.

"Definitely not," George replied. "We're too entrenched here to think of starting again elsewhere. No, what we want to do is firstly establish some sort of picture of the world we're on and then check for a thousand or so miles around here to see if there is any change in the vegetation or the wildlife. It would also help if we could discover coal or minerals. We desperately need things like cement, clay to make bricks, a better supply of salt than we can get from the sea. All that and a host of other things that would make life easier."

"There's one other thing," remarked Elaine. "We can also establish once and for all if we're the only human inhabitants. Though we've seen no signs to date doesn't mean that some other ship may have landed here in the past, or even since we've been here."

"If we're all in agreement, then, I suggest George and Dave make the initial flight," said Colin. "Dave's our cartographer and photographer, so he's the natural choice for this trip. We'll split the remaining flights between us next Sunday. For today, as soon as this meeting's over, we should get the remaining lifeships out of the hold and check them over."

"I think you'll find number one is kaput," I said. "I had a quick look at it after the crash and saw it was damaged. That's why I took number two instead."

My prophecy proved to be correct. Number one had broken loose from its cradle, presumably at the moment of the collision, and the front and one side were dented and cracked. We decided to leave it in situ, drain the fuel tank and let the engineers dismantle it where it was. The four remaining ships seemed in good shape, so we flew them to a point about a quarter of a mile from the main ship and made our checks. Each had a full tank of fuel. The survival room and the provisions cupboard in each had already been cleared and the seats taken out from the main cabin, so no further preparations were needed. They were ready to fly.

I had deliberately avoided being alone with Nicola at any time, from discretion rather than choice. Then three days later my personal problems were solved in the most unexpected way. The evening gathering had been short and I had completed my nightly rounds before half past eight. Returning to our ship I was surprised to find Susan in tears. My immediate assumption was that that it had something to do with her pregnancy, but I was wrong. I comforted her as best I could while asking her what was the matter.

Eventually she calmed down and dabbed her tears dry. She looked directly at me for the first time since I'd come through the door. In a low tone she said: "I don't know how to break this to you, Matt. I've been tearing myself apart these last few days because I feel so guilty."

Again I assumed that her concerns were for the baby; that she'd damaged it or that she'd lost it in some way. I soothed her again.

"Whatever it is, you can tell me," I soothed. "I promise I won't be angry or upset."

Then it came out with a rush. "Michael and I are in love. I want to leave you and be with him. I wasn't going to tell you at all because I didn't want to hurt you after all you've done for me, but I can't go on being torn apart like this."

I looked at her for a long minute without speaking, then I asked her: "You're absolutely sure about this, are you?" She nodded without saying a word, and I took her hands in mine.

"You make me feel so ashamed," I said simply. "I'm equally guilty. I've fallen in love with someone too."

She looked at me closely. "It's Nicola, isn't it?"

"How did you know," I asked in surprise.

"I've seen the way she looks at you," she replied. "It didn't take me long to realise she was in love with you. The one thing I couldn't work out was how you felt about her."

"Not to change the subject, but does Michael know about the baby?"

"Yes, of course," she replied. "He's not worried about it. In fact he said that family life as such is going to be very different here than what we've known in the past. All the children in the future will have more communal care than parental care anyway." That was something that hadn't crossed my mind until now but I quickly realised the truth therein. Young Michael obviously had a good head on his shoulders. But now it was decision making time. I thought quickly.

"Unless you want to leave right now, I suggest we make the moves in the morning – **and** announce to everyone what we're doing. That way we'll avoid any gossip. In any case I think people will understand. You and Michael are close to each other in age, as are Nicola and I, so it's a more sensible arrangement. I suspect we won't be the only couple to split up. Now, there's a cabin almost ready, it just needs a few finishing touches tomorrow, so you and Michael can move in there and Nicola can come in here. Is that O.K. with you?"

Her eyes shining, she gave me a hug and a kiss. "That's fine. I just wish I'd known about you and Nicola earlier. I'd have saved myself some sleepless nights. Can I go and see Michael just now and tell him. You can see Nicola at the same time."

It took me a while to track her down, but I finally ran Nicola to earth in the catering cave, where she and Dorothy were cutting up fish for the following morning's meal. I drew Nicola to one side and quietly told her what had transpired. Impulsively she flung herself into my arms and kissed me. When I turned round I saw Dorothy watching us with raised eyebrows. There didn't seem any point in dissembling, so I told her what was happening.

"It's no secret," I reassured her. "We plan to tell everyone in the morning anyway, so you don't need to keep it to yourself."

After the girls had moved their respective belongings, which in any case were few, Michael drew me aside the next morning. "I can't say I'm sorry about what's happened," he told me. "I'm too happy at the way things have turned out. But I do apologise for not having the courage to tell you myself and for leaving it to Susan. I also wanted to assure you that I will take as great a care of your unborn child as I would one of my own."

I clapped him on the shoulder. "I know you will. More importantly right now, take good care of Susan. She's a very special girl."

I think I walked on air for the rest of the week. For certain I hadn't realised just how much the complication in my domestic life had been preying on my mind and affected my concentration. Apart from the joy I got from her physical presence our union reawakened Nicola's interest in the day to day running of the community. Whereas before she had shown no curiosity about the daily round I now found that she was more than willing to discuss things and give her opinion when I propounded my problems to her. There was a new zest and a new sparkle about her, too. I didn't need to ask if she was happy. I certainly was. In one aspect though I couldn't change her mind. I wanted her to join the committee, but she was adamant.

"I meant what I said to the others the day we got here, Matt," she emphasised one evening just before bedtime. "I'd had enough of space and I'd had enough of responsibility. Foolish maybe, but I had these dreams of finding the right man, marrying, settling down, raising a family and leading a normal life." She laughed. "Now my dreams have come true, even though the circumstances are a lot different from those I'd envisaged!" She laughed again. "So how about getting to work on the family aspect?"

The Far Side of Nowhere

"You've forgotten something," I reminded her. "You're not married yet. Will Saturday suit you?"

We didn't make a big deal out of it. After all, there was no chance of her getting a wedding dress, or me a suit for that matter. I did wear my best uniform for the occasion, though. It was a simple religious ceremony with all the camp present. We had no rings to exchange, but Nicola had one that she wore on her right hand, so she removed that and I solemnly placed it on the third finger of her left hand at the appropriate moment. Afterwards Dorothy provided a meal of bread and fruit!

CHAPTER FIFTEEN

The first thing I did when our committee gathered at Central the next day was to tell them of my altered circumstances. Dave was the first to congratulate me.

"You've made history again, Matt," he said with a grin as he shook my hand. I looked at him enquiringly. "You were the first person to arrive on this world, now you're the first to get a divorce."

"Hardly a divorce. Susan and I weren't officially married. Call it the first separation."

Then we got down to business. George and Dave had made three orbits of the planet on the previous Tuesday and another two on the Wednesday, all from different angles. From the photographs they'd taken Dave had made up a fairly accurate map of New Britain. There were four continents, all of approximately the same area and not too dissimilar in shape. One vast ocean spanned the rest of the world apart from the two polar ice caps, which were marginally smaller than those on Earth. Our various encampments were shown clearly on the picture of the continent that we were on and it confirmed what our amateur astronomer William Haddow had said some months before. Our present position equated roughly to that of central Spain on Earth.

"On the second day we landed at a couple of places on the continent furthest away from here," George reported. "They were about two thousand miles apart, one just north of the equator and one a couple of thousand miles further south. Maybe you won't be too surprised to find that the vegetation and the wild life were exactly the same as we have here. There were the same trees, shigs, gecks, the same birds and the same butterflies. The only difference was the temperature. At the equator it was just over a hundred degrees, further south about seventy-eight. We spent an hour or more at each place looking around but we couldn't find a single new thing to bring back to show Eileen."

The Far Side of Nowhere

"Not only that," Dave added. "I've blown up some of the photographs we took of the other two continents and they look exactly the same too. I think it's a fairly safe bet that apart from what might be in the sea we've seen all that nature has to offer right here."

One of the interesting things to emerge from the map that Dave had drawn was the geography of the continent we were on. To the north of our present position the coastline ran in a largely straight line all the way to the north coast. To the south, however, it ran straight for about three hundred miles and then swung westwards. This meant that if we travelled some four hundred miles due south we would find ourselves almost the same number of miles from the sea.. Another thousand miles further south the coastline gradually drifted eastwards again, so that by the time it reached the southernmost tip of the continent it was once more directly south of us.

Colin spoke up. "George and I have discussed this already, but we'll hear your views before making a final decision. In the light of what he's told us it seems pointless to do any detailed exploration of any of the other continents. We suggest that we make four trips on this one, two this week and two next. One should go to the north, one due east, one south-west and one south-east. Personally I don't think we'll find anything of interest, but we might just strike lucky and discover coal, oil or minerals. I'm not too hopeful though."

We agreed with his reasoning and left him to allocate the flights. "For this week I think Elaine and Dave can tackle the northern safari while Matt and I head south-east. Next week George and I will head east and Elaine and Matt south-west. Tuesday for the first trip this week and Wednesday for the second. That way if one survey discovers something that needs further investigation we can follow it up immediately. Take-off from here, let's say nine a.m. That suitable to everybody?" There was no dissension.

Monday brought another problem in its wake. Returning from their daily hunting safari Harry and June reported that they had sighted a herd of mammoths heading our way. They were still three miles off, but advancing steadily and would reach the camp some time the following day. Breaking out the six remaining stun guns I called for three more volunteers and we went out to try and turn the herd. Reasoning that the previous method had been successful and kept them away for several months I laid down similar tactics. Somewhat reluctantly I gave the order to kill two of the beasts. I didn't like doing so, but when the babies arrived we would need a supply of the mammoth hides and we had no idea of when the herd might be within reach for a third time.

Once again the manoeuvre achieved our objective. We waited for an hour, and by then the herd was a mile distant and moving steadily away from us. The two dead beasts we left for a working party to come and cut them up and bring the hides, horns and hooves back to camp. The rest of the remains I ordered to be buried. Whether the flesh would decompose in the assumed absence of any bacteria was a question I couldn't answer, but with luck it would enrich the soil. In two or three years' time I estimated that our fields would extend to this point.

Wednesday morning quickly arrived and I was at Central well before nine. Dave was hanging around waiting for me and gave me a rundown on the survey that he and Elaine had made the previous day.

"A big fat nothing," he told me with some disgust. "We went due north almost up to the polar ice cap and landed there on a small island. There was no vegetation and no wild life, not even a fish to be seen in the sea, which was lightly frozen anyway. Then we zigzagged back, landing three times in different scenery. One spot was in a valley of a mountain range, the peaks being three times as high as those behind Landfall. We thought we might find some traces of metals, maybe even gold, but we didn't. It was the same story in the other two spots, just the plants, birds, fish and animals we've seen already. The only worthwhile data that we've brought back is that the mammoths seem to prefer a colder climate. They're much more numerous the further north you go, right up to where the grass ends and the icy wastes begin."

A speck in the sky as we were talking heralded the arrival of Colin, using his flying belt. Once landed he wasted no time, but led the way to one of the three lifeships lying beside the wreck of the *Sunrise*. "You take the controls, Matt," he said. "Thirty miles plus on a flying belt has lessened my appetite for being a pilot."

Once I'd taken the lifeship up to five thousand feet we held a quick discussion and decided to head east-south-east in a straight line until we reached the opposite coastline. Then we would follow the coast south until we were south-south-east and zigzag back to base. We wouldn't land on the outward leg unless we saw anything that might be worthy of closer inspection. The cockpit of the lifeships was a semi-circle of plexi-glass, giving a good all round view. The pilot's seat being on the right-hand side, Colin scanned to his left with a pair of binoculars, while I did the best I could with the naked eye on my side.

The countryside over which we passed showed little variation. Mostly it consisted of a flat plain, with here and there a range of low hills and the occasional river or small lake. Flocks of shigs were everywhere, though we only saw two herds of mammoths the whole day. There were woods a-plenty, both deciduous and coniferous, and on one occasion Colin spied a vast forest in the distance, stretching some forty miles.

We reached the coast after just over two hours of flying, a distance of some two thousand, eight hundred miles. Here we got our first surprise of the day. Instead of the rocky seashore that bounded our ocean to the west, we found mile after mile of sandy beaches, reminiscent of the Mediterranean. I landed the ship carefully on the sand and we spent nearly half an hour inspecting this new phenomenon. I had hoped we might find some new species of seaweed or some crustaceans amongst the sand, but there was nothing.

"It's a pity this is so far away," Colin remarked with a sigh. "This would be valuable when we get around to trying to make glass. There's very little sand anywhere around Seashore. I suppose we could come and collect a load now and again as long as the fuel holds out. Grab a sample to take back to Eileen and we'll be off again."

Airborne once more we swung out in an arc over the sea before returning to the coast and heading southwards. There were one or two small islands close to the shore from time to time, but none we deemed worth landing on. Colin was holding our rough map, and when he estimated that we had reached a point south-south-east of base he gave me the nod to head back inland. It was at this point that we started our slalom. Very soon I had to take the ship up to seven thousand feet as we encountered a range of hills with peaks rising to about six thousand feet.

The first leg of my zigzag had been southwards. I had turned north and was halfway through the second leg when Colin gave an exclamation.

"I thought I saw something glinting in one of the valleys down there," he said. "Circle round Matt and when I give the word take it down into the valley."

I did as he instructed, and as I banked I distinctly saw a flash of silvery metal on the floor of a long narrow cleft in the rock. There was just enough room to put the ship down, but long before we came to earth our suspicions were confirmed. With some excitement we got out for a closer look. Bits of metal, both large and small, were scattered over the ground

"It's the wreck of a space ship," Colin announced breathlessly as we walked around the bits and pieces. "A small scout ship by the look of it and... " here he broke off to pick up a chunk of the wrecked ship's hull. "I thought so. It's Russian. This must be the scout ship that they sent into a black hole when the *St. Petersburg* went missing."

"That's a thought," I said. "I wonder if the *St. Petersburg* is on this world somewhere."

"Unlikely," Colin replied. "It was even bigger than the *Caledonian Sunrise*. Those photographs that George and Dave took were pretty all-encompassing. There's no way they'd have missed something that big. If my memory serves me right these Russian scout ships had a four man crew, but I can't see any sign of bodies."

I wandered away from him and then called him over to where I stood. "Here's the reason, I guess," I said. I indicated a section of the hull about fifty feet in length and thirty feet wide. In the middle was a gaping hole as if someone had fired a large shell through it. "Looks like they were hit by a meteor or some chunk of space debris. Those scout ships of the Russians were just a single compartment. The crew must have died the instant they were struck and the bodies sucked out into space."

In another place we found among the wreckage some of the provisions the stricken ship must have carried. These consisted mainly of tinned meat and fruit, coffee, dried milk and unsurprisingly half a dozen bottles of vodka which by some miracle had survived the impact intact.

"This is going to be interesting," I remarked. "How do you divide six bottles between a hundred and eighty people?"

"Easy," Colin replied. He picked up the bottles one by one and smashed them against a nearby boulder. I looked at him with raised eyebrows. "What did you do that for?" I asked.

He looked sombre. "My father was an alcoholic and I've seen the misery that addiction to drink can cause. If we took that vodka back and handed it round it might give some people ideas about making their own booze and get them dependent on alcohol. I suppose it will happen anyway in the fullness of time, but I'd like to delay it as long as possible. Which reminds me, you might tell Eileen to keep a close guard on that yeast she's producing. If anyone queries it tell them we need all the yeast she can make for bread and there's none to spare. Thankfully there's an absence of yeast spores in the atmosphere on this world, so there's no natural source of fermentation."

We gathered up the remaining provisions plus a few chunks of metal for analysis. The Russian ship was probably twice the size of our lifeships, so there was no way we could load all the salvage. "Someone can bring the engineers here soon," Colin said. "They can break up the bigger portions and ferry all the scrap back to Central. With what's in the *Sunrise* once we've broken it up we've got more than we need at present, but the time will come when we run short. This will be valuable then. What's left of the instruments and the drive will come in handy too. I don't see anything else of interest here, so let's head home."

Back in the air we soon left the mountainous region behind us and then it was back to the all too familiar terrain. We landed briefly a couple of times, once beside a fair-sized lake, but apart from noting that the fish that we could see therein were the same as those in Narrow River we spied nothing to interest us. It was close to six o'clock by the time we reached Central. I left Colin to recount our day's adventures to the others and headed back to Landfall for the evening meal and the night's meeting.

My trip with Elaine the following Tuesday proved even more exciting. We followed a similar pattern, heading due south in a straight line. We didn't go as far as the south coast of the continent. After three thousand miles we turned due west until we reached the coast and then started the zigzag. About halfway home we extended one arm a couple of hundred miles out to sea. Elaine was at the controls and just as she turned landwards again my binoculars picked out a chain of islands in the distance to the north. After she changed course to due north I soon spotted that there were six islands extending from the coastline out to sea. The outer three were quite small, then came two large islands and one slightly smaller one. When she took us down for a closer look I discovered that it was low tide and that the two largest islands were joined by a narrow, natural causeway. Each was some fifty miles long, roughly like a flattened egg in shape, and thirty miles at the widest point. Both they and the island nearest the shore were thickly covered by trees, but what really made us excited was that they looked totally different from the three types of trees we'd seen on New Britain to date. Spying a clearing in the middle of one of the islands just large enough to accommodate the ship Elaine landed.

"Thank heaven these things land and take off vertically," she exclaimed as we touched down. "A couple of feet either way and we'd have been hanging out of the trees!"

It was almost true. When we opened the door and stepped outside we had little more than two yards of space to walk around in. But our concentration was on the trees in our vicinity. Our first impressions were confirmed immediately: these were totally different from the clover and dandelion trees. They were all of the one variety and in shape reminded me of cypress trees back on earth. The leaves were long, triangular in shape and very slightly serrated at the edges. They were also a much darker shade of green as well. Here and there were small bunches of tiny red berries about half the size of a redcurrant. The other difference between this forest and the ones we knew was that there were no bushes to be found, only smaller trees of the same species.

"Let's get a couple of samples of the leaves and the fruit for Eileen to study," Elaine suggested.

"Do that," I said, "while I have a look around and see if there's a young tree small enough to uproot and take back with us. It will be interesting to see if they'll grow anywhere else."

I hunted around for ten minutes but the smallest tree I could find was some six feet high. I pulled at it with all my strength but couldn't budge it and we had no spade on the ship. Then I had an idea. There was a couple of hunting knives in the ship. Taking one I cut off three twigs some four feet long, put some damp soil into a container and planted the twigs in it. Eileen could stick them in the ground to see if they'd grow. If they didn't we could always return better prepared and collect a tree with roots.

I took the ship up and headed back to the coast. The nearest island to the shore was also thickly wooded with the same trees. The channel between it and the shore was very narrow, at one point passing between two rocky cliffs. Just as I approached the shore Elaine gave a cry. "Matt, down there. Look."

I looked where she was indicating and couldn't believe my eyes. A river ran down into the sea and to the north was an area covered with what I can only describe as skeletons of trees. Even more amazing was the sight of a number of small animals, most of whom were stationary and gazing

Bernard Stocks

up at us. Taking the ship half a mile from the ghost forest I landed with the cabin facing it and we both trained out binoculars.

"I don't believe it," Elaine said in a hushed voice. "They're cats!"

I studied them closely. "They're very similar," I agreed. "But their ears are round instead of pointed and the tails are shorter, about half the length of a normal cat's tail. And look at the eyes. I've never seen a cat with purple eyes before."

Other than that there was no difference. All the beasts that we could see were short-haired, but there was a variety of colours similar to those of Earth cats. I spotted black, white, grey, ginger, silver and a metallic blue plus combinations of these. There was a uniformity of size, too, equivalent to a small adult earth cat.

"Matt, they're starving," Elaine said with a catch in her voice. "And there's a lot of dead ones, too."

This was true enough. I could see over a dozen corpses, including a litter of four kittens, their pathetic little bodies rigid in death. Those that were alive were pitifully thin and I could see the bones sticking out under the fur. Here and there a litter of kittens were pulling desperately at a mother's teats. Then a thought struck me and I scanned the bare upper reaches of the trees. I saw two or three cats perched precariously near the top of different trees, vainly trying to reach the few remaining leaves.

"There's the problem," I said. "The leaves are their food and they've stripped the trees."

"We must do something to help them," pleaded Elaine. "Can we get them on the ship and ferry them across to the island?"

"I doubt if we could coax them into the ship," I opined. "It could be dangerous, too. There must be five or six hundred of them. If they decided to attack us we wouldn't stand a chance. They must have sharp claws to be able to climb trees and hang on the way those three are doing."

As I spoke Elaine drew my attention to the shore. Three of the beasts were sitting at the water's edge. One was a ginger colour slightly bigger than the others we'd seen, and he was flanked by two tabbies. But what held my attention was the way Ginger's head turned from one to the other of his two companions. It was for all the world as if they were... I whistled quietly. "If I didn't know better I would say they were talking to each other," I said.

"That's what I was thinking," Elaine replied. "If so it means they're classified as an intelligent species and covered by the First Directive."

"Bang goes our chance of a change of diet then," I remarked intending humour.

"Don't you think of anything apart from your stomach," snapped Elaine. "This is important. These could be the only surviving specimens of the planet's master race."

"In which case why are there so few of them?" I asked.

"How the hell do I know?" Elaine replied with some irritation. "Maybe the trees have died out over the years until only these few are left."

As we argued the ginger cat, braver than his fellows, was sliding into the water, obviously attempting to swim across to the island. But the current was too strong and after he'd gone less than five yards he was swept away. We moved back away from the shore and watched other groups of the beasts for about a quarter of an hour. At the end of that time we were ninety-nine per cent certain that they were communicating.

"One thing we can do is bring some food across to them," I said decisively. "Take us over to that island there and see if you can find somewhere to land. If not take us back to the clearing on the larger one. We'll bring back as many branches as we can carry. That will keep them going for a day or two; meantime we'll report back and see if we can find a permanent solution."

Elaine took off and quickly found a cove in which we could land. Armed with knives we spent the best part of an hour lopping branches from ground level. When the lifeship was full we flew back to the ghost forest. Being careful not to come too close to any of the cats we spread the branches we had culled over as wide an area as possible. Any time we came too close to the cats they retreated, watching us warily all the time. At one stage I laid some branches close to two of the dead bodies. Luckily one was male and one was female. Using gloves and a box I picked up the corpses to take back for Eileen to study. When we finally returned to the ship and went inside, one or two of the live beasts, braver than the rest, ventured cautiously to the nearest branch and started to eat. The rest soon followed, apart from two or three that did not seem to have the strength to move. Just before we took off again I studied the terrain through binoculars.

"Can you remember if there was any dynamite on the *Sunrise*?" I asked Elaine.

"I think so," she replied. "Most long distance space ships I've been on carried some for emergencies. Why, what did you have in mind?"

"You see that channel between the two cliffs?" She nodded. "If we can put a charge of dynamite at the base on one side or the other or both the rock should fall into the water and make a causeway. That will get the cats on to the first island and solve the problem for a long while. Even better, if we can then find a way of connecting that island with the two larger ones we can just about guarantee their long term future. I'll speak to Paul and Walter when I get back. If they agree we'll bring them out here tomorrow to see whether the idea's feasible."

We abandoned any notion of making further zigzags and followed the coastline for the rest of the way home. Though we still kept a sharp lookout we saw nothing of further interest.

CHAPTER SIXTEEN

As soon as I got back to Landfall I handed my specimens, animal and vegetable, over to Eileen. She showed great excitement at our discovery and immediately asked to be taken to the site the next day. Then I sought out Paul and Walter, our two engineers. I gave them a full account of what we'd found and asked about the dynamite. They weren't sure, but a quick radio link-up to George at Central established that there was indeed a small supply on the *Sunrise*. I told him what I intended. He was in full agreement and was quite happy to let me take a lifeship back to the site the following day. I made the necessary arrangements with Paul, Walter and Eileen.

Around eleven the next morning I landed a quarter of a mile away from the skeleton forest and we all studied the scene through binoculars. It was immediately apparent to me that the majority of the cats were more lively than they had been the previous day. Nearly all the leaves had vanished from the branches that we'd left and I suggested that before we did anything else we should get them a fresh supply of food. Eileen asked to be left at the site, so having warned her not to stray too close to the group I took off again. On the way to the first island I hovered over the narrow channel between that and the mainland to give the engineers a view of the cliffs. They had brought the dynamite with them. As Paul had remarked: "If the job is feasible there's no point in making two journeys."

After a good look at the layout the two conferred in low tones. "The cliff on the island is leaning inward, so that's not going to be much help," was Paul's opinion. "The one on the mainland, though, is inclined slightly seawards. If we put charges close to the base and about a third of the way up most of the rock should fall into the sea. Whether it fills the channel or not is in the lap of the gods."

Before moving on I studied the island through binoculars. It didn't take long to find what I was looking for, a stream running down to the sea twenty or thirty metres from the south side of the island's cliff. There would have been no point in getting the cats across if there was no water for them on the other side. Then we took another full load of branches back to the mainland and distributed them around. The cats were still wary of us and retreated whenever we approached. For the first time I heard a noise coming from them. It was difficult to define precisely, but it resembled a low growl made from deep in the throat. Eileen confirmed that they were indeed communicating with one another, both by sound and by the movement of their bodies and tails. Once all the branches were laid out Paul and Walter went off to inspect the cliff. They suggested that we left them to it. "There's no real danger," Walter explained, "but I'd rather there was no one else around while we're handling explosives."

Eileen and I watched in fascination, from a safe distance of course, as the cats attacked the food we had brought them. While doing so she gave me a summary of what she had found out when dissecting the two bodies I had brought back.

"Their internal arrangements are very similar to the shigs," she told me. "They also have two livers and two stomachs, two kidneys, but only a single heart. The reproductive organs are identical to those in Earth cats. I can confirm, too, that they are definitely vegetarian. When you told me about their lack of food and that several were dead I wondered if they might have had cannibal tendencies and fed off the bodies, but there's no indication of that at all. I saw no traces of fish in the stomachs either. Living so close to the water I thought there was a chance that they would catch and eat fish, but obviously not."

About an hour after the engineers had left us we heard two loud explosions some thirty seconds apart. After waiting for a couple of minutes to make sure there were no more to come we hurried down to the shore and walked along to the spot where the cliff had been. It was no longer a cliff. There was a heap of rock where it had once stood. Once we got close we could see that the channel was just about closed.

"We've a bit of work to do by hand to fill in the places where the water is still flowing over the top, but it shouldn't take too long," was Paul's greeting as we came within speaking distance.

"Won't there be a build up of water on this side?" I asked him. "If there's water flowing over the top of the pathway the cats won't attempt it."

"Look for yourself," replied Paul. "There's enough spaces in the rock that's under water for it to get through without coming over the top." This was true. Although the water level was appreciably higher on one side it was still a foot or so below the uneven top of the causeway that had been formed. There were still gaps towards the island side, and these we proceeded to fill with loose rock. Once there was a dry path to the island we spent another hour levelling out the traverse as best we could. It was still very uneven in places, but at least the cats would have a dry passage across.

"The only thing we've got to worry about now is how to persuade them to cross," I said when we'd finished the job to our satisfaction.

"Simple," Eileen observed. "We go and gather what's left of the branches and lay a trail down to this spot and across the causeway. It may take a while, but eventually one or two will lead the way and the rest will follow. To be on the safe side I think we should retire once we've laid the trail, though I'd like to stay and watch from some hidden point."

We quickly found a spot along the shore from which she could watch both the causeway and the main group before we moved the branches into the trail she had suggested. The area down to the shore we spread very thinly to encourage them to move on quickly. Once Eileen was safely bestowed at her post I took off with Paul and Walter to the far shore of the nearest island, where we landed on the beach. The channel between this and the large double island was at its narrowest point here, not much more than seven metres. Trees grew down almost to the water's edge.

Walter did some quick measuring of the biggest tree in the vicinity. "No problem," he pronounced. "All we need to do is cut down this tree, lop off most of the branches and then drop it across the intervening space in the same way that we've built out bridges. That's a job for Dan and his team. Paul and I have almost finished making the first butter churn and the first boiler for making cheese and we'd like to get back to that as soon as possible."

Before we left the spot I searched around until I found two embryo trees each about three feet high. I'd brought a spade and containers with me and we dug these up. Thankfully the roots only went down a short way so the job was not too difficult. I also picked a handful or two of the ripest berries, intending to pass them on to Cassie to see if they would grow. Then we returned to the mainland. Eileen was still at her post and gave us her report.

"The first two or three cats have just crossed," she reported. "They were a bit tentative, but now one or two more are following. It won't be long before they're all over."

We watched for a while. It was a slow process, but the group were soon nearly all close to the shore and a steady stream began to move across the causeway, eating as they went.

Back at the denuded forest we found two mothers, one with three kittens and one with four. It was obvious that they were too weak to move. Much against my instincts Eileen insisted on doing something for them. Putting on a pair of heavy gloves and taking one of the detachable shelves from the storeroom she approached the first cat cautiously. I was at her side with a stun gun ready in case of trouble. Very gently she laid the shelf on the ground and lifted the mother on to it, all the time holding her so that she could see her kittens. The mother struggled slightly, but she was too weak to do much, other than make the growling sound. Then Eileen lifted the kittens one by one and placed them beside their mother. Between us we carried them back to the ship, then did the same for the other mother and kittens. I took off once more, landed on the island well away from the cats who had recently crossed over, and we offloaded our cargo at the side of the stream. We cut some branches and laid them on the ground so that the two adults had easy access to food and water. Before heading for home I flew over the large double island to let Eileen see it.

"That should keep them going for a hundred years or more," she said happily. "Maybe even for ever. If they only multiply in the way that the shigs do, just enough babies to make up for deaths, the trees should regenerate as they move backwards and forwards."

George and Colin were at Central when we got back. I suggested to them that someone else should take Dan and his team on the next trip. They agreed and I left specific instructions with them as to how to get there and what needed to be done. Their trip to the east that day had yielded nothing of note and Colin said to me with a light laugh: "If there's any more exploration trips I think you should be on them, Matt. You seem to find something interesting every time."

Nicola and I were settling down to married life. It needed some adjustments on my part. Susan had been an easy person to live with, undemanding and ready to let me lead the way. Nicola was cut from a different mould. She'd been the product of a broken home and was determined that her children would not have a similar experience. She insisted from the start that we should always be completely honest with each other, discuss our differences openly and criticise each other's faults where necessary. This had its good side, as it meant I could discuss the running of Landfall with her and rely on getting a constructive response. I suppose the biggest difference was that whereas with Susan I had come and gone without question Nicola wanted to know where I'd been and what I'd been doing all the time. It felt a bit restrictive at first, but I soon got used to it.

About this time Dr. Wallace became a regular visitor to our lifeship after the evening meeting. At his insistence we were soon calling him Stephen instead of giving him his formal title. We suspected that he was lonely, despite having the company of Michael and Emma during the day. Nicola, ever more direct than I, asked him point blank one evening why he didn't take a partner.

"There's not a lot of choice now that you've teamed up with Matt," he replied gallantly.

"Eileen's still unattached. You could do a lot worse, you know."

"I'm years older than she is," he protested.

"I doubt that Eileen will be worried about that," Nicola retorted. "In fact the more I think of it, the more I believe it would be a perfect match. You're both scientifically inclined."

"Stop matchmaking and let Stephen decide his own future," I warned her. "Next thing we know you'll be starting a dating agency or a wife-swapping circle!"

Her words must have borne fruit, however. Within the week Eileen had moved into the doctor's lifeship. Nicola wore a self-satisfied smirk for days afterwards even when I remarked that it meant we had one less cabin to build.

"Haven't you any romance in your soul, Matt McNeil?" she said witheringly.

"Come to bed and I'll show you," was my response to that.

By the end of the first week in October the grain harvest was complete and all the threshing had been done. Halfway through we had encountered a major problem. There was a shortage of sacks and other containers. With much reluctance I had to deploy the clothing group into making more sacks out of shig skins. If there'd been any other solution I would have jumped at it, if only to husband out precious supply of cotton. Three women were now working full time making flour with the coffee grinders. One day a week they diverted to making oatmeal. The maize we reserved for the chickens and the barley went to Dorothy and her team whole to be used in cooking.

One or two of the men came to see me one evening to ask if they could have some of the barley for brewing purposes. With Colin's warning imprinted on my mind I turned down the request on the grounds that all the yeast we produced would be needed for bread making. They weren't too pleased, but accepted my decision.

We'd tested the berries from the trees found by the cats' home area, but they tasted vile and caused sickness in the two volunteers who risked eating them. The nuts produced by the dandelion trees were just about edible but not eaten. They were about the size of a large hazelnut, but hard and bitter tasting. But they soon became a valuable asset. Always keen to experiment Dorothy roasted them, then ground them to a coarse powder. From this she made a very passable hot drink. We came to call it coffee, though it was a long way removed from that delectable beverage. With milk and later syrup added it tasted a little bitter and had an unrecognisable flavour but it soon became popular.

The first butter had been made using the churns that the engineers had designed. Although small quantities of salt were coming to us from Seashore Dorothy decreed that it should be reserved for making cheese and not used for butter or in cooking until supplies increased significantly. Her team had made some cheese already and it was maturing.

The one item of produce that defeated us was the sugar beet. We started lifting the crop once the grain harvest was in, but I soon called a halt. The problem was that none of us knew how sugar was made from beet. I had a vague idea it resembled the production of salt, that you boiled it in water for an unspecified time, then removed the solid stuff and evaporated the rest. For our first attempt we cut up about two pounds of beet, boiled it for an hour in a pot with two gallons of water. Then we strained the liquor into another pot and continued boiling. After three hours we were left with a solid dark brown layer on the bottom of the pot. It resembled toffee in appearance, but resisted all attempts to break it up. Boiling it with more water had no effect. Eventually we had to throw the pot away. From then on we stopped the evaporation at the point where the liquid had become a thick sweet syrup. Containers being in short supply we were only able to make up small quantities at a time and the bulk of the harvested beets had to be stored in one of the caves.

Any decisions that I made regarding crops and animals were always taken in consultation with Peter Gibson. At his insistence we dug up the rest of the potatoes at the end of November, distributed their shares to the other settlements and put our own into store. The carrots we treated likewise, but all the other vegetables were left in and used as required. Tomatoes and lettuce were long finished by then and I had reassigned half of Cassie's group to other tasks. Those that were left were busy making flower pots and seed trays from the riverside mud ready for next year.

By the time December was a few days old the outside work had dwindled. We had earlier agreed in committee that it was advisable to keep everyone as busy as possible so my biggest headache around this time was in finding work to be done. I trebled the size of the clothing group, gave Dorothy a couple of extra pair of hands to help with the butter and cheese making and allocated more staff to the building section. The last cabin had been completed on the second of the month and the group had turned to making furniture to supplement that we'd received from the *Sunrise*. Todd Paterson, our one remaining joiner, had decided that any additional rooms to be added to the cabins should be left until the spring.

Before that, however, there was a little matter of an election to take care of. Our six months in charge was up on the first of the month. The evening before I reminded the assembly of the fact and added a rider. "On this occasion I insist that we have a proper secret ballot. All of us on the committee were flattered to receive your vote of confidence last time, but in a situation like that it's only too easy to go along with the crowd. Remember that this time the people you elect will be in charge for a full year. Therefore I propose to give each of you, including the children, a slip of paper on which you can write down the name of the person you wish to vote for. As before, Dr. Wallace does not wish to be considered, but apart from him you have a free choice. Once all the votes are in the box I will ask for two volunteers to count them and announce the result."

There were no dissenting voices this time. When the votes had been counted I was flattered again, having gained all but seven. Four votes had gone to Paul Cooper, two to Dorothy Cole and one to Eileen Wilson. I thanked everyone and, in the style of all good politicians, assured them that I would do my utmost to work in their best interests. On the radio link to Central later that evening I learned that Colin, Elaine, George and Dave had also been returned with large majorities. Our committee was unchanged.

Bernard Stocks

A few days after that meeting Nicola was sick two mornings running. We were both pretty certain of the reason and a visit to Dr. Wallace confirmed that she was pregnant. That brought the expectancy total for Landfall up to twenty-six. I remembered something that Dave had said a few weeks before, and thought wryly that I would be making history again. I'd be the first in the world to father two children! In the same week we also learned that Elaine was pregnant as well. I tried to visualise what Landfall would be like by the following spring and to foresee what new worries twenty-six babies could produce. I failed!

At Dr. Wallace's insistence everyone in our community was given a full medical during the first two weeks in December. "With winter approaching I want to make sure that we're all in good condition," he told me by way of explanation. "We don't have the luxury of influenza inoculations and medicine for treating colds and flu are in short supply. The uneven diet we've been forced to adopt hasn't helped, either. If I find that anyone is at risk I can have them put on more suitable duties. As far as the mothers to be are concerned I think they should be restricted to work they can do sitting down from now on. Once I've seen everyone at Landfall I'll set up camp at Central for a few days and check out the rest of our teeming population."

When his check-ups were completed I was pleased to hear him say that the whole group was in good shape. "The physical work that most of them have had to do has been a beneficial factor," was his view. "No-one is carrying any excess weight, there are no weak hearts among us as far as I can ascertain and no-one with high blood pressure apart from two of the expectant mothers. Even with these two it's not much above average. Providing we're careful we can hope to come through the winter virtually unscathed."

CHAPTER SEVENTEEN

Our last committee meeting of the year, held on Christmas Eve, turned out to be the longest we'd ever had. It was George's turn in the chair.

"I'd like to start this meeting by getting a summary from each of us of the present position of each location," he began. "After that I think we should set some objectives for next year and discuss plans for achieving those objectives. Would you like to get us going, Matt?"

I started off by sketching our position with regard to pregnancies and recent developments, including the doctor's health review. Then I went on: "I've made a rough inventory of our food supplies. On my calculations we'll run out of the main commodities during the second week in January. There'll be some odds and ends left of winter vegetables such as brussels sprouts and parsnips and maybe a little in the way of flour, oatmeal and barley. Other than that I'm afraid it's back to shig meat and fish. We do have milk and the occasional egg, though, so we're not quite back to square one. We also have one advantage over last year. Peter Gibson tells me that the climate is such that we can begin planting next year's crops at the beginning of February, which of course means that we'll have provisions two months earlier."

"We have to find some way of preserving food, particularly fruit," Colin broke in. "One year of a restricted diet isn't too serious, but if it continues year on year it's bound to have an effect on our health. The question is, how do we do it? The cold store on the *Sunrise* isn't nearly big enough."

"Easier said than done," I ventured. "I've already spoken to the engineers about it. They tell me that there'd be no problem in refrigerating one of the cargo holds. The shortage of containers is the main stumbling block. I'm no expert, but I'm pretty sure you can't just dump a load of fruit or vegetables on the floor and expect them to keep fresh for up to six months. They have to be cooked and sealed."

"That means that one of our aims for the near future is to find a way of making glass," said George.

I quoted the engineers again. "They know how to make it, and there are odd pockets of sand that can be used on the seafront to the south of Seashore. But without coal or oil they're unable to generate the high temperatures required. They're giving thought to the matter, but so far haven't come up with a solution."

"Couldn't we make containers from the river mud?" asked Elaine.

"We could," I replied. "But unless we can find a way of glazing them I'd hesitate to use them. We can experiment with that, of course, but I wouldn't fancy eating anything that's been stored in them for a while. If we could find a way of glazing them it would be a different matter."

"Let's leave that point for the moment," said George. "If you're finished, Matt, I'll call on Dave to tell us about Riverside."

"Things are progressing well with us," Dave reported. "We've developed a first class team spirit and become a good, tight group. I've organised along similar lines to Landfall and as a bonus Trevor has decided to settle with us. He has friends among our people. We've sixteen cabins completed and occupied and eight fields stripped and ploughed. We should have added another couple to that by the time we're ready to start planting, provided the weather is kind to us. The pigs and other livestock are settling in well. We've encountered one rather serious problem, but I'll leave George to tell you about that, as it affects him too. There's an inexhaustible supply of fish in the river and plenty of shigs nearby, so our basic food supply is assured."

"Thanks, Dave," said George, turning to Colin and Elaine. "Who's going to speak for Seashore?" They looked at each other before Elaine pointed at Colin.

"Looks like it's me," he said with a smile. "Here goes. For obvious reasons we're not as far advanced as the rest of you. We've five cabins built and occupied with two more nearing completion. That'll take us just over half way. Our final population will be twenty-four, but Elaine and I will probably opt to stay in the lifeship. We've only two fields ready, with possibly two more to add next month, so we'll be relying on supplies from the rest of you for a large part of next year. We're already making a small quantity of salt, but it's a laborious process. At the moment we have to bring the seawater to the evaporating tray by hand, and we've only one tray. Once everyone is in residence the engineers will provide more trays and they've designed a pumping system which will speed up the process. My guess is that by the middle of next year we will be able to supply all the needs of all four locations."

George then gave a rundown on the situation at Junction. "We're running parallel with Dave right now. Fifteen cabins are occupied plus two more halfway to completion. We've also got eight fields stripped and ploughed, plus another couple being stripped. Our livestock is thriving too. Which leaves the problem that Dave touched on. Briefly, the power supply is not satisfactory. As you know, we're both linked to the generator here at Central, with wires that are simply lying on the ground. We've already been cut off three times because shigs, while they're grazing, have bitten through the cables. The offending beasts were electrocuted, of course, but that's no consolation when you're having to examine nine or ten miles of countryside to find where the break is. If you're all in agreement I'm proposing that we move two of the remaining lifeships to Riverside and Junction and take our power from the generators in them. I've discussed it with Paul Cooper and it's an easy job to make the reconnection. Before he does he'll put in some wind turbines here so that there'll be ample power at Central for as long as we need it. Does anyone object?"

Nobody did and George moved on to the next item; plans for the forthcoming year. Before he could go further Elaine interrupted.

"There's one overriding factor that we have to keep in mind before we even start to discuss this," she pointed out. "In case you'd forgotten, everything that we do next year will be overshadowed by the birth explosion. I don't know how much you guys know about childbirth, but let me remind you that you don't have a baby one week and then put it in a crèche and go back to work a week later. In most cases it's going to be the best part of six months before the babies can be away from their mothers for any length of time. That means our work force is going to be considerably reduced. Matt, in particular, is going to suffer. He'll be losing over a third at his busiest time."

"I hadn't forgotten that aspect," George told Elaine gently. "I've got it right down here in my notes. The first thing I would propose is that the people Matt has loaned to us for field preparation should be returned to him immediately. Apart from Seashore we've matters well in hand and our own groups can take it from here. Perhaps you'll let them all know when you get back tonight, Matt, and thank them for their contribution. We will, however, need to retain the building workers. Once the cabins are all finished Dan has some ambitious plans for improving our surroundings. Colin has the full details."

"I do indeed," Colin confirmed. "Dan was down at Seashore all day yesterday and we spoke while he was working. He's proposing to build a school and a cookhouse at each location. They won't be anything fancy, just larger cabins than the ones he's building now. In fact, he's talking about four times the current size, one-roomed for the present of course, for the schools and three times for the catering hut. The design will be such that the inside can be subdivided later if needed and additional rooms can be added. I don't need to tell you what an asset the school in particular will be. Apart from educational use it will serve as a meeting place. We haven't all got a handy cave available," he concluded with a humorous glance at me.

"I'm sure Dan will include Landfall in his plans, cave or no cave," George said.

"I wouldn't say no to a schoolhouse eventually," I reflected. "At present we don't need one as we've only the six children. But I can't see Dorothy moving to another prospective kitchen. She loves her cave too much. She even turned down a cabin and has elected to continue sleeping in the cave beside her beloved pots and pans."

"Before we move on there's another item I want to bring up concerning the children," said Colin. "I think it would be a good idea to retain as many different surnames as possible. We've only got around a hundred and seventy just now and it would be a pity to lose any through marriage. This will have to be approved by a majority and can only be on a voluntary basis, but my suggestion is that sons take the surname of the father and daughters that of the mother. We might even be able to persuade those couples already married to use this system as well. Perhaps you can put it to the masses at the next meetings you hold. One other thing. We've got three Smiths, three Patels and two Purdies. I'm going to have a quiet word with them all and see if some can agree to adopting new and unused names"

None of us could see any reason to argue and the motion was adopted. Colin seemed pleased, but quickly moved on to his next request. "I'm sorry to harp on about it, but I'd still like to get access to the other side of Broad River. It may not be a vital matter right now, but it will have to be considered sooner or later. The engineers and I have been looking over the *Sunrise* for a suitable strip of metal and we think we've found it. There's a bulkhead just behind the damaged portion of the bow that will give us a piece of metal of the strength and dimensions required. We've worked out a way to get it out of the ship once it's cut. From there we'll attach it by chains to one of the lifeships and either drag it or fly it to the river. It shouldn't be too difficult for the pilot to drop or drag it to the right spot on the other side."

George looked round the table. "Has anyone any objections?" he asked. We all shook our heads. "Then I suggest we go ahead next week. Providing the lifeship doesn't break up during the transfer we can leave it at either Riverside or Junction as the power supply point. Have you worked out exactly where to site the bridge, Colin?"

"We've picked out a couple of suitable spots. Both are closer to Riverside than to Junction. Ideally we'd have liked to put it halfway between the two, but the river begins to widen about four miles from Riverside and I don't think we can get a long enough piece of metal from the bulkhead to put it any nearer Junction. Would you let Paul know, Matt. He's going to organise a gang to do the cutting and removal of the metal from the ship. Tomorrow's Christmas Day and I'm going to propose later on that we make it a holiday for everybody, so let's say Tuesday."

"Will do," I confirmed. "I'll probably come with him. I'd like to see how it's all done."

From there we moved on to discuss what crops we should plant in the coming year. Various plans were mooted and discarded and after a fair amount of good-natured argument we decide that everyone should grow everything.

"I'm sure the time will come when it will pay us to specialise and have certain crops in certain locations," George summed up. "But for the next two or three years I think it is more sensible to make each community as self-supporting as possible. We'll keep a close eye on stocks, so if any one community does run short of anything the others will help them out. And as we've already mentioned we'll all have to help Seashore this year. If you should hear anyone complaining about that just remind them that Colin's lot are the only providers of salt for all of us. Now we've got that out of the way are there any new initiatives we should put in hand. That will probably mean loading a few more tasks on to the engineers, but let's hear them anyway."

"Before we start there's something I'd like to bring forward," I said. "I'm not being parochial, believe me, but it seems that all the ideas and all the advances are coming from us at Landfall. Now from what I've seen of the crowd that George brought here there's a fair spread of intelligence among them. Why aren't they coming up with thoughts of their own?"

The others all started to speak at once until George held up his hand. "Let me answer that one, please." He turned to me. "I see where you're coming from and it's something that Colin and I have talked about once or twice. I'm no psychologist, but I think the main reason is this. All the people that the rest of you brought were awake and conscious at the time of the crash. They knew, or had a rough idea, of what was happening from that moment on. Now just think for a moment about those that I brought. They went to sleep on Earth fully expecting to wake up and find themselves on Paladia, being greeted by friends and relations. Instead they discover they're floating in space in a wrecked ship with less than a fifty-fifty chance of staying alive. It was too much to take in and it's left them bereft of initiative. All they want to do right now is follow orders and try to adjust. I can see signs that it's happening, but it will be a slow process. Eventually I think you'll find their brains will be back to normal and they'll start thinking things out for themselves."

I still thought that there should have been a few at least of the newcomers coming up with suggestions but I left it at that. As predicted, most of the ideas we pooled involved the engineers. I pointed out that they already had their hands full. They were supervising the production of milk churns and boilers for making cheese. Although they had the design they still had to make a prototype spinning wheel. Among new items we required were the means to mill grain in larger quantities than the coffee grinders could manage. On the same principle we wanted a machine to grind the ever-growing pile of shig bones into fertiliser and cattle feed.

"Is there any chance they can fix up some kind of heating in the cabins?" Elaine wanted to know. "It's becoming monotonous at this time of the year having to wear the thermal sleeping bags when we're not working. If I remember rightly there was some talk soon after we arrived about putting pipes through the cabins and passing hot water through them."

"They're still working on that one," I told her. "There simply isn't enough pipework to go round, and most of what there is will be needed for your seawater pumping system. Walter's been trying to design some form of electric convector heater, but he can't finalise it until we see how much wire we'll have left for the heating element."

Dave had been fairly quiet up until then, but at last managed to get in a matter of his own. "I think it would be a good idea if we co-opted one of the children on to the committee. I feel that they should have a voice at the top table. After all, it's their world we're building. Although we talk to them from time to time it's only natural for them to be a little overawed and unwilling to put forward ideas. If they had a representative of their own they'd be more likely to communicate with him or her."

George and Colin looked doubtful, but Elaine jumped in before they could speak. "I think it's a great idea," she enthused. I nodded agreement, and she went on; "That's three to two, so the motion's carried."

"How do you intend to elect this person?" Colin asked, still looking sceptical.

"For this coming year I think we should just appoint someone," she replied. "And I've got the very person in mind, Monica McCallan. She's fourteen, Irish, very mature and gets on well with all the other kids. Even more important, she's not afraid to speak her mind in front of adults. When we hold next year's elections we can then let the under sixteens vote for their own member."

Though both Colin and George put up token opposition they were outvoted and soon gave in with good grace. That gave me the chance to ask a question that I had been waiting to pose.

"Cassie tells me that the embryo fruit trees and bushes will be ready for transplanting around the beginning of March. You all know the number that we have, about one hundred and sixty of each. Do you want to divide them between the four locations?"

It was immediately obvious that I was the only one to have considered this matter. None of the others had any clear views, but after I pressed them George eventually made his mind up.

"We've all got plenty of seed, thanks to the survival rooms in the lifeships. You've only got twelve months' start on us, so if the other three agree I suggest you keep all yours and we'll start our own. I'm sure if you have a huge surplus ahead of the rest you'll share it out."

"As long as we've got the clover fruits and the oval fruits we're well stocked in that direction anyway," was Colin's opinion. "O.K., it would be nice to have a bit of variety, but we'll just have to be patient."

"There'll be some rhubarb and some strawberries coming this year," I said with a smile. "We'll share it out and with any luck there'll be two strawberries and one stick of rhubarb per person."

By the time the meeting came to an end darkness had long fallen. The others all elected to stay at Central overnight but I decided to head for Landfall and home. I'd never attempted the journey at night before, but the regular trips of altabs and lorries had left a faint but narrow track. The small searchlight on the front of the altab had a range of about twenty metres and I was fairly confident of my ability to navigate the six miles. In the event I found it easy. I spent most of the evening informing the group of the decisions we'd taken during the afternoon and then briefing the engineers in greater detail.

Christmas day was a muted affair. There'd been some talk of getting some branches from the conifer forest and setting them up as Christmas trees but in the end we decided that it would be a pointless exercise. We had no decorations to put on them and no presents to give. For a brief spell in the morning we all rushed around shaking hands, kissing and wishing everyone in sight a Merry Christmas. One that was over boredom set in. If the weather had been more clement I think most of us would have worked a normal day. As it was a thin sleety rain and a cold north wind made outdoor conditions unpleasant.

CHAPTER EIGHTEEN

It took four days to put the bridge across Broad River. I felt a bit guilty at absenting myself from Landfall for that length of time, but the whole operation was so fascinating I couldn't tear myself away. The first thing the engineers did was to mark off a section of the chosen bulkhead some fifty metres long by five metres high. One side of this rectangle was as close to the outside wall of the ship as possible. Then they cut away the part of the ship's hull through which the sheet of metal would have to pass. After that they drilled three holes through the side of the proposed sheet to accommodate the chains that would attach it to the lifeship.

From somewhere in the *Sunrise* they'd collected sixteen small runnels, each some three inches long. At intervals along the top and bottom of the marked area small rectangles were cut out and the runnels welded on. Only then did they start to cut out whole thing. This was a slow business. The metal of the bulkhead was about three inches thick and the oxy-acetylene cutters had to be recharged at frequent intervals. By Thursday evening only one side remained to be cut.

First thing Friday morning George piloted one of the lifeships into position, taking Walter Butter with him. The chains were attached to the metal sheet and to the lifeship, then Paul started to cut the remaining side. He and Walter were in constant communication by radio from that point on. When only half a metre of metal remained attached Paul directed Walter to tell George to raise the lifeship until the chains were horizontal to the ground and just to take the strain and no more. At the same time he warned everyone in the vicinity to stand clear. Carefully he cut through the last metre. When the final blob of red hot metal fell to the deck he gave the word for the lifeship to move forward.

By this time we were all outside and at a safe distance from the action. Thankfully it was a dry day though cold. As George accelerated we all held our breath. Slowly the sheet of metal emerged from the side of the *Sunrise*. As soon as it was clear it toppled over, but the chains held and as

George pulled away the bottom edge trailed along the ground. The lifeship banked and set course for the river at a bare thirty miles an hour. Those of us that had an altab at hand followed on, though keeping a good fifty metres clear of the lifeship and its cargo.

The metal sheet made a broad furrow as it dragged along the ground. Several shigs in its six mile journey escaped death by the narrowest of margins. One or two did, in fact, get bumped, but appeared to suffer no lasting ill effects. George took the lifeship to a point just over the south bank of the river and waited for Paul to arrive. On our side there was a good three metres to spare. Visibility to the rear from the lifeship was restricted, but Walter gave his opinion that they were well over the river's bank. Using binoculars Paul confirmed this and gave the order to land.

After a long look through the glasses Paul turned to the rest of us and gave a sigh of relief. "There's at least two metres of clearance on the other side. With some confidence, ladies and gentlemen, I can now announce that we have a bridge across Broad River. I'm sure it's solid, but just to be on the safe side I'll cross it by myself. When I give the signal, and only then, the rest of you can come across. Walk in single file in the middle of the bridge when you do."

Five minutes later the whole group was standing on the south side of the river and Paul gave the order to disconnect the chains. I noticed a very slight tremor in the metal as we had crossed, but the whole thing felt as solid as a rock underfoot. Once the chains had been taken off Paul made a close inspection of the ground surrounding the end of the bridge before pronouncing himself satisfied.

"Forgive me for indulging myself," said George when everything had been done and he'd vacated the pilot's seat, "but I'm going to walk across and back before I take the lifeship on to its new home at Riverside." He did just that.

As we walked back ourselves I said to Colin: "You'll be pleased that's done."

"Pleased and relieved," he answered. "Until they started on it I hadn't realised how potentially dangerous the operation was. I still believe we're justified in doing it though. It may not be apparent in the next year or two, but future generations are going to be grateful we had the foresight to do it while we could. I can't think of any other way in which we could have bridged the river, so we had to do it while we still had a sufficiently big piece of the ship to use." Although I'd contributed nothing to the operation I shared his sense of pride.

New Year's Day was a facsimile of Christmas Day, except that the weather was dry and most people opted to work. There was some talk of a large party walking to Central to exchange good wishes with the other groups, but with so many of the women pregnant the idea was abandoned almost as soon as it was mooted. We didn't bother to hold a committee meeting on Hogmanay. As George said when he informed me of the decision by radio, we'd dealt with all the important issues the week before. The only additional item was that Elaine had approached Monica McCallan and that the latter had welcomed her attachment to the committee.

The first baby was born on Wednesday the third of January. It was a girl, and according to Dr. Wallace's best estimate she was some three weeks premature, weighing in at exactly six pounds. "Thankfully she's healthy and quite sturdy," Stephen told me afterwards. "I'll keep her and her mother with me for a couple of days for safety's sake, but there's not the slightest cause for concern."

Both Michael and Emma had assisted the doctor and the former told me later that they'd received a running commentary of instruction as the baby was being delivered.

"Dr. Wallace said that we might have to work on our own if more than one baby arrives at the same time," he said with a worried look on his face. "I just hope we see a couple more before that becomes a reality."

We had to wait until the fifteenth before the next happy event. This time it was a boy, just under nine pounds, and the mother had gone the full term. Two days later I learned that I wasn't going to make history as the first father of two on the new world. One of the mothers gave birth to twins, one boy and one girl. Though they each weighed under five pounds Stephen gave them a clean bill of health, though he kept them with him for three days.

"There must be something in the air here," he said with a grin when I went in to see the new arrivals. "Mother and babies are in great shape. If all the rest follow the pattern I'm going to have an easy time."

Susan's baby was born on the twenty-fourth, a fine boy weighing eight pounds, nine ounces. I was working on one of the far distant fields at the time, but Michael came out to tell me. He'd been present at the birth and reported that though Susan had suffered some pain the birth had been straightforward and though weak she was feeling fine. He insisted that I should go back with him to see the baby right away.

It was an eerie feeling as I stood looking down at my son. I found it hard to analyse my emotions. There was pride, certainly, at having fathered such a healthy looking specimen of babyhood, plus a certain sadness in knowing someone else would have the pleasures of being with him constantly. I also felt some satisfaction that I would be close to him as he grew to adulthood, even if I was to have no part in shaping his destiny.

"We've been discussing names," said Michael after I'd held the baby for a few seconds. "With your permission we'd like to call him Matthew." Susan nodded in agreement.

"I've been thinking about this for the last few days," I told them, "and I'd rather you didn't. For the boy's sake I think I should distance myself from him as much as possible so that there's no conflict of loyalties. It's better all round if he grows up thinking that Michael is his real father."

"He'll find out sooner or later," Susan protested in a weak voice. "Everyone in the community knows he's your son and someone sooner or later will mention it in his presence."

"I didn't say he should never be told," I explained. "You'll both be the best judges of when the time is right to tell him, but I think you should leave it until he's old enough to understand, probably when he's around nine or ten. It's not just a case of telling him who his real father is. You'll have to explain why you and I separated and why Michael is now with you and I'm not. By the time he's ten he should have some idea of what love is and how people react to it." We left it at that and later in the day Michael sought me out to tell me they had decided to call the boy Donald, after Susan's father.

By great good fortune we only had one real crisis during the baby boom. That was on the evening of the thirtieth, when three women went into labour within minutes of each other. Stephen Wallace only had room for two of them, so Nicola and I spent an hour cleaning the survival room in our ship and turning it into a ward. We took the healthiest of the three women and Michael and Emma faced the task of delivering the baby. The two worked well together, despite the fact that they weren't exactly the best of friends. There was still some resentment on Emma's part which Michael found hard to cope with. A couple of times Emma sprinted over to the doctor to seek advice, but just after midnight the baby, a girl, arrived in the world. Michael was exhausted and soon left, but Emma insisted on bringing in her sleeping bag and remaining with mother and child. For a thirteen-year-old she was showing remarkable resilience.

"Are you sure you're not too tired," I asked her.

"No, I'm fine," she replied. Then, with a wink she added: "But I don't think I'll be able to go to school tomorrow."

As he'd suggested before Christmas Peter Gibson set the start of planting for the first of February. Although our work force had diminished the weather was on the whole kind to us and we made good progress. Peter and I had drawn up a timetable, starting with the potatoes and some of the vegetables, to be followed by the grain crops. The crofting group started sowing their seed at the same time. The mood in the camp was quite good, despite the fact that we were back to the basic diet of shig meat and fish. Once a week there were a few brussels sprouts or parsnips, but the wheat, oats and barley had run out. Most of the milk was going to the new-born and the eggs to the six children. The cheeses that Dorothy had made were still maturing and by common consent we decided to leave them until bread was on the menu once more.

By the end of February twenty-four mothers had given birth, leaving only Nicola and one lately confirmed pregnancy to add to the population eventually. Dave and Fiona were now proud parents, too – a baby boy in their case. Two days later the news came over the radio that Elaine had presented Colin with a baby girl. Some of our mothers insisted on doing some work in the intervals of caring for their offspring, begging me to find jobs for them. I added most of them to the group making clothing. The work was light and could be interrupted at any time and we needed much more in the way of clothes for the babies. Although it was somewhat early Dorothy was experimenting in the making of baby food with what little raw material she had.

I had a period of depression around the last week of February. Though I tried to hide it Nicola soon realised that something was wrong and tackled me on the subject one evening as we were getting ready for bed. At first I was reluctant to discuss the matter, but she persisted and in the end I poured my heart out.

"It's Susan's baby," I told her haltingly. "Although it's my baby too I don't feel any emotion towards it. I had a surge of pride when I held him just after he was born, but since then I'm no more drawn to him than to any of the other children. It's making me wonder about our own baby, yours and mine. Will it be the same then? Maybe I just don't have the seeds of fatherhood in me."

"I had a feeling that was what was bothering you," she said after a pause. "Call it wifely instinct. As it happens I studied a bit of psychology at school, so I know something about the subject. I may be wrong, but I think it's just part of your general personality. You're the type of person who concentrates on today and tomorrow. You tend not to look back on what's happened and what cannot be changed, except to learn lessons from the past. I think that when you and Susan split up it closed a chapter in your life. Baby Donald is part of that closed chapter. You've accepted that you'll never be part of his future and you've dismissed him from your mind. Our baby will bring a different scenario. You'll be here, with me and the baby, all the time. You'll be part of his or her growing up, holding it, seeing it all day and every day. I don't think you'll have any trouble being a father then."

I thought this was a pretty shrewd assessment. I just hoped her analysis was correct. It still worried me, but from then on I was able to put it to the back of my mind.

Monica McCallan proved a worthwhile addition to our committee. Before the first meeting that she attended she buttonholed me and asked if it would be all right for her to visit Landfall on a regular basis. "I've made arrangements to go to the other sites once a week," she informed me. "Although there's only six at Landfall their views are just as important as anyone else's. George has given me an altab for my own use so transport's not a problem." I told her that would be fine by me. During the meetings she showed herself to be all that Elaine had foretold, sensible, mature and not afraid to state her opinions.

One meeting that stands out in my memory took place on the second Sunday in March. Dave was in the chair that day and after the main business was concluded he had a suggestion to put to us.

The Far Side of Nowhere

"I've been thinking for some time that we should do a little more exploration," he began. "We've had a good look at this continent, and George and I landed on the furthest one from here when we did our mapmaking orbits. But we've never set foot on the two continents to the east and west of us. I propose that we do so in the next couple of months, with maybe one flight to each. Somewhere on this world there must be coal, oil and metal. We're never going to find them if we don't look for them."

Colin objected almost immediately. "What good will it do, Dave? We've the photographs that you took and they show there's no difference between any of the continents. Even in the unlikely event that you do find coal or oil we haven't enough fuel to bring it here in the quantities we need. In fact I don't think we're justified in using up more fuel just for the sake of exploration. Our supply isn't inexhaustible and I think we should keep a healthy reserve for emergencies."

Dave didn't look too happy at Colin's response, but he put a brave face on it. "What do the rest of you think? Matt?"

"Sorry, Dave," I said. "I agree with Colin on this one. Even if you found oil and we had the means to bring it back here it wouldn't be much use to us. Crude oil contains too many impurities, and good though Paul and Walter are even they couldn't put an oil refinery together. Supposing you did find a coalfield? What are you proposing? That we should move the whole community to a new site. That's just not on. We've spent too much time and effort getting a foothold here, and in any case we couldn't move the *Sunrise*. We've come to depend too much on the wreck to leave it behind."

"I agree with Dave," Elaine spoke before being invited. "While we've got fuel left I think we should see what there is to be seen. Look what two of our trips on this continent brought forth. We didn't spot the Russian scout ship or the forest of the cats from the photographs. Who knows what else we might find? For all we know another spaceship might have come through that black hole and crash-landed. We might not be the only human beings on this world after all. The photographs didn't show up the scout ship."

"That was because it was small and partially concealed in a deep valley," Colin pointed out. "I'm sure a full sized ship would have shown up."

"What about you, Monica?" Dave asked.

"I think we should," our youngest member stated. "But it's for selfish reasons only. I'd like to go on a trip to somewhere new."

"Three to two in favour," said Dave, looking happier. "That just leaves you, George."

"I'm going to split it down the middle," George said after a pause. "I don't think we should go, for two reasons not given so far. Firstly, Dave, you speak glibly about finding coal and oil. Think back to your days of walking around on Earth. How many coalfields or oilfields did you see on your travels? Coal and oil are invariably hidden underground and there are no signposts telling you where to look. Even if it was there you wouldn't find it. For all we know we could be sitting over a coal mine right now. The other reason I'm against it is this. We all know that the lifeships are very safe, but accidents can happen. Suppose you crash and put your radio out of action. It could be weeks before we find and rescue you."

Colin spoke out unexpectedly. "How about a compromise? One flight, to the continent west of here. Take two or three days, explore thoroughly and then come back and call a halt to any further jaunts."

It seemed like a reasonable solution. George had one final proposal to make. "Obviously you and Elaine should go, Dave, as you're so keen. I think Monica should go too. But I suggest that you take Matt as well. He seems to have a nose for rooting out the unexpected. If he's willing, that is. But I would leave it until the nights get lighter. Say the end of May or the beginning of June."

Dave looked at me. "O.K." I said. "I'll go along, providing Nicola doesn't object. But I'd like to make it two days only. Nicola will be in the latter stages of her pregnancy and I don't want to leave her for longer than I can help. I'd like to take Eileen along as well. If there are any new life forms to be found it would be invaluable to have her on the spot." And that was how we left matters.

Before we finally left the subject George had a rider to add. "This discussion has given me an idea. I was only joking when I said that we could be sitting on a coalfield right now. But the more I think about it the more I believe we should take steps to find out. We'll liase on the matter, but I think we should pick two or three spots well away from the cultivated and grazing areas. Whenever there's a surplus of labour we can put people on to digging down as far as they can. There may be all sorts of interesting things to find right under our noses. In the meantime, start thinking what use we can put some deep holes to."

CHAPTER NINETEEN

I wanted to make the first of April, the first anniversary of our arrival on New Britain, a public holiday. But when I put it to the community at the meeting the night before I was voted down. The general view was that we had no means of celebrating the occasion and that we'd all be sitting around for the day getting bored. My second suggestion was adopted, however, and in the morning we held a short service combining Protestants and Catholics. Our two religious leaders, if I can call them that, offered prayers of thankfulness for our survival and we sang a couple of well-known hymns before heading off for our daily duties.

That evening, when I was taking my usual tour around the camp, I stopped at the furthest point of the cultivated fields and gazed at the scene. I felt a glow of satisfaction as I took in the fields, now green with their various crops sprouting above the ground. Our four cows were grazing peacefully in another direction. The bull had been left with them all winter and we were sure that all four were with calf. Thankfully Peter Gibson had looked after the bull while it was there. I was far too scared to go near it, a feeling shared by most. Eight or nine of the sheep had given birth and the lambs made a homely sight as they gambolled about their mothers. In the distance in the other direction the two rows of cabins were visible. I could just make out Harry and June on the riverbank catching fish for the morning meal.

I'd been there for some ten minutes when I saw the giant figure of Dan Dunn approaching.

"Surveying your kingdom?" he asked with a smile.

"Something like that, Dan," I told him with an answering grin. "Not my kingdom, though. It's ours, yours, mine and everyone else here at Landfall, plus those that have moved on. Everyone's worked so hard."

"You've played a major part, though," were Dan's reassuring words. "We couldn't have accomplished half of what we have without the right guidance and the right planning which you and the other members of the committee supplied."

"We've had a lot of luck as well," I said. "Not least the arrival of the wreck of the *Sunrise*. George deserves a medal for that salvage job. We had a foothold on the planet before then, no more than that. The contents of the ship trebled our standard of living and our long term prospects of survival."

"It still needed a guiding hand to put it to its best use, though," Dan pointed out. "But enough of the past. Where do we go from here?"

"If the first year was about survival, then next year's key word should surely be consolidation," I replied. "Barring disaster our food supplies are more or less assured. It's now down to you and the engineers and whatever new ideas you can come up with. I gather you're ready to start on your larger cabins."

"That's right. All the cabins are built in all four locations and we've added a small amount of basic furniture to supplement what we've taken from the wreck. We've been cutting timber over the last few days and we'll be making a start on the Riverside and Junction cookhouses tomorrow morning. I want to see how they turn out before we move down to Seashore or start on the schoolhouses."

We'd been so intent on our discussion that neither of us had noticed Paul Cooper had joined us.

"Boasting again, Dan?" he asked by way of announcing his presence.

Dan laughed. "Just taking a craftsman's pride in his work, the same way that you do. I haven't seen much of you and Walter these last few days. What have you been up to."

"We've been down at Seashore setting up the salt extraction plant," Paul replied. "With the nights getting lighter we decided to stay there until the job was done, so we bedded down with Colin and Elaine. We just finished at lunchtime today and spent the afternoon checking that everything was working. I'm pleased to say that it is."

"What exactly have you done?" I asked him.

"First we found an inlet where the sea runs fairly deep. Then we set up a pump, electrically driven, of course, to bring up the water as and when required. We'd previously constructed half a dozen open trays which could be electrically heated, plus lids to cover them in the event of rain. We set the trays up as near to the sea as possible, pumped water in to a depth of six inches and then boiled it off until only the salt remained. I'm afraid it's a time and labour consuming method, but it's the only thing we could think of. Luckily the salt concentration in the seawater is high, so the half dozen trays should be enough to supply all our needs. If not we'll just have to put more trays in."

"What's next on the agenda?" I asked him.

"Before we went to Seashore we'd just finished making a spinning jenny. I'll get Peter to get some wool from one of the sheep tomorrow and we'll try it out. If it works we'll make one for each of the other three settlements. After that I've got an idea for providing heating in the cabins."

"Want to tell us about it?" asked Dan. "Or are you keeping it a secret till you see if it will work?"

Paul laughed. "It's no secret. I'm sure it will work, though I'm not sure how well. Basically it's a system of warm air heating. We'll set up boilers at each end of the two rows of cabins and run a pipe through them all. The hot air generated by the boilers will be pumped through these pipes. In each cabin there'll be a valve in the pipe to let air into the cabin. We'll put some sort of grating or flap on the openings so that the occupants will have some control over the heat coming in. The only thing I'm not sure about is whether the flow of air will be strong enough to reach the cabins at the end of each line. There's no way of estimating that, so it will have to be trial and error."

"Sounds good to me," I commented. "Will it be up and running before next winter?"

"In Landfall, yes," Paul replied. "But there is a snag as far as the other communities are concerned. We've only a finite amount of piping that can be taken from the main ship and the lifeships. I'm not sure if we're going to have enough for four such systems. As far as I can estimate we should just make it and no more, but I could be wrong. The main worries will be sixteen or seventeen years down the line, when the babies being born just now start wanting cabins of their own."

"You're getting as bad as Colin for looking too far ahead," I reproved him. "By that time you, or somebody else, may well have found another way of doing it. We may even have found coal by then. Any progress on the matter of food preservation?"

"Not yet, I'm afraid," he answered. "But I've been speaking to George about it. By the end of the summer we'll have refrigerated one of the cargo holds and cleaned it thoroughly. We'll experiment by dumping a large quantity of clover and oval fruits just as they are – maybe even picking them just before they're fully ripe. Then we'll see how long they stay edible. We can do the same with some of the vegetables and things like tomatoes. It's trial and error, but it's the best that we can come up with at the moment. At worst it will prolong the supply for a few extra weeks."

Darkness had fallen by the time I got back home. For some time now I'd stopped using the term lifeship and accepted that it was indeed my home for the foreseeable future. Nicola was waiting up for me.

"I was beginning to think you'd abandoned me," she laughed. "Where have you been?"

"Talking to Dan and Paul, and meditating," I replied. "It's only a year ago today that I put this ship down on the surface, yet already it seems as if I've spent the greater part of my life here. Everything that went before is just a distant memory. But mainly I've been looking forward, trying to see what the coming year will bring."

"There you go again," she said triumphantly. "Another chapter of your life has just closed and by the morning you'll have put it out of your mind."

"Stop psychoanalysing me and come to bed," was the only reply I could think of.

Our four cows all calved within a week of each other. Peter Gibson had dealt with the lambing on his own, but the delivery of a calf was too much for one man to cope with. Dr. Wallace, Michael and Emma gave a hand with all four. Two were cows and two were bullocks.

"I think we'll keep both of the bullocks just to be on the safe side," decreed Peter. "We'll maybe need the services of the older bull again next year, but after that we can rely on our own. We've ten lambs, four male and six female. Three of the rams we'll fatten up during the year and have them on Christmas Day. I don't suppose we'll be able to kill any of the turkeys, so roast lamb for Christmas dinner will be a real treat."

Our other professional farmer, Gavin had had a hectic time during the spring. He'd had to race around the other three communities to deliver lambs and calves as and when required. It made me realise how much we needed at least one vet. Before one of our committee meetings I scrutinised the list of people we had compiled to see if anyone had any experience in that direction. I drew a blank. But when I brought the matter up during the meeting itself I quickly found a volunteer.

"I'd like to become a vet," Monica declared immediately. "Are there any books in the ship's library on the subject?"

"I'm afraid not," Elaine told her. "I checked some time ago. If you're serious we can maybe arrange for Dr. Wallace to give you some tuition, but it will be a matter of learning as you go along."

"I've got a better idea," I put in. "I'll get Eileen to give you a crash course in zoology. Once you've picked up the basics then you can tap the doctor's surgical knowledge. You can skip the rest of your regular morning schooling. You'd be finished with that by the end of the year anyway."

"I've a friend, Laura Hodge, who's the same age as me," Monica said. "I'm sure she'd like to do the same. Can we both study together?"

"Definitely," I told her. "Ideally we could use four vets, but two is a start and hopefully you can pass on your own skills eventually to someone else. In the meantime, once you're confident you can split the four communities between you."

Eileen, when I approached her on the subject, was more than willing to take the two of them under her wing. At first I suggested that the two girls moved to Landfall, but their families weren't too keen on the idea. We compromised by putting an altab permanently at Eileen's disposal so that she could spend as much time as possible with the two of them at Junction.

From time to time she gave me progress reports, all of which were in glowing terms. Her verdict was that both girls would make excellent vets. They were good with animals, willing to learn and above all were desperate to succeed.

We had other additions to our livestock during April and the early part of May. Several of the hens became broody, so we stopped gathering eggs for a while. By mid May thirty-eight chicks had arrived in the world. Never have chicks been so well looked after. As soon as they left the eggs chicks and mother hens were transferred into the cave where Dorothy and her team did the cooking. We debated leaving them outside and hoping for the best but it seemed risky when we had a cave handy that was always warm and free of drafts. It may not have been very hygienic, but the quicker we could build up our stock of poultry the sooner we could have a sufficient supply of eggs. The fact that we could kill and eat the surplus cockerels wasn't far from my thoughts either.

We lost a few unfortunately, but twenty-nine survived. Sixteen were hens, thirteen cockerels. Peter dashed my hopes of a meal of roast chicken that year, however.

"The most we could afford to kill would be ten," he said. "That would mean one bird between eight people. You'd get about two mouthfuls each. There'll maybe be a few more chicks during the summer, but even then I wouldn't want to kill off any cockerels for a year at least."

About this time Cassie and her team were setting up their orchard. To be strictly accurate they planted three orchards and one vineyard. One orchard was of temperate fruit such as apples, pears, plums, cherries and damsons. The second was more tropical in nature: oranges, lemons, grapefruit and figs. Number three comprised some three dozen nut trees. We had sweet chestnut, hazelnut, almond, walnut and brazil nut saplings all looking healthy. I bemoaned the fact that we had no peanuts to plant.

"Just as well," remarked Cassie when I complained to her. "None of us would have a clue how to grow them. My regret is that there are no cashew nuts. They were always my favourite. I could have lived on them quite happily. By the way, I'm keeping around forty of the saplings back for the time being in case we lose any of the ones we've transplanted. If all goes well I'll either put them out in September or hold them until next spring. I'm also planting our reserve stock in the next couple of days."

I felt sorry for the crofting group during the operation. The site that we'd chosen for the orchards was over a mile away from the main camp and all they had to transport the young trees was a rickety cart that Dan had put together the previous summer. Cassie was worried that the shigs might find the embryo trees suitable for eating. To try and keep them away she ordered that most of the turf between the trees should be uplifted and replaced face downwards. It seemed like an excess of caution to me but I didn't want to interfere.

Bernard Stocks

In truth there were not that many shigs in the immediate vicinity of the camp at that time. Harry and June were having to travel two miles or more to keep us supplied with food. I asked them if they wanted me to organise a drive to bring another herd closer.

"Maybe next year," was June's response. "It's no hardship at the moment now that we've got full use of a couple of altabs, and you need all the workers you can muster just for the day to day jobs. From close observation I've learned that the shigs are pretty obstinate beasts. They take a hell of a lot of shifting if they don't want to move."

My first observation when Cassie took me out to view the completed orchards was that the young trees seemed very far apart. She laughed. "In three or four years' time you'll accuse me of having planted them too close together! Once they start to spread it's surprising how the space between them shrinks."

At the beginning of May we had another worrying few days due to the weather. As in the previous year we had what I would describe as a monsoon. Heavy rain fell continuously for three whole days, causing a certain amount of flooding. But once again the storm was followed by a long spell of hot sunshine. The fields quickly dried out and all our crops flourished. By mid May potatoes were on the menu once again, quickly followed by lettuce, cabbage, spinach and rhubarb.

It was in May, too, that we made our abortive attempt to find out what if anything was hidden in the ground beneath us. As soon as I had some spare capacity I picked a spot well away from our farmland, one that was right out in the open. We marked out an area about three metres square and started digging down. The earth that we removed we used to put a bank around the hole to prevent anyone or any animal falling in. A metre or so down we hit a layer of thick black clay. From that point on we had to bale water each time we dug, lengthening the operation considerably. Eventually, when we'd gone down some five metres and expanded gallons upon gallons of sweat we struck solid rock. With some thankfulness I ordered the hole to be filled in again. In the unlikely event that there was coal or oil underneath it would have been beyond our resources to gather it. Before replacing the top layer we took some of the clay back to camp to try and mould it into bricks or pots. We soon discovered that once it dried it became brittle and whatever we made simply fell apart.

Similar operations had been going on at the other three settlements, all with negative results. At Seashore they struck rock three metres down. At both Riverside and Junction they managed to dig down for over seven metres, but soon found that, presumably due to the close proximity of the river, the holes filled with water overnight. We had no pumps to spare to deal with this and had no option but to abandon the project. George had half-heartedly proposed that we should try again twenty or thirty miles south of Broad River, but we felt we couldn't really spare the manpower for what would probably turn out to be another wasted effort.

It was round about this time that we at Landfall finally abandoned the nightly meetings. General opinion was that they had become both boring and unnecessary, a view which I'd held for some time. Latterly they had become more of a social gathering, but as it gave everyone a chance to unwind after a hard day's physical labour I kept them going as long as there was a demand. From that point on we only held two meetings a week. One was on Friday to discuss the issues that anyone wanted me to place before the committee and one on Monday when I reported back on the outcome.

CHAPTER TWENTY

It was in May that our committee finally managed to produce a draft constitution for approval. When finished it took up three full pages of small print. Because of our dwindling stock of paper we only made four copies. We'd been discussing the terms since the early part of January and there'd been many arguments, some quite heated, before we reached agreement. The opening section dealt with the election of the committee and even this didn't go through without a hitch. As discussed previously, elections would be held annually at the beginning of December; the committee would number five adults and one member under sixteen to be elected by that age group only. Then Dave pointed out a snag.

"The youngest of the settlers is nearly seven now; the oldest of the new generation just a few months. That means that by the time our seven year old is sixteen there'll only be ten year olds available to replace him."

"Some ten year olds can be very mature," was Elaine's contribution.

"We can't be sure of that," objected Dave.

After much discussion our solution was to make a minor amendment and phrase the constitution to read 'one member under sixteen providing that a suitable candidate is available'.

The section on religion went through fairly easily. We decided there should be no organised religion: everyone should be free to worship in the way they chose. In reality it was the only conclusion that could be reached. The three Patels plus one of the black women were Muslims. About a quarter of the population were Catholic and about the same number Protestant. There was one Buddhist, one Baptist and the rest had no leanings towards any form or group.

The biggest problem, as we had anticipated, was law and order. As we all had next to nothing in the way of possessions it was unlikely that theft would be an issue for many years to come. Kidnapping and terrorism were highly unlikely too, as was fraud. But assault, rape and murder could occur at any time. Thankfully there'd been no trouble at Landfall, but at Junction

George had had to intervene in a couple of fights, one of them between two women which became quite ugly. With the greatest reluctance we agreed that we would have to set up some kind of small prison, probably within the wreck of the *Sunrise*. In the absence of a police force it would devolve to the committee members to act as warders.

The committee was deeply divided as to how we should treat rape and murder. The obvious solution would have been to deal with these as we had dealt with the previous incident and simply banish the offender or offenders to some far distant spot and leave them to fend for themselves. But as Colin pointed out our fuel was running out and the time would come when the maximum distance we could send anyone would be that which the lorries could cover. That was less than sixty miles. Elaine, Monica and I all favoured the death penalty: the other three were implacably against it. Elaine's counter proposal for rape was castration, but that suffered a similar division.

"Rape is a notoriously difficult thing to prove conclusively," was George's view. "The very nature of the offence means that there are almost never any witnesses. There is always the suggestion that in the first instance the victim was willing and then changed her mind at the last moment. If it was a clear cut case then I would agree that castration is a suitable punishment, providing Dr. Wallace agreed to carry it out, but it's a racing certainty that any such case that comes before us will not be like that."

Colin suggested public flogging, but got no support at all. The problem seemed insoluble and in the end we had to fudge the issue slightly in the following terms. 'While fuel is available anyone convicted of rape or murder will be removed to a distance of at least one thousand miles and left to fend for themselves. When it is no longer possible for this sentence to be carried out a person so convicted shall be confined for an indefinite period.' Even this compromise was only carried on a four to two vote.

Elaine was the bitterest opponent. "We're storing up trouble for ourselves," she stormed. "Supposing someone molests a child and we've reached the stage where we can't deport them. Do you think the rest of the community would let it rest at a jail sentence. First thing we know there'll be a lynching. What do you do then?"

As gently as he could Colin pointed out that none of us were happy with the situation, but that it was the best that we could do. That led us on to the next bone of contention and one that I hadn't given a thought to.

It was George who brought the subject up. "As far as I can make out there are no gay people among us, but of course one can never be sure. Should we make a statement on homosexuality in the constitution or just rely on common sense?"

Once more there was a difference of opinion, but by a four to one majority we decided not to pursue the matter. Monica abstained on the grounds that she didn't know enough about the subject to give an opinion. Elaine was the loudest voice in the argument, saying that while gay people should be accepted without reserve she was utterly opposed to gay marriages.

"The bible is quite clear on the subject," she stated firmly. "It is a sin in the eyes of God and therefore we cannot condone such a union. I don't suppose the problem of gay people adopting children will come up during our lifetime, but I'd be against that as well."

George was happy enough with the decision but added a rider. "It would be a good idea if we kept our eyes open. If any of us suspect that someone is gay we should let the committee know immediately. Then we can monitor the situation and be ready to step in should there be any discrimination."

The final part of the constitution dealt with future development and I cannot do better than to quote it verbatim.

"The committee will at all times work to improve living conditions and provide the best possible environment for future generations. The next ten to fifteen years will be devoted to consolidating our four existing settlements, building up our herds and flocks of livestock and ensuring an all-year-round supply of a variety of foods. By the end of that period plans should be laid for additional settlements on the south side of Broad River and to the east of Riverside. Our children will spearhead this expansion. From then on each generation will settle more and more of this world. The aim of every one of us should be to give them a solid base on which to build."

We all took copies back to our respective constituents. As we only had one copy each it took a while before everyone had read it, but apart from one or two minor criticisms it received an overwhelming vote of approval.

Once we'd put the constitution to bed Dave reminded us about the proposed survey of the neighbouring continent. I was in two minds as to whether or not to go, but Nicola insisted that she would be fine. She added that if the others wanted to make it a three-day trip I was to go along with them. In truth she looked both healthy and happy. Pregnancy obviously suited her and she flushed with pleasure every time the baby gave a kick. I managed to get hold of a walkie-talkie and made her promise to call Stephen Wallace if she felt the slightest thing wrong. Her final request the morning I set off was to bring her back a prawn curry!

"I'd kill for a prawn curry right now," she told me quite seriously. As I kissed her goodbye I reminded her that the previous week all she'd wanted was a knickerbocker glory!

Monica's parents weren't over keen that she should go with us, but with some help from George she eventually talked them round. Eileen came along as an observer and expert, while Dave, Elaine and myself shared the flying duties. We set off at nine o'clock on the morning of the first of June. Dave took the controls for the hop across the ocean and less than three hours later we landed on the north-east tip of the western continent. At this point we were only just over a hundred miles from the Arctic Circle. Having come from a temperature of over eighty degrees it was quite a culture shock to emerge from the ship into a near freezing atmosphere. Our plan was to zigzag over the whole continent from north to south, landing and exploring six or seven places as widely apart as possible. All the time we were airborne we would keep a close watch on the terrain below for any unusual features.

We stayed for about an hour at our first port of call, exploring over an area of about two or three square miles. We needn't have bothered. Most of the land surface was rock. Only a few odd tufts of grass grew here and there was a complete absence of bushes and trees. The foreshore was very similar to that at Seashore with little or no sand. Though we gazed into the sea at various points there was no sign of any fish.

For the second leg of our journey I was pressganged into taking the controls. The theory was that our only previous discoveries had come when I was the pilot. I headed west-south-west for well over two hours until we hit the west coast of the continent. There was nothing there that looked different to the terrain at Seashore, so after a quick discussion we agreed not to land there but start the next zigzag and touch down about five hundred miles inland. I did so close to a range of mountains, the main peaks of which rose to around four thousand feet. Not only was it a good deal warmer here than at our previous landing, but there was also plenty of life to be seen. Depressingly though it was only too similar to where we were living. The grass, trees and bushes were the same, herds of shigs were omnipresent and when we found a nearby river the fish were the same, too. Close inspection of a small forest a mile away unearthed a large colony of gecks. The girls wanted to climb the lower reaches of the nearest hills but Dave and I talked them out of it. Most of the rock faces were pretty sheer and the danger of a fatal fall was only too obvious.

Airborne again we carried on in the same direction until we hit the east coast. By this time it was after six o'clock, though because of the time difference between the continents the local time was probably around one. After a quick discussion we agreed we would stay there for the night, retiring early to avoid possible jet lag. We'd landed at the edge of the beach, which was quite sandy, though less than half a mile away we could see low cliffs. Once we got to them we quickly found an outcrop of rock stretching out some thirty metres into deeper water. Dave had had the foresight to bring along a home made fishing net, quite a large one at that. We walked along the outcrop, three on one side and two on another. About halfway along Eileen, who was in the lead, gave a yell. The rest of us crowded round. There in the water was another of those monstrous flat fish that we had seen on our first ever visit to Seashore.

Dave looked at the fish and then at his net. "It's too big," he sighed. "We'll never get a fish that size into it. Even if we did the net would probably break under the weight. Let's see if there's any smaller ones about."

Almost at the end of the outcrop we saw one. It was about half the size of the previous specimen, probably a growing baby. Very quietly Dave moved to the very edge of the rock and slowly and carefully slid the net under the fish. With a quick snap of the wrists he scooped it out of the water. It was still a fair size, at least two feet across its widest point and half as long again. Monica wanted to cook and eat it, but I vetoed that suggestion immediately.

"We haven't tested it," I warned her. "It could easily be poisonous to humans and we're a long way from a doctor. Leave it with Eileen for dissection and study."

Once again we found nothing unusual in our surroundings, though we roved a fair distance. About five o'clock in estimated local time we'd had enough. We were tired and hungry, so we broke out the supplies we'd brought with us, shig meat and potatoes, collected driftwood for a fire and prepared a meal on the banks of a small stream that meandered down to the sea not far from where we'd landed. After that we talked for a while and then turned in.

I awoke at first light next morning. Though I'd slept soundly through the night I had a long minute in which I was totally disorientated. I couldn't understand why Nicola wasn't in the sleeping bag beside me. Then reality dawned and I sat up. At first I thought all the others were sleeping peacefully; then I saw that Monica was missing. I sat up with a jerk, unravelled myself from the bag and went outside. It took me five minutes of searching before I found her, sitting on the beach and gazing out to sea.

"If you want to do this again, please wake one of us and tell us where you're going," I scolded her. "I know that we've not found any danger anywhere on this world, but you could have had an accident quite easily."

"I'm sorry, Matt," she said, full of contrition. "But I was so excited I couldn't sleep very well. I didn't want to disturb the rest of you, so I crept out and came down here. It's so beautiful, the sea. I could sit here for hours."

We went back to the ship, by which time the others were stirring. After a quick meal we lifted off again and headed for our next proposed destination. This was a spot on the equator near the central portion of the continent. Early on in the flight we crossed two more mountain ranges, but some eight hundred miles from the equator these gave way to endless rolling plains. Shigs were everywhere and we spotted three or four large herds of mammoths. At one point we passed over a huge lake shaped like an flattened hourglass, some hundred or so miles long and eighty miles wide at its widest points. At the equator itself the land was as flat as a pancake as far as the eye could see. The grass was burned brown and there were very few shigs about. The outside temperature gauge registered ninety-three degrees and we weren't yet at the hottest part of the day. Two wide and sluggish rivers flowed from east to west within a mile of each other.

I set the ship down close to a large forest of deciduous trees, hoping for some shade. As we disembarked the heat struck us like a blow in the face and we quickly moved into the forest. I noted that the vast majority of the trees were clover trees, with very few dandelion trees or bushes about. The same species of birds and butterflies were present in profusion. We noticed that much of the fruit on the clover trees was ripe and that gave me an idea.

"Let's spend a couple of hours or so here and load the ship up with fruit to take back," I suggested. "It'll be at least a month before ours at home are near to picking."

The others agreed willingly. We had to climb the trees to get at the harvest, but that was no problem. At the end of two hours we had a vast mound of the yellow fruits and had all eaten our fill while we were up the trees. Our haul almost filled the survival room.

"That will do us," I said as I surveyed our winnings. "There should be enough there for everyone to have a dozen each."

Apart from the forest there was little else to see in the vicinity. Dave half-heartedly suggested that we should go and have a look at the nearest river, but by now we'd all had enough of the stifling heat. It was just after one o'clock when we lifted off again and headed south-west to the far coast.

There was nothing of any great interest once we did reach the coast. The surroundings were depressingly similar to the other coastal spot that we'd visited. Dave managed to catch another of the baby flat fish.

"This should stay fresh until we get back to Central tomorrow," he said. "We can then get it tested to see if it's edible. Sooner or later the crowd at Seashore will start to thinking about making some kind of boat and fishing offshore. Testing this now will let them know if it will be worthwhile or not."

Our final hop that day was to a point some hundred or so miles from the south coast. We didn't see much point in going to the coast itself as it was odds on that it would be similar to the north. Instead we set down in a wide valley in the middle of a mountain range. A crystal clear stream flowing briskly down the middle provided us with water and a shallow cave gave shelter from the stiff breeze. For over two hours we wandered around, hoping to find something unusual even if we weren't sure what. Dave had a wild notion that there might be gold in the stream and spent most of the time in a minute examination of the banks. He was disappointed.

As we sat down to our evening meal Elaine voiced the thoughts that had been in all our minds. "We haven't found anything because there's nothing here to find. It's been a pleasant couple of days but totally unproductive. Colin and George were right. We've wasted our time. I vote we head home first thing in the morning." No-one demurred, though Monica looked a bit sad.

"Fine by me," was my comment. "But someone else can do the driving tomorrow. By the way, if it's possible to find it I'd like to fly over that island that we left the two rapists on, just to see if there's any sign of life. It's marked on that world map that Dave made, though I'm not sure how accurately it's been placed."

Elaine volunteered to pilot the ship home. More by good luck than judgement she managed to take us over the island in question. We circled low over it three times while looking for signs of life, but there were none. At the spot where George and I had deposited our prisoners there was evidence of occupation: two crudely constructed huts and the remains of several fires, but if the two men were alive and awake they didn't show themselves. I was pleased to see that there were no signs of them having attempted to build a boat.

Shortly after one in the afternoon Elaine landed the lifeship at Central. There was no sign of anyone around as we collected our altabs and Elaine her flying belt. Dave proposed to head for Junction and report to George before going back to Riverside; Elaine would of course brief Colin. Monica wanted to come back to Landfall with me for a session with our six children, but I insisted that she leave it.

"Your parents will have been worried while you were away," I added. "It's best you go and see them before doing anything else." She wasn't happy about it, but she saw my point and complied without further argument.

CHAPTER TWENTY-ONE

Anna Jane Holt, named after Nicola's two sisters, entered the world at exactly seven a.m. on the twenty-third of July and weighed in at a healthy eight pounds one ounce. I was present at the birth, though my only contribution was to hold Nicola's hand throughout. The full medical team was present and I marvelled at the calm demeanour of both Michael and Emma. It wasn't a difficult delivery, though it proved painful for Nicola in the absence of any anaesthetic. I think it was the greatest moment of my life when Emma wrapped a cloth around the infant and handed her over for me to hold. As I cradled her in my arms I was engulfed by a wave of love and tenderness for both her and Nicola. I suddenly understood what Nicola had been trying to tell me in the last few months. This was different.

Donald, Susan's baby, was always in my thoughts as Susan's baby and the fact that I was his biological father only registered dimly on the borders of my consciousness. Anna was our baby, Nicola's and mine. She would share our lives, be with us every waking hour for many years to come. We would see her through the good times and the bad, protect her as best we could and try and guide her to adulthood with as little trauma as possible. That was the moment the doubts I'd had of my fitness for fatherhood finally dissolved. I vowed there and then that I would love and protect my wife and daughter to the utmost of my ability.

I did no manual work that day. I gave what orders there were to be given and dealt with personal enquiries impatiently. I just couldn't bear to leave my wife and new daughter. Nicola was still quite weak, but insisted on breast feeding the mite. Under her instructions I changed the cloth that served duty as a nappy whenever it was required and received the constant stream of visiting well-wishers with as much patience as I could muster. Even at that early stage in her life Anna gave every sign of being a good baby. She whimpered once or twice during the day and the night that followed, usually when she needed to be changed, but no tears were shed and she never actually cried. She slept in Nicola's arms, waking at roughly four-hour intervals.

I had to force myself to go back to work the next morning. Nicola said she felt stronger and able to cope, though she practically had to drive me out. As it was I came back at hourly intervals to check that all was well. I really needn't have worried. One or other of the medical team visited regularly, as did Dorothy to bring milk in case it was needed. Even so it took me a week or more to reach the stage where I could stay away most of the day and retain my peace of mind.

Anna had timed her arrival perfectly. The baby boom in the other three settlements had started at the end of May and for the month of June and the first two weeks in July we hardly ever saw Dr. Wallace, Michael or Emma. They based themselves at Junction ready to race to a potential birth at a moment's notice. One or other would come back to Landfall if requested, but these were always flying visits. By the time we had need of their services the worst was over, though all three looked tired and drawn for a couple of weeks afterwards.

"We had one tragedy," Stephen informed me when at last he came to visit for an hour. "One of the babies at Riverside was stillborn despite all our efforts. It was a girl, two months premature. If I'd had an intensive care unit and full facilities we might have saved her, but as it was there was nothing I could do. Michael and Emma were magnificent. There was one occasion when three mothers went into labour almost simultaneously at each of the locations. I sent Michael to Riverside, left Emma at Junction and went to Seashore myself. George fixed up a radio link so that we could keep in touch constantly. All three babies arrived without a hitch and all healthy. Those two are going to be good doctors in a few years' time."

By the end of July, and the second baby boom, the population of New Britain had risen by another fifty-one souls. It bade fair to rise again the following year. Already four of the existing mothers at Landfall had fallen pregnant once more. I suppose it was to be expected: evening entertainment on our embryo world was non-existent!

By now we were well into the harvest, and it was a good one. Though we still had to do the cutting and threshing of the grain by hand the engineers had provided us with a machine that worked at ten times the speed of the coffee grinders. Once again I had to divert the clothing section into making sacks. Our storehouse cave began to look very healthy indeed as we stockpiled for the coming winter. The difference from the previous year was that the other three settlements now had their own supplies. We did send a certain amount to Seashore to supplement their requirements, but ninety per cent of everything we grew now remained at Landfall.

We still hadn't come up with a method for preserving vegetables, but as soon as we had a surplus of clover and oval fruits we started filling the refrigerated cargo hold on the *Sunrise* that the engineers had set up. One of the Junction contingent was given the job of checking daily and noting the condition of the contents. Apart from fruit we were going to test some of the vegetables for durability as well. Our chickens had continued to remain broody during the summer. By the beginning of August forty-nine chicks had survived and the early arrivals were growing by the day. Twenty-three were cockerels, persuading Peter to accept that, after all, we might be able to put roast chicken on the menu around Christmas time, if the birds had grown sufficiently.

The livestock was thriving in the other settlements too. Twelve of the fourteen sows had given birth, all with fairly large litters. Four of the resultant piglets only lasted a few hours but the rest were growing rapidly, all sixty-three of them. Roast pork in the not too distant future suddenly became a real possibility. The flocks of turkeys, ducks and geese had more than doubled in size. The restricted diet that we were forced to provide did not seem to be having any ill effects. Even the normally pessimistic Colin was pleased with our progress, though his eyes were still firmly fixed on the distant future.

"If we can get three more years as good as this one," he remarked as we talked together one day, "we can relax and let nature take its course. Conversely, one bad harvest or an outbreak of disease among any of the animals and we'll be back to where we started. We have to make sure that everyone stays focussed and keeps grafting. Remind them that we can never have too much of anything, but we could easily have too little."

All too soon winter was upon us again. The mood, in Landfall at any rate, was much more upbeat than it had been the previous year. A lot of that was down to the improvement in the diet, but there was also a quiet satisfaction apparent. All around us we were seeing the results of the hard work that had been put in. Our living conditions were still quite crude, the lack of adequate toilet facilities in particular, but they were improving. There was no longer a feeling of desperation or of worries as to whether we could survive.

As I had done before I made a special effort when drawing up the duty rosters to ensure that everybody had a full day's work. With a decent grinding machine now to hand I diverted the three coffee grinders entirely to producing our substitute coffee and used the main machine in its spare moments for grinding up the shig bones for fertiliser. Our policy from the time we arrived on New Britain had been to throw nothing away and with most of their allotted tasks completed the engineers had turned their attention to experimenting with all the waste that had accumulated. They had no difficulty in using any metal scrap; now they were trying to recycle the mound of paper and cloth. By mid December they'd devised a process for making a paper substitute. I never quite understood how it worked, but they boiled up waste paper, some cloth and some dried leaves from the dandelion trees in a small quantity of water, producing a soft pulp. One of the items salvaged from the *Sunrise* had been a trouser press. Using this they squeezed out the water from the pulp and pressed it flat. Once it had dried out the result was somewhat akin to parchment, but it could be written on without difficulty. All we needed now was a way of making writing implements.

The spinning machine that the engineers had designed and made was now in use all day and every day. We had a fair stock already of rough wool and had started making cotton. The latter wasn't very strong and broke easily but with patience it could be used for sewing. Only one field, at Riverside, had been devoted to growing cotton that year, but each settlement would devote a field to that crop in the future. The one disappointment was that, despite all our efforts, we had been unable to find any materials for making dyes.

The flat fish that we had brought back from our expedition to the western continent proved not only edible but delicious. The flavour defied description but was certainly superior to the river fish on which we'd been existing. Colin commissioned Dan and his team to build a small boat which could be used for inshore fishing and from the moment it was launched it provided a steady supply of what we came to call simply the flat fish. The cod like fish we had seen on our first seaside trip also proved edible, though not as tasty.

During the autumn Paul and Walter had been busy installing the crude central heating system that they had designed into the cabins. It worked after a fashion, though the amount of heat lost was probably greater than that gained, even though all the pipes were lagged with shig skins. It took them two or three attempts to come up with a reasonably efficient grating inside the cabins but once they had done so it was possible for the warm air to be switched off. Along with Walter I checked each cabin's temperature early one morning in December when there'd been a slight overnight frost. Those nearest the boiler at each end were around the sixty-five degree mark, those furthest away registered fifty-nine. It was not perfect, but at least it took the edge off the cold.

Christmas that year was a slightly more festive occasion. Peter Gibson duly provided the lambs for Dorothy and we sat down to a meal of roast lamb, roast potatoes, broccoli, mashed swedes and brussels sprouts. For a starter Dorothy made soup from the offal and bones from the lambs and she surprised us all with a dessert of stewed clover fruit mixed with oatmeal. It may have been a far cry from the traditional turkey dinner, but after a constant diet of shig meat and fish it tasted like manna from heaven!

Predictably our final committee meeting of the year was a long one, but decidedly upbeat. Colin was in the chair and summed up our individual reports. Land under cultivation had more than doubled, with twenty-two fields ready at Landfall for the following year, twenty each at Riverside and Junction and ten at Seashore. The last-named was now producing enough salt for all our needs. Our livestock was multiplying at a more than satisfactory rate and providing our cold store proved effective we would have a supply of fruit, cereals and vegetables for most, if not all, of the winter. The orchards that Cassie had planted were thriving. Many of the young trees were now over five feet in height, and only two had died. The ones that she had held back for emergencies were nearly as tall and would be planted out in the following spring. Dan and his helpers had completed schoolhouses and catering huts for three of the locations and was planning a schoolhouse for Landfall early in the New Year. As I had foretold, Dorothy insisted on keeping her cave.

The schoolhouses in the end turned out to be more than four times the size of our cabins and could hold up to forty children. Dan had made benches rather than chairs for them on the grounds that benches were easier to make and less wasteful of materials. Over thirty cabins were now boasting two rooms and work was proceeding to bring the remaining ones up to standard.

"I've one or two matters I'd like to bring up," said Colin as he concluded the review. "Before I do, has anyone any points they'd like to raise?"

"I've got one," George jumped in quickly. "I'd like to regularise the use of the two lorries. At the moment they're making daily trips between the four locations and Central. To my mind this is wasteful. I've noticed on several occasions that they're carrying very little on them. One a week or so ago took one small bag of salt from Seashore to Riverside and went back with one sack of potatoes. I know the lorries can be recharged every night, but sooner or later some of the working parts are going to wear out and we'll have no way of replacing them. My suggestion is this. We'll base one lorry at Seashore and one at Junction. Each lorry will make two trips a week only, say on Tuesdays and Fridays. The one at Seashore will bring salt and sea fish to Junction. The second lorry will deliver to Riverside and Landfall and pick up its cargo from both places plus anything needed from the cold store at Central on the way back. Its load can be transferred to the first lorry and taken back to Seashore. We can radio our requirements to each other on Monday and Thursday evenings." Nobody raised any objections to this proposal and no other issues were raised.

After giving us ample time for reflection Colin took up the running again. "To my mind this is a significant turning point in our affairs. We have achieved our immediate aim of getting a foothold on this world and ensuring our continuing food and clothing supplies. Incidentally, we've done that in much less time than I anticipated. In my own mind I've dubbed that as phase one, survival. Now we are entering phase two, which for want of a better word I'll label expansion. I feel that it's the right time to consider the broader aspects of life. I know that the birth rate will continue to be high and reduce our workforce, but even with that in mind there are things we can set in motion to improve the quality of life."

"We have been fortunate so far in having capable engineers, joiners and builders, plus a first class doctor among the survivors. I know that we have allocated some of the children to study under them and we have our two trainee vets. I don't think it's enough and I propose that we call for volunteers among those in their twenties to understudy the experts on a full time basis. Ideally we should have at least one doctor, one nurse and one engineer in each location. But there are other trades and professions that are not represented and which are necessary. We have made provision for two vets, but four would be much better. We need a dentist. So far Dr. Wallace has attended to any dental emergencies, but with the increasing population and his teaching duties dentistry will be low in his list of priorities. We need a skilled mechanic. As George has pointed out, the lorries will not last for ever, neither will the altabs. We need a metallurgist. If and when we do find metallic ore it will be of no use to us if we have no means of extracting and purifying it. I'm sure you can think of other skills that are needed. The people we choose, or the ones that volunteer if you prefer it, will have to be self-taught in the main, but there are manuals and text books on many subjects in the ship's library to help them."

"I also think we should start to think about non productive skills. We have no music and no art. Admittedly there are no musical instruments, but I'm sure someone has the skill to make a flute or something similar out of wood. Given music, even in its most rudimentary form, we can hold dances and concerts to relieve the boredom of the long winter nights. I admit that painting is out of the question given the absence of dyes, but there must be some among us who can sculpt from wood or river mud to provide toys for the children and ornaments for the homes."

"Hang on for a minute, Colin," I protested. "I agree totally with the essence of what you're saying, but already you've committed around twenty of our workforce. Not only that, they're twenty of the youngest and strongest. Providing food, looking after animals and catering still needs to be done mainly by hand. You've pointed out yourself that our workforce is already reduced. We'll be throwing too big a burden on too few people if we adopt your proposals."

"I'm not suggesting that we do it all at once," Colin came back quickly before any of the others could intervene. "My proposal is simply that we make a start. We can put it to our constituents and see what response we get when we ask for volunteers. Then we allocate gradually, one here, one there, all the time observing the effect on day to day working. There are savings to be made in that, too. We can slow down the rate at which we're increasing the land under cultivation. An extra two fields per year per site should be more than sufficient from now on. The building sections can be scaled down slightly, too. Everyone who wants one now has a cabin, and long before the end of next year every cabin will have two rooms and basic furniture."

Colin paused for breath and Dave grabbed his chance. "Like Matt, I agree with the theory, but you're forgetting one thing. In three years' time over fifty children will be ready to start their education. In five years' time there could be more than double that number. The four or five professional teachers we have at the moment aren't going to be nearly sufficient. Before we think of anything else we have to recruit and train at least another four, if not more. By all means make a start on what you suggest, but please let's take it very, very slowly."

Nods from George and Elaine showed that they agreed with Dave, as I did myself. Colin looked disappointed. I turned to Monica.

"You've been very quiet today," I told her. "Have you any thoughts?"

"A few," she admitted hesitantly in her soft Irish voice. "I think Colin's idea is brilliant, but I also agree with what the rest of you have said. So instead of looking for volunteers only among the ones in their twenties why don't you look at the under sixteens. Not all of them are working with adults. In fact some of them haven't a clue as to what they want to do. Why not look for your volunteers among them instead?"

This seemed like a good suggestion. Not for the first time Monica had shown wisdom beyond her years. We batted the subject around for the best part of an hour and in the end came up with a compromise. Monica would sound out the younger element. The rest of us would put the proposal to our regular meetings and gauge the response. Once we knew the majority view we could then implement the proposal at a suitable speed.

George had a final point to raise before we closed the meeting. "Dave and I have been talking recently about exploring the land to the south of Broad River. Weather permitting we'll take a couple of altabs and spend some time on Saturdays just roaming around. If any of you want to join in let us know and we can divide up the countryside between us."

Elaine and Monica jumped at the prospect and after a moment's thought I added my name to the list. Colin was unenthusiastic. "I don't know what you're hoping to find. I thought we'd already come to the conclusion that one bit of this world is identical to every other bit."

"It won't do any harm to map out our immediate neighbourhood," George pointed out. ""It won't be long before we start running short of one or two things. We're using up the coniferous wood at an alarming rate, for one thing. The herds of shigs are thinning out quite fast, too. It may be easier to bring in new supplies from south of the river than cast around on this side."

"I suppose it won't do any harm," was Colin's rejoinder. "Come to think of it, if we ever decide to add a fifth site it might be a good idea to situate it on the south side of the river."

I found myself alone with Elaine for a few minutes at the end of the meeting. "Can't you get that man of yours to keep his feet on the ground?" I asked her jokingly. "Before we know it he'll have our grandchildren signed up for their jobs."

Elaine sighed. "You know what he's like, Matt. He always wants to run before he can walk. He has a vision of how this world should look in a hundred years' time. Unfortunately he wants to do it all in the next five years instead."

"I suppose it's just as well that one of us is far-sighted," I observed. "Personally I'm quite happy to get through a month at a time. We've still only got a toehold on the world."

Somewhat to my surprise the majority of the people at Landfall were in favour of Colin's suggestion and there was no shortage of volunteers. I noted down all the names, but warned them that progress would be slow. Some, however, were so keen that they offered to study in their own time providing that I could get them the requisite books from the ship's library. I also discovered for the first time that we had several among us with musical ability. Before the end of that evening a small group had got together to experiment in the production of musical instruments.

Having mentioned to the committee that I was going to do so I brought in two new directives at Landfall on New Year's Eve. With immediate effect Saturday afternoon would in future be a voluntary working affair similar to Sunday. I added the rider, however, that at busy times like the harvest period this concession would be suspended. I had no worries about work not getting done. Sundays had shown that most people preferred to do some work, if not a full day, rather than sitting around doing nothing. My second new measure was to authorise a midday snack for those who wanted one. Our stock of flour was high, as was our reserve of butter. The meal would consist of two slices of bread and butter per person, with cheese twice a week if supplies permitted. This proved a popular innovation: almost from our arrival there had been complaints about the two meals a day system.

We were, in fact, producing more butter and cheese than I had budgeted for. Nearly all our new mothers were breast-feeding their babies and the drain on the milk supply was much less than I had anticipated.

Just before the evening meal that day Eileen came to the lifeship in a state of suppressed excitement. She handed me a cup containing a few brownish coloured crystals.

"Taste that," she commanded. I did so, and a smile spread over my face.

"It's sugar, isn't it?" I said. "How did you manage to make it?"

"Dorothy and I have been experimenting for some time," she explained. "It started when she found a jar of the sugar beet syrup that had been put aside and forgotten. When she opened it she found that the top couple of inches was solid, but that it broke easily into pieces. She came and told me and since then we've been trying various boiling times. We're not quite ready to go into production, but we've almost got the correct consistency now. It's a question of how far to reduce the syrup, then putting it into trays and skimming off the crystals as they form and blow drying them. I've spoken to Paul Cooper and he's going to make up some trays and hot air blowers for us which will connect to the central heating boilers."

"Pat on the back time, Eileen, for you and Dorothy," I said. "You've taken us another step forward. I'll radio the others and pass on the information. If you see Paul before I do, you might ask him to make four sets of whatever equipment he designs."

If this Christmas had been a more joyous celebration than the previous one, New Year was sombre by contrast. A cold and cutting north wind, bringing with it frequent flurries of snow, made it a miserable evening on what I still liked to think of as Hogmanay and the day itself proved no different. Though many of us stayed up, or at least awake, to see out the old and see in the new at heart we all felt depressed.

CHAPTER TWENTY-TWO

It seemed that all at once nearly everyone was wearing the home made shig skin gowns – I use that word for want of a better description – that our clothing section had been making in quantity. They were warm and comfortable to wear, though drab in appearance. Not for the first time many of us wished that we had found a way of making colourful dyes. The wintry weather continued until midday on the third, when the wind swung round to the west and temperatures rose. The snow was replaced by a thin intermittent drizzle, rendering all but the essential outside work impossible. The mood in the camp was improving though, but on the evening of the fifth tragedy struck. William Haddow, our amateur astronomer and weather forecaster, died suddenly.

I wasn't there at the time, so I had to rely on an eye witness account. The evening meal had just finished and William was in conversation with three or four others when he suddenly gasped, put a hand to his chest and crumpled to the floor. Someone raced to fetch Dr. Wallace while the others checked for a pulse. It was still there, but very faint. On arrival the doctor applied artificial respiration for more than five minutes. William appeared to recover briefly and even opened his eyes and tried to speak, but another violent spasm shook his body and he was gone. Sadly his body was carried to the doctor's surgery and Stephen came to report to me.

"There was nothing I could do," he told me. "If he'd lasted a little longer I might have got him back to the surgery and used the defibrillator on him, but two attacks in that short space of time is invariably fatal." He became brisk. "Now with your permission I'd like to carry out a post mortem. I've two reasons for asking. One is to satisfy myself that it was indeed heart failure and that if so whether the deterioration in the heart was caused by our recent diet. If that's the case we're going to have to radically rethink our way of life. Secondly it will be part of the learning curve for Michael and Emma. As the population ages there will be times in their future careers when they will have to perform autopsies. This will

The Far Side of Nowhere

give them invaluable experience." I told him to go ahead and do whatever he thought necessary.

The post mortem took place the following morning. Although the prospect filled me with dread I decided that I should be present. I won't go into details; suffice to say that it was a gruesome business and I was relieved when it was over. Stephen gave me a verbal report on the spot. "I'm no expert in forensic medicine, but as far as I can determine the cause of death was an aneurysm, which basically is an air bubble in the blood stream. This can cause a blockage in the supply of blood to the heart and bring on an attack. Thankfully it's a very rare occurrence: poor old William was just plain unlucky. As you heard me say to Michael and Emma, his other organs were in good shape, so at least we can set our minds at rest as far as food and water on this world are concerned."

William had been our oldest inhabitant at sixty-six. He was one of the few among us who had not taken a partner since arriving, so it devolved upon me to make all the funeral arrangements. This meant a quick decision on where we should site our cemetery. I suddenly remembered a spot at the head of the valley, just where the two ranges of hills joined. Although I'd only been there a couple of times I had been struck by the beauty of the place. It was a small but pleasant meadow three or four metres higher than the surrounding landscape and enclosed by young conifer trees. Between it and the start of the hill country proper lay a large pool formed by the water draining off the hills from which our Narrow River commenced its flow. The only question was whether the earth was deep enough for a grave to be dug.

Calling on Dan for assistance I grabbed a couple of spades and we made our way there. Dan approved my choice immediately.

"It's big enough to cater for our needs for a long time to come," he stated. "When you look around it's probably the only place close to camp where we could site a cemetery. Just about all the available space is under cultivation from Cassie's lot, or taken up by the cabins. We'd need to go a couple of miles away at least to find another site and then it would be out in the open. Let's see how far we can dig down." We chose a spot at the northern edge of the meadow and got to work. Half an hour later, and with a sigh of relief, we laid our spades aside. We were nearly two metres down before striking rock.

"While we're here we might as well complete the grave," I said to Dan. "We're three-quarters of the way there already." He agreed, and in another twenty minutes we had completed our self-imposed task.

"I'll start making the coffin right away," Dan promised as we started back. "I might have it finished by nightfall, but to be on the safe side can you make the funeral the day after tomorrow?"

Every last person in Landfall, young and old, joined the funeral procession as it wended its way from the camp to the cemetery. Though quiet and somewhat reserved William had been a popular figure among us. Colin, Elaine, Dave and George had come by flying belt and altab to mourn with us. Six men including Dan Dunn and myself bore the plain wooden coffin on our shoulders. Though not an overtly religious man William had been a Protestant and Joyce Haggart had prepared a touching funeral ceremony. To begin, those of us who knew the words sang the twenty-third Psalm, 'The Lord's my Shepherd' and this was followed by a short prayer. As we lowered the coffin into the grave to the familiar recital of 'Ashes to Ashes' there was muted applause, continental style, from those assembled. Four of the mourners began the task of filling in the grave as Joyce offered another prayer. Then we sang 'Abide with me'. I thought this would end the proceedings, but to my embarrassment Joyce turned to me and asked if I would like to say a few words. This was something I had not expected and I had nothing prepared. Hastily I composed myself and faced the mourners.

"This is the saddest day and the biggest blow we have had to face since we arrived on New Britain," I began. "I don't have to tell you that William was a respected and much loved member of our community and he will be sorely missed. But I think I can claim to have known him well enough to say that he would not want us to grieve too long for him. If he could he would be telling us now that there was much work still to be done and that we should get on with it. We must never forget him though and I would welcome suggestions as to what kind of monument or memorial would be most fitting. We must ensure that his name will be remembered by future generations."

I wasn't very pleased with my effort but it was the best I could think of on the spur of the moment. We were just about to begin the walk back to camp when Dan called a halt. Paul Cooper handed him a sack which, when opened, revealed a wooden cross that Dan had made. It must have taken him a fair amount of time, because it had been sand-papered smooth. Carved into the horizontal part of the cross were the words 'William Haddow R.I.P.'

Solemnly Dan thrust it into the newly dug soil at the head of the grave.

It was the best part of a week before the black cloud of depression lifted from the camp. Indeed, if it hadn't been for the children the mood would have lasted a lot longer. But by now all the toddlers were crawling and many could walk and even run a few steps. Several of them had uttered their first words. They provided endless amusement for their parents and those around them. Nicola and I felt a bit jealous. Our little Anna had only just cut her first teeth.

At the first committee meeting in February Dave outlined his plans for our exploration of the south side of Broad River. He'd already put in a lot of preparation. He handed each of us an almost blank map on which he'd drawn a semicircle.

"Given the range of the altabs, the semicircle has a radius of thirty-five miles, with some space on the outside." he explained. "When you get to the outer limit use binoculars to mark in anything you can see beyond the thirty-five mile range. I've spent most of my spare time in the last three weeks going along the north bank from Riverside to Seashore. With binoculars I could see about six miles of the southern side, so as you'll see I've filled in all the features there already. We'll cover the rest of the area in easy stages. Now I want to make this as comprehensive as possible, so we'll include everything we see. Disregard single trees or groups of three or four. Anything from five to twenty trees in a group mark as a copse. Twenty to a hundred we'll call a wood and anything over that a forest. Add a letter 'C' or a letter 'D' to indicate whether trees in a particular group are coniferous or deciduous. Mark in any streams or other features and any high ground or ridges as well. Shigs don't normally stray very far, so we can show the herds as we come across them, mammoths too if there are any." Turning to Colin he asked: "Have you changed your mind about joining in?"

"No, I'll leave it to the rest of you," that worthy replied. "Elaine's keen to go and one of us has to stay and look after the baby."

"Right, then," Dave continued. "We'll make a start next Saturday. Meet at the bridge across the river at twelve noon. I'll arrange to have fully charged altabs waiting there. We'll work in twos and I think for the sake of propriety Monica should be with Elaine at all times. For the first trip Matt and I will make up one team and George can go with the girls. We'll switch round on subsequent days. You'll notice that I've marked two segments on the map with dotted lines. On the way out keep to the northern side of the line as far as possible. Then turn south and move in as near to a circular direction as you can estimate for six miles and come back along the southern side of the line. Now we're not going to have any radio contact, so although you might want to separate every so often to check something always be sure to remain within sight of one another. From what I've seen the terrain is pretty flat apart from near the coast. Otherwise if someone breaks down it may take a long time to find them. Any questions?"

Luckily the following Saturday was dry and not too cold, with a light breeze blowing from the west. Dave and I took the segment nearest the river. It was quite slow going as there were a number of copses and a couple of woods on our outward journey, not to mention several herds of shigs. A couple of times we came to small streams meandering across our path. For the most part these were shallow and easy to cross, but there was one that was too wide and too deep at the point we encountered it and we had to detour to find a place to cross. It was a full two hours before we reached our furthest point and turned south.

Before heading back we swept the countryside to the east with binoculars and filled in the details we spotted outside the semi-circle on

Bernard Stocks

Dave's map. For the most part the view ahead was flat, so at a guess we recorded another seven or eight miles in that fashion. We found nothing unusual or of any great interest on our trip back to the bridge. We were the first there and it was a full twenty minutes before we spotted George and the girls heading towards us. While they got their breath back Dave told them of our results.

"We can contribute a little more," George reported. "About five miles outside your semi-circle we saw a large lake through our binoculars. It was almost square in shape and I would guess it was about ten miles long and nine miles across at its two widest points. It was fringed by trees, the same ones we've already seen. When we turned we headed roughly south for eight miles before setting out to come back here. A few miles south of where we turned we spotted another wide river running from east to west. At its nearest point I would estimate that we'd reach it at just about our thirty-five mile limit. Other than that it's the same old story: shigs, trees and bushes plus one small herd of mammoths."

The following Saturday was wet, cold and dismal. I was quite relieved when Dave radioed through to call off the second expedition. By then we'd started planting our crops, and I was tired and out of sorts anyway. But the sun was shining a week later and I found myself looking forward to the day as I rode down to the bridge. On this occasion Dave and George paired off leaving the girls with me to travel almost due south. The outward trip brought little to enthuse over apart from the largest herd of shigs that I'd seen to date. As George had predicted we came to a wide river after just over thirty-four miles. If anything it was even wider than Broad River, slow flowing and teeming with fish.

I turned to Elaine. "For heaven's sake don't tell Colin about this or he'll be wanting to put a bridge across it," I said jokingly.

"Don't worry," Elaine smiled. "I think the last one cured any desire he might have for building bridges. He confessed to me afterwards that he'd died a thousand deaths while we were putting the one across Broad River. At first he was terrified the metal plate would fall and crush those working on it. Then once the lifeship started towing it he foresaw it crashing and killing all on board."

We turned west along the riverbank for about ten miles. Just before we started the journey back I stopped for a couple of minutes to fill in the map with a small wood we were passing leaving the girls to go on ahead. Before I was ready to resume I heard a shout from up ahead. Looking up I saw Monica waving furiously. My immediate thought was that Elaine had had an accident, but as I got nearer I could see her pacing cautiously back and forth over a thirty metre span. To mystify me even further, every few steps she bent down and seemed to sniff the ground.

"What is it?" I asked when I got within shouting range.

"Does this smell remind you of anything?" she and Monica queried almost in unison.

I took a cautious sniff for myself and recognised the odour right away. "That's the smell of peat," I said wonderingly.

"That's what I thought," said Elaine. "It seems to run about fifty metres from the river and I make it about half a mile wide."

I took the trowel out of the altab's saddlebag and carefully cut into the soil. As soon as I broke the turf the smell became almost overpowering. Underneath it was rich and dark brown in colour and certainly looked like the peat I remembered from my younger days. "I'll cut out a few squares to take back," I said with some excitement. "We can dry it out and see if it is really peat. If it is then this could be a really significant discovery. We might even be able to use it to make glass."

We always carried a couple of sacks on these trips, so I cut out enough pieces to fill one of them. Before filling in the map and leaving the spot we double-checked the extent of the area, though Elaine had got it right the first time. The journey back to the bridge was all depressingly familiar, but the three of us were cock-a-hoop at having discovered something new. Dave and George had little to report, but shared our excitement when we gave our bulletin.

Back in Landfall I put the suspected peat out to dry and went looking for an engineer. Eventually I tracked down Walter Butter and told him of our discovery.

"Sorry to dash your hopes," he said when I'd told him my thoughts. "Although peat burns at a higher temperature than wood it still doesn't generate the temperature needed to melt sand and make glass." I must have looked as disappointed as I felt, because he added a rider. "It's an important discovery none the less. If there is peat then the chances of there being coal somewhere in the vicinity are greatly increased. I suggest you put it to the committee that if and when they can spare the labour it might be worth digging down at various spots nearby." With that I had to be content.

On the third and last expedition I was paired with George. The segment nearest the coastline was always going to be the more interesting so at Dave's insistence we tossed for it. George and I won. It was almost a relief to get away from the flat plain that we'd covered on previous trips and get in amongst the foothills that fringed the ocean front. These hills extended inland for seven or eight miles and for the outward journey we skirted the edges. Once we came to Wider River – that was the name Dave had given it - we followed its northern bank to the sea. Although the hill country was rocky there were several passes that were easy to negotiate on the altabs. Without proper surveying equipment we couldn't be accurate in gauging the height of the hills but they were lower than those encompassing Landfall, probably not more than six hundred feet at their highest point.

Two interesting points arose from our day. The first was that all the trees we saw were coniferous, unlike the area around Seashore where both species were in evidence. There was the occasional oval or square bush to be seen here and there and there were far fewer shigs. I suppose we should have expected that, as grazing was much poorer than on the plain. We made several diversions into valleys and even climbed one or two of the hills looking for any evidence of metallic ore, but found nothing.

Most of the way back we hugged the coastline and that provided our second discovery of the day. Almost halfway between the two rivers we came across a wide beach of silver sand, over three miles in length. All of the shore had been of shingle up to that point and when we rounded a bend to be greeted with that magnificent beach we thought at first it was a mirage. But it was real enough. The sand was firm and we could ride the altabs along it without difficulty.

"Can you picture this in two hundred years' time?" I asked George as we stopped to drink in the view. "It'll be crowded with day trippers, girls in bikinis, stalls selling ice cream and probably a fun fair or two. Pity we haven't got any donkeys to breed."

"Unfortunately we won't be here to see it. It won't happen in our time," he replied with a note of regret in his voice. "It could have other uses, though. If we can find a way of making glass we won't have to look too far for our raw materials."

Beyond the beach was the all too familiar shingle and that stayed with us all the way until we reached Broad River. Visibility was good and we could see Seashore clearly beyond the other bank. Two or three people were at work near the cabins and waved to us as we turned east and made for the bridge.

Dave and the girls were there before us and had something to report as well. "We found another patch of peat, about the same size as the last one and about six miles further west," Dave commented. "But even more importantly we came across a couple of pieces of what looks to be a dark kind of slate. Now where there's slate there's often coal, so we've marked the spot. As soon as the planting's finished we'll get a squad out there and dig down. Even if we only find slate there are possibilities in using it for building and roofing if there's enough of it."

Dave summed up the whole enterprise at the end of our committee meeting the following day. "I think this has been a well worthwhile effort," was his opinion. "We now have a detailed map of over four hundred square miles of countryside beyond our present domain. This will be invaluable when the time comes to spread ourselves on the south side of the river. We've confirmed that there are ample supplies of timber and of shigs and we've found peat and sand in reasonable quantities. There's an outside possibility that we may also have found coal."

"There's one other point that I should mention," George broke in. "We still can't be absolutely certain that we've encountered everything that this world has to offer. I know we haven't found anything hostile yet, but that doesn't mean that it may not be there. But we can now confirm that we are safe from three sides. We only have to worry about the east and we've even covered that to a distance of over twenty miles."

Colin had the final word. "As you know, I wasn't over enthusiastic about this whole thing, but I apologise for my doubts. I realise now that it was indeed worth doing and I congratulate all of you on doing it so well." I thought that was very handsome of him.

CHAPTER TWENTY-THREE

The first of what Dr. Wallace termed the 'second round of babies' arrived in late March. Thankfully for the medical team the new arrivals were well spaced out this time. The smallest gap between births was four days. Two days after the first I awoke one morning to realise that Nicola was not in her usual place beside me in our sleeping bag. An unusual sound made me look round and I spied her at the door of the lifeship being sick. I went to her and put my arm around her gently.

"Does this mean what I think it does?" I asked her.

She nodded. "I was sick yesterday morning just after you left. And my period is a fortnight overdue. Looks like Anna's going to be getting a sister or a brother before the year is out."

A wail from behind me told me that the said Anna was awake and hungry. Nicola said she was up to breast feeding her, while I prepared some of the pureed food that Dorothy had provided for all the youngsters. I never did find out exactly what went into it, but the babies all seemed to be thriving on it.

"I'll get Stephen to give you the once over some time today," I told Nicola. "Meantime take it easy and yell if you feel off colour or feel anything unusual."

"I'll be fine, don't worry." she told me. But I worried all the same.

By the end of the summer our population in Landfall had risen by another eleven, with three more pregnancies confirmed in addition to Nicola's. Susan and Michael became the proud parents of another boy at the end of June. Without making it obvious I'd watched Michael with Donald, my son, whenever the opportunity arose and was satisfied with what I saw. He couldn't have been more loving and attentive to a son of his own. Part of the reason, I think, was that he and Susan had a very strong and loving bond. In Michael's mind Donald was part of Susan and that was all the reason he needed for accepting the boy into his heart.

The Far Side of Nowhere

About the end of April a pressing matter led me to a conference with Dan and the two engineers one evening. Along with the other members of our committee I'd been concerned for some time about toilet facilities. There were none in the cabins, of course and people were still using the chamber at the back of one of the caves or the chemical toilets in the lifeships. The latter use was disturbing for the doctor and Eileen and for myself and Nicola. We were prepared to put up with it for the general good, but unfortunately two of the four ships were almost demolished and chemicals for the other two were running low.

"We've got a possible solution, but you're not going to like it," Paul Cooper began. "First off, there's no possibility of putting individual toilets in the cabins. We just don't have the necessary raw materials. The best we can offer is a public toilet. Dan has plans for a raised structure which he'll tell you about. We can make it big enough to take five or six individual cubicles."

Dan broke in at this point. "My idea is to build a cabin on stilts. We'll drive a suitable number of supporting posts into the ground, and make a platform on top about eight feet high. Then it's simply a matter of putting together a hut about the same size as one of the catering huts we've made at the other locations. Steps or a ramp will lead up to the door of the hut."

"The problem, of course, is how we dispose of the waste material," Paul pointed out. "As you'll remember, the ventilation shafts in the *Sunrise* are about a foot or more square and there's plenty of them. We'd connect them up to each individual cubicle: no problem there. It's the next bit that you're going to object to. We can only spot two methods of ultimate disposal. One is to make and use a large skip on wheels. Whenever it becomes full it's taken away and spread on the fields as manure. The second option is to discharge straight into the river."

I looked at him in horror. "We use the river for drinking water and we catch our fish from it. And the crowd at Junction do the same. We can't pollute it."

Walter Butter made his first contribution. "The situation isn't as bad as you might think. I've done some calculations, rough ones admittedly, that suggest the dangers are minimal. There's a high volume of water passing down Narrow River, as you can tell from the swiftness of the current. Doing what we've just suggested will only raise the acidity and pollution factors by about one part in two million. By the time the water reaches Junction that reduces to one in four million. Remember, too, that this is natural waste. It's not as if we're pumping harmful chemicals into the water."

"Most of the solid waste will fall to the river bed anyway," Paul explained. "In fact there is an advantage to be gained. It will nourish the weeds that the fish feed on. Obviously we'll have to make sure any water we take for drinking or washing comes from well upstream of the emission point. Equally obviously Eileen is going to have to sample the water here and at Junction on a regular basis just to make sure it remains pure. The slightest hint of danger and we can stop. By that time we may have come up with something better. But at present that's the best we can offer."

"I'll need to discuss this with the committee," I said doubtfully. "This affects other areas so it's not a decision I can take on my own. It's the drinking water aspect that concerns me most. As you know, the fish stocks are running low anyway, and more and more of our fish is coming from the sea via Colin's lot at Seashore." This was true. Apart from the giant flat fish we now had two other species from the sea. Using strong rafts four of the Seashore group were able to fish quite far out from shore. There was the large cod like fish we'd seen earlier, but in deeper water lived another breed. This was an almost perfect sphere about a third of a metre in diameter with delicately flavoured pale pink flesh. "I suppose you're proposing a similar system for the other three communities."

"We are," Paul replied. "In fact their need is greater than yours, so we'll probably start with them. With the amount of water in Broad River pollution there will be even less for Riverside and Junction. We haven't looked closely into the possibilities at Seashore as yet. It might be feasible to run the waste from there straight into the sea."

Another objection occurred to me at that point. "I know the ventilation shafts are wide, but there's still a possibility of blockage. How do you propose to deal with that?"

"There's a number of pump mechanisms still left in the *Sunrise*," said Walter. "We can fix up hand pumps and hoses in each toilet and ask people to flush out after usage."

I still wasn't convinced but promised I would take the matter to the committee. I suggested that either Paul or Walter should be present the following Sunday to answer any questions or concerns that the other members might have.

May was a busy month for all of us. For the first time we decided to shear the sheep. This wasn't an easy task. All we had to work with were three hand held hair clippers, battery charged. Though there weren't that many sheep each one took an hour or more and it was the best part of a week before the job was completed. No sooner was that behind us when Harry and June reported that they had almost exhausted the shigs in the area and that we would have to drive in new flocks. The nearest were some five miles away.

Reluctantly I gave the order to abandon all other work for a day except for the catering group. Half a dozen remained at the edge of our cultivated area to prevent the shigs encroaching on our fields. Everyone else walked the five miles to the east. The herd we were attempting to move contained some five or six hundred beasts. We spread out in a line nearly a mile long and with sticks and the occasional light burst from a stun gun started to move the reluctant herd towards camp. It was a slow business and it was four hours or more before we had driven them to where we wanted. The next day we repeated the exercise with another similarly sized flock to the south of camp.

A couple of evenings later I was relaxing after supper and playing with Anna, who was just taking her first steps. Nicola was outside washing out some of the baby clothes. After a few minutes I heard her talking to someone, then Eileen came in. I knew right away by the look on her face that she had made some new discovery. She held her hands out of sight behind her back until she was fully within the ship, then brought them round for me to see the contents. In each hand was a square of woven wool, one green, one a dark pink. I asked her how she had managed to colour them.

"You remember those two trees and the cuttings and berries you brought back from the cat country," she began. "Dorothy and I have been doing some experiments and we've found that we can make a green dye from the leaves and a red one from the berries. They're permanent, too. Both these scraps have been washed four or five times and the colour's just as strong as when we dyed them first. They don't work so well on the shig skins, unfortunately, as they're black to start with, but if we had more raw materials to work with I'm sure we could colour them as well."

"Well done," I said. "It'll be nice to get a bit of colour into the clothes we're making. All we need now is yellow and blue and we've got the full range. I was planning to pay a visit to the islands where the cats are. I suggest you come along plus another couple and while we're there we can dig up as many young trees as the ship can carry. If there's any spare space we'll take cuttings as well. We'll split what we get with the other sites and start new forests solely for those trees. In about three years' time we should have all the leaves and berries we can use."

With a great deal of reluctance the committee agreed to the proposals for the public toilets. Though we talked round the subject for nearly two hours none of us could come up with a better solution. Instructions were issued for Eileen to test the water in Narrow River at Junction twice weekly once the one at Landfall was installed and working and that in Broad River once every two weeks at selected points. Also at Landfall a board would be put up defining the lowest point of the river from which drinking water could be taken. Work began on them almost immediately and all four were completed by the end of October. Walter's calculations were soon proved to be accurate. All the water samples taken showed only the slightest deviation from one hundred per cent purity.

All too soon the harvest was upon us and yet again it was a good one. Our cold room at the *Sunrise* had been far more successful than we had hoped. Even the fruit had lasted much longer than we had forecast and had only run out in the middle of April. We therefore commissioned a second cargo hold to be converted. This was larger than the first and the two combined bade fair to give us an all year round supply of both fruit and vegetables.

Bernard Stocks

Our visit to cat country one Saturday was a pleasant day out, or at least it would have been but for the hard labour of digging up over a hundred young trees. Dave and Colin joined Eileen and myself on the trip. We took our supply from the outermost of the islands. We didn't want to tap in to the area that the cats were currently in for one thing and there was always the possibility that now they were well fed they might attack us if we got too close. We landed briefly on the island they were now inhabiting and were pleased to see them all looking sleek and fit. Though they showed no signs of wanting to attack us we kept a reasonable distance from them.

Our second child, a boy, was born on the tenth of November. It was another easy birth and Nicola said it had been less painful than the first. I wasn't sure if this was the truth or if she was just putting a brave face on it. Her hand held tightly on to mine throughout and her facial contortions belied the truth of her statement. We named our son Malcolm John McNeil, after my father and brother.

Anna was fascinated with her baby brother and hardly ever strayed from the side of his cot. By now she was walking and talking and a real bundle of energy. She seemed to have inherited her mother's blonde hair and blue eyes together with my nose and chin. While Nicola was feeding the baby Anna would stand at the door of the lifeship and would call out to anyone passing by: "Come see my baby." She always described Malcolm as 'my baby'. Frequently around that time I looked a couple of years ahead and wondered how we would cope with two energetic youngsters. When I mentioned the matter to Nicola she laughed and said: "By that time there might well be a third either here or on the way!"

It had been another hot summer, the sunshine alternating with the occasional spell of heavy rain, and our orchards had thrived. Most of the trees from the first planting were around three metres tall by the end of the growing season and Cassie forecast that we could expect the first few flowers and fruit the following summer. The soft fruit bushes that we'd planted around the fields had made similar progress. Ourselves, Riverside and Junction had added three new fields by the end of the year and Seashore five. There were enough male turkeys surplus to requirements to provide our Christmas dinner and pork was on the menu for New Year's Day. All these advances were noted at our final committee meeting of the year.

"Our next target," said George in his summing up, "should be to stockpile a year's reserve of those crops which will keep. Cereals, potatoes and root crops come into that category. We've been lucky so far, but the possibility of a crop failure one year is always present and now is the time to insure against such an eventuality. It will probably take us a couple of years but it's well worth doing. If nothing else it will give us peace of mind. None of us wants to go back to the basic shig and fish diet, I'm sure."

At a suitable moment I brought up another important matter. "The engineers tell me that they're running short of raw materials," I reported. "They've used up just about all of the spare lifeships and they want to know if we'll give the go ahead for the dismantling of what's left of the *Sunrise*."

"Shouldn't be a problem," Colin responded first. "We'll need to retain the two cargo holds as cold stores and I think it would be a good idea to leave one or even two of the remaining three for future use. I presume they will leave the generator in place. We've salvaged all the movable gear that we can so there's no reason for leaving it any longer." Everyone agreed with this.

We'd all been returned to our places on the committee with big majorities in the elections at the beginning of December but it was at this meeting that Elaine announced her resignation. She and Colin had just celebrated the birth of their second child at the beginning of December and she felt that the family's needs should take priority.

"Using a flying belt with one baby is hard enough," she commented with a light laugh. "Using one with an active child <u>and</u> a baby is out of the question."

By unanimous vote we appointed Monica in Elaine's place. She was due to turn sixteen in the following March and having more than proved her worth we didn't want to lose her. Under pressure Elaine agreed to stay on until then.

"Instead of being the voice of the under sixteens you can now be the representative of the teenagers," I told Monica.

CHAPTER TWENTY-FOUR

We didn't leak the news of Elaine's withdrawal from the committee until the day after Monica's sixteenth birthday. Naturally we had to get general approval for Monica's appointment and this was by no means certain. However, when we put it to our respective meetings we got sixty per cent support and she was duly elected. She had endeared herself to adults as well as the younger generation and the fact that all the other members of the committee wanted her to stay weighed heavily in her favour. I was not only pleased for Monica herself. I had been worried in case an election would have thrown up another male, making the committee totally male dominated. I did not think this would be a good thing; in fact I would have liked an equality between the sexes as being more representative. I brought the matter up at our first committee meeting after Elaine's waygoing. While the others agreed in principle I had no support for writing such a requirement into the constitution.

Colin summed up the general feeling. "As the population increases and the committee gets bigger, then is the time to consider some sort of equality. For the present it's not vital and everyone seems happy with the set-up as it is. We'll keep a finger on the pulse of public opinion just to make sure there's no dissatisfaction."

Monica's replacement as the voice of the under sixteens was voted for by that group only. Having regard for my worries about inequality I was pleased when they elected another girl. Christine Lowrie, a fourteen-year-old originally from Carlisle, won by a narrow margin. Though not quite as mature and outgoing as Monica she had a sensible head on her shoulders and like her predecessor was popular among her peers.

This, our fourth year on the planet, was memorable in a number of ways. Mid April brought us our first hurricane. At least that's how we referred to it though we had no means of measuring the speed of the wind. It was certainly a good deal stronger than anything we'd encountered up to that point. My personal estimate was close to eighty miles an hour but

I could have been way out. For six solid hours the gale howled about us as we sheltered in caves and cabins. Intermittently heavy showers of rain and hail made life even more miserable. Just after nightfall the wind dropped suddenly and the rain came down in sheets for another four hours.

Hardest hit were the younger children. They had been so used to playing outdoors all day that being cooped up for hours on end made them fractious and for the first time difficult to control. Tempers became frayed and normally placid parents flared up uncharacteristically. I couldn't do much to help alleviate the situation as Nicola and I had our hands full with Anna and Malcolm.

Before breakfast the following morning Dan, Paul, Peter, Cassie and I made a tour of the whole site to check the effects of the storm. We started with the cabins which thankfully showed no damage; a tribute to the design and workmanship that Dan and his team had provided. We next inspected what remained of the coniferous forest to the north of the camp. By now this was reduced to between forty and fifty trees. Two had been uprooted and in falling had caused a breakage in one other tree.

"No problem," remarked Dan. "We'll get busy today cutting up and shaping the three. It just means we'll be building our second schoolhouse a couple of years ahead of time."

The orchards had suffered too, but not nearly as much as we had feared. Eight young trees had been uprooted altogether and Cassie opined that there would be no difficulty in replanting them. Some of the soft fruit bushes surrounding our ploughed fields had met a similar fate – one blackcurrant bush had been blown over a quarter of a mile. The crops that we had planted in February and March came through unscathed mainly because they had only just shown through the ground and nothing was more than three inches high. By great good fortune none of the trees and bushes in the deciduous forest had been affected.

"Looks like we've been lucky," commented Paul. "All the same, I hope yesterday was a one-off and we don't get any more days like it."

Even before the hurricane we had decided to start the schooling of the three-year-olds in the middle of April. On the third Monday of the month therefore Landfall Primary School, as we'd decided to christen it, was formally opened. The school roll consisted of twenty-four pupils and two teachers and classes at the start were from ten until noon and two until four. Several of the mothers had volunteered to help as well. The teachers, with Dan's help, had made up a vast number of wooden blocks inscribed with letters and numbers. In the absence of writing materials these would be used to teach spelling and arithmetic. Much of the time was given over to play. Old favourites like 'I spy' and 'blind man's bluff' were trotted out and several new games had been thought up by teachers and mothers.

I popped in for a short while on that first afternoon just to see how the children were settling down to the new regime. They all seemed quite happy despite the sudden restriction on their previous complete freedom, though whether this would last once the novelty wore off was anybody's guess. I'd wanted Anna to attend even though she wasn't yet three, but Nicola had overruled me. "Let her have her freedom for a little while longer," she advised. "She's no trouble to look after; in fact in her own way she helps me with Malcolm and I don't want to lose her just yet." In truth Anna doted on her younger brother and he seemed just as taken with her.

Naturally I had to give a full report on the school's opening at the next committee meeting. The other three areas wanted to be aware of any problems prior to the opening of their own schools in July or August. Monica was in the chair for the first time, looking nervous but coping well. Once I'd fielded a number of questions George raised his hand.

"I've been giving some thought to the development of the children," he opened. "We've got plans for their educational needs, but so far we haven't considered their physical wellbeing. I think, and I hope you'll all agree with me, that we should consider some form of sport as part of the curriculum. Firstly I'd like to see fifteen minutes of exercises either first thing in the morning or at the end of the afternoon session, or both. Secondly I'd like to see something that will promote competition. Right now we don't have the ability to make a ball of any kind, so things like football and cricket are out of the question. But there's no reason why athletics shouldn't become part of the daily life of both the children and adults. It would be easy enough to lay down a running track for field events, starting with foot races. The joiners can make us hurdles and high jump stands and a sandpit and a board are all that's needed for the long jump. For safety's sake I think we should omit throwing events, for the time being anyway. What do the rest of you think?"

"I think it's a great idea," I said with enthusiasm. "Apart from being of immense value to the children's development it will provide something for the adults to do during the summer and at weekends. Of course not everyone will be interested in competing, but all the communities have shown great team spirit and I'm sure those who don't take part actively will willingly assist as officials." The others were just as keen as George and I and we quickly got down to more specific planning.

"Are you suggesting just the one running track, say at Central, or one for each township?" Dave wanted to know.

"I think we should aim for the latter," George replied. "Maybe later we can add one at Central. If the idea becomes popular that can become a sort of national stadium where the four locations can compete against each other."

The voice of caution that was Colin sounded the first pessimistic note. "Do we have the manpower available to do all this?" he queried. "Don't get me wrong; I'm all in favour, but I don't want to see more important work suffer accordingly."

Dave was indignant. "I'm sure we're all intelligent enough to make sure that doesn't happen. But with this year's crops all planted we've all got some spare capacity just now. Even Dan and his merry men are under employed."

The motion was adopted unanimously and received a warm welcome when I recounted the plans to the evening meeting at Landfall the next day. Volunteers were immediately forthcoming and a start was made that week. Unfortunately the nearest available site was over a mile and a half from the main camp, but this was ideal for the purpose. An area slightly larger than a football pitch formed a natural bowl with grassy mounds on three sides for spectators. Dan committed himself to building two cabins to act as changing rooms as well as making hurdles and high jump stands. Unfortunately there wasn't a supply of water nearby to provide possible showers or even provision for washing. Naturally there were no toilet facilities, but a sizeable copse of bushes nearby would cope with dire emergencies! As an example of the height to which the enthusiasm for the project was running one volunteer even suggested that we cut steps in one of the surrounding mounds and laid wood down to form terracing!

Measurement of the running track was left to the two engineers. In common with the accepted practices of the time we had left Earth our elliptical track measured four hundred metres. We had no way of painting lines to form lanes, but we overcame this by laying lines of small white stones for two hundred metres. Races longer than two hundred metres would be run in lanes for that distance then runners could have free access to all areas of the track. The high jump and long jump pits were sited in the middle of the track.

A committee of three, all volunteers, was formed to oversee all competitions and make such rules as they considered necessary. They quickly drew up a programme that included races over one, two, four and eight hundred metres plus one, two and five kilometre events. There was a suggestion of a ten kilometre event as well but it didn't receive much support. Hurdle races would be over one and two hundred metres. For the next couple of years the children would race over twenty-five and fifty yards, graduating to longer distances and the hurdles and jumps when they got older. Also for the children we introduced novelties like three legged, sack and egg and spoon races.

I asked Colin to come over on the second Sunday in July to formally open the Landfall Stadium. For the occasion we put up two poles joined by a ribbon at the starting line. Colin made a short speech hailing what he called 'this historic event' and solemnly cut the ribbon. In less than a month Riverside, Junction and Seashore all had their own tracks and a start had been made on the one at Central. I wasn't altogether in favour of this last venture. Although I could see the attraction of having inter area rivalries it would mean most competitors and spectators would have to walk six or seven miles to attend, the two lorries being required for the

Seashore contingent. I doubted that competitors could give of their best after such a hike to get to the track.

It was round about this time that we laid down the general principles for the future education of our children. They would remain full time students until their thirteenth birthday. After that they would spend three hours in the classroom in the morning and in the afternoons they would take up a type of apprenticeship in whatever line of work they desired. Opportunities would be given them to change direction after six months if they were not happy. The committee also suggested, having discussed the matter at length with the teachers, that school should be continuous throughout the year with no holidays except for Saturdays and Sundays. Needless to say, this decision was welcomed by the parents, many of whom already had another child under school age. Several indeed were expecting a third addition to their families.

At the same committee meeting we made another important decision with an eye mainly to the future. It was Dave who first brought the matter up, but once he had done so I was amazed that none of us had given it some thought long before.

"I've noticed a bit of clandestine activity in the bushes among the younger element," was how he phrased his introduction to the subject. "Now I know that we want to increase the population as quickly as possible, but if we're not careful girls will be falling pregnant at eleven and twelve. Should we not lay down a minimum age of consent?"

There was a long pause before Colin broke the silence. "You're right, of course. Question is, how do we enforce it once we decide what age it will be? I hardly need to remind any of you of the ongoing problems there have been on Earth."

"The simple answer to that is that we can't," I opined. "All we can do is to lay down the law and try and achieve agreement by education. That can come from both parents and teachers. But you'll never stop young people from experimenting with sex, and we've no means of providing contraception. I don't know what the best approach would be. Maybe some sort of scare tactics about the effects that under age pregnancies could have on future health and well-being. Maybe Dr. Wallace will have some ideas."

"I agree broadly with Matt," said George. "Much as it goes against the grain to make a law that we can't enforce I still think we have to make the effort. For once, however, I think the final word should be left to Monica and Christine. They're much closer to the issue than the rest of us." Turning to the two of them he went on: "I realise this will probably be embarrassing for you both, but it is important. I promise that none of us will make judgements on you."

Christine was blushing and looked tongue tied, but Monica took it in her stride. "I've got a boy friend as you know and we've been having sex for over a year now. I've been firm about the timing of it, mainly because

I don't want a baby for another couple of years. I suppose too that sixteen was imprinted on my mind. Although it's not a subject that I've talked about much with the others I think you'll find that everyone over twelve here has had some sexual experience. It would be surprising if it were otherwise. After all, there's not much else to do here in the evenings. Would you agree, Chris?"

Swallowing audibly and speaking in a low voice, Christine agreed. "I think Dave and Colin are both right, though. There should be an age limit, but some at least will ignore it."

We talked round the subject at length and eventually settled on fifteen as being both the age of consent and the minimum age at which couples could marry if they so wished. I would have preferred to see it set at sixteen, which was the accepted age in most countries on Earth, but I was outvoted.

"Even on Earth children are maturing, both mentally and physically, at a much earlier age than in the past," George pointed out. "I would guess that the maturing process will be accelerated here, given the conditions under which we're living. In time we may find that fourteen is a more appropriate figure."

For a few weeks after our decision was made public I tried to keep an unobtrusive eye on our handful of younger teenagers. I didn't see anything untoward, which meant that either they had accepted the ruling or that they were just too clever in hiding their activities from me!

Nicola and I had persuaded Dan to make us up some of the letter and number blocks and we had managed to teach Anna some simple sums and spelling. In this way we hoped that she would be on an equal footing with the other children once she started school. We tried to make it like a game and she seemed to enjoy it and proved an apt pupil. She entered the school properly at the end of July. The morning she was due to start, however, brought the first real rebellion that we had experienced with her. For some reason she had assumed that Malcolm would be going with her. The tantrums started when it was explained to her that this wasn't possible.

"But who's going to look after Malcolm when Mummy's busy?" was the theme of her objections amid a flood of tears.

"I think Mummy will be able to cope," I told her as gently as I could. "It's only for a short time each day, and you'll be back at three o'clock." But she just would not be consoled. Eventually I had to put my foot down and become stern with her.

"All of us here, adults and children alike, have to do things we don't want to," I said. "We have to work in the fields or cook or make clothes; you have to go to school. You want to be as smart as all the other children, don't you?"

It took a lot more of the same before we finally managed to coax her along to the schoolhouse over half an hour late. Even then Nicola had to promise to come in with Malcolm during lessons. When I came in at five o'clock that evening she was a little happier. I asked her how she had enjoyed her first day at school.

"It was all right," she answered gravely. "But it would have been much nicer if Malcolm had been with me."

For the first couple of weeks Nicola made a point of looking in at the school at intervals. Gradually she reduced the frequency of her visits and after about three weeks stopped altogether. By then Anna had settled down and we had no more problems.

It was about this time that Paul and Walter came to see me one evening. I could tell by their faces as they walked through the door of the lifeship that they weren't bringing good news. Paul's first words confirmed this.

"We're running into difficulties watering the fields. The biggest headache is here in Landfall because the new ground that we're opening for cultivation is further and further from the river. The other areas will suffer too, though not quite as drastically. As you know, up until now we've been able to pipe water from the river to water the fields, but now we've run out of both pipes and pumps."

"Any suggestions about what we can do?" I asked.

"We've thought round and round the problem for a few weeks," Walter contributed. "Frankly we can only see one answer and that's going to mean a lot of hard work. We'll have to dig irrigation canals from the rivers to encompass the fields. I reckon there's two years' work in the job and we'll have to keep extending them as we increase the area under cultivation."

"The scheme does have a couple of advantages," said Paul. "Firstly it will free up pipes and pumps for other uses. More importantly it will solve the problem of sewage disposal. Instead of having the outlets to the toilets going into the river they can go into the canals. This will serve a double purpose. It will remove any possibility of contaminating our drinking water and at the same time fertilise the fields."

I thought quickly. "You're right. It is the only solution. Start drawing up your plans for the canal system. I'll notify the committee on Sunday and the others can start working out the needs for their own areas. As soon as you're ready I'll set up a working party and we'll get weaving."

We started work the following Monday. Each canal, and there were initially five planned for Landfall, would be a metre wide and a metre deep. Naturally we dug the main part of each one before digging out the section adjacent to the river. It was a slow business. The soil we excavated had to be disposed of, often some distance from the place where we were working. But by rotating the personnel around other jobs we didn't get too many complaints – just a lot of sore backs!

Our first proper athletics meeting at Landfall was held on the first Sunday in September. Luckily it was a perfect day for sport: dry, sunny and not too warm. We started the day with the children's events, moving on to the adults after a break for lunch. Around thirty adults competed and as I had expected there was no shortage of volunteers to act as officials. Apart from the normal races and jumps we laid on some for 'veterans' over forty. Though not having much prowess as an athlete Nicola insisted that I ought to compete rather than officiate, so I entered for the eight hundred and fifteen hundred metre events. I surprised myself, coming fourth out of six in the former and third out of five in the latter. The family honours went to Anna, however. She had entered into all six of the children's events, winning two, coming second in three and third in the remaining one.

The day was voted a huge success and provided talking points for most of the following week. By popular demand we decided to hold a meeting once a fortnight and from that point on nearly two dozen men and women took up some form of training routine. Though nobody seemed worried about the lack of prizes I prevailed on Paul to make some small cups from our precious supply of metal and we used these for the various events. The other three locations reported similar enthusiasm and we held our first 'World Championships' in late October, with the four townships competing against one another. Paul surpassed himself in making a fairly large cup to be awarded to the winning town. This turned out to be Junction, though the final points tally between them, ourselves and Riverside was very close. It was George who made the most telling contribution, winning both the jumps and the two hurdles events. With a much lower population to draw from Seashore finished well adrift of the pack, but it didn't seem to diminish their enjoyment of the day. Sport had arrived on New Britain in a big way.

On the domestic front we were blessed with another excellent harvest and the livestock continued to multiply. There'd been a little blossom early in the year on some of the fruit trees and bushes in our orchards and surrounding our fields at Landfall and come the end of summer we'd gathered no less than six apples, four pears, five plums and a handful of gooseberries and blackcurrants. Needless to say they were all given to the children. Cassie gave her opinion that it would be two more years at least before we started getting terrestrial fruit in decent quantities, but it was an encouraging start. In the meantime we still had the native fruits to supply all our needs in that direction. All the cabins now had two rooms and it was planned to increase this to three over the coming twelve months for those families with more than one child. The public toilets that

Bernard Stocks

the engineers and joiners had provided were working well and our water supplies remained unaffected. All in all we were making good progress in our efforts to establish ourselves on this world.

CHAPTER TWENTY-FIVE

Yesterday was the tenth anniversary of our arrival on New Britain. There are times when the years seem to have flown and others when I feel I have spent a whole lifetime here. Most of our efforts are still geared to the production of food. With over two hundred and fifty children under nine the demand is ever increasing. Nicola and I have four of them ourselves: three girls and a boy. Mairhi and Martha arrived at roughly eighteen month intervals after Malcolm. The largest family is one of four boys and two girls in Riverside. There are two families of five, one of them containing two sets of twins. One of the many things that we have to be thankful for is that all the young ones are exceedingly healthy. All have good eyesight and hearing, too. Of course advances in optical and aural science over the past forty years means that all the adults carried these attributes. Nowadays it is an easy matter to correct congenital problems soon after birth and to deal speedily with those occurring later in life. It is good to find that we seemed to have passed these improvements on to our offspring. We just do not have the materials or the skill for making spectacles and hearing aids.

Each of our four main settlements now boasts four farmers, two to tend the fields and two to look after the livestock. Each year we have extended the land under cultivation by at least two fields per location. Our biggest source of pride, however, is our orchards. The three we originally planted at Landfall have long since merged into one and Cassie has started two new ones some three miles from the camp. All the temperate trees and bushes have been giving us fruit in ever increasing quantities and now supply nearly all our needs. Many of us still have a taste for the clover and oval fruits, though, and still pick, eat and store them. Our tropical fruit trees have been a little slower to develop, but we've had oranges, lemons and grapes in small amounts for the last two years and this year we're hoping for figs and grapefruit, possibly even a few olives.

Bernard Stocks

Our livestock is multiplying at a satisfactory rate but we are still heavily dependent on shig meat and fish for our dietary needs. Over the past year we have had pork, lamb or beef about three times a month and chicken or occasionally duck once a month. For the past three years, though, we have had turkey at Christmas and goose at New Year. The shigs in the vicinity of all four camps are much thinner on the ground and once a year at least we have to drive in new herds from a considerable distance away. Most of our fish at Landfall now comes from the sea, but Riverside and Junction rely on the river for theirs. Despite the heavy requirements the amount of fish in Broad River never seems to decline.

We are still no nearer finding a supply of metallic ore. The coal seam that Dave discovered proved very small and was quickly used up. Thanks to an invention by Walter Butter we are now able to make small amounts of an inferior type of glass, most of which is used to make bottles and jars. It is becoming important for us to find new supplies of metal as we have used up nearly all that we could salvage. All that is left of the *Sunrise* is the four cargo holds that we converted to cold stores and a small room that holds the generator. We have kept one lifeship flying for emergency use but our supplies of fuel are low and that will probably go the way of the rest in the near future.

Despite all our efforts we have not been able to find materials to provide blue and yellow dyes. Once the cat trees became established there was a plentiful supply of green and red so those two colours were used on everything. It soon became accepted practice that the men wore green and the women red and the same distinction was applied to baby clothes. After careful experiments we did, however, manage to produce three or four different shades of each colour, so baby girls were given the traditional pink and the palest green hue was used for the baby boys.

Colin's original request for people to consider making crude musical instruments eventually bore fruit. Once the first two or three flute type reeds appeared the interest in such pursuits quickened and soon we had two dozen or more. The more enterprising among us managed to put together contraptions that vaguely resembled guitars and violins. The sounds produced were somewhat raucous at first but either they improved or our ears became attuned to them. Over the last couple of years we've discovered some songwriting talent among us and nowadays we have frequent dances and the occasional concert.

Another leap forward came when someone with an inventive turn of mind managed to make a football out of mammoth hide. It bore an uncanny resemblance to the ball used in the very early days of football, with a leather case and an inner core made from a shig's bladder. Though a trifle on the heavy side, it came through a successful trial with flying colours and soon we had a steady stream of new balls at our disposal and football became a regular pastime for many of us, women included. We already have an under nines league up and running and there is talk of an adult league being formed in the near future.

One thing for which we are all thankful is that death has cast its icy fingers but lightly upon us. We lost one man at Junction in a freak accident two years ago. He was felling a tree when it twisted unexpectedly in mid air. He was unable to get out of the way in time and was crushed beneath it. One other baby at Riverside was stillborn and we lost a one-day-old boy here in Landfall. He was born two months prematurely and despite all Stephen Wallace's efforts just did not have the strength to survive. We laid him to rest beside William Haddow in our little cemetery. That was a sad day for us all.

In general the health of all four communities is excellent. According to our good doctor the reason is plain. "Though all of us have to work hard we're doing so out in the fresh air," he explained. "The human race wasn't made to sit in stuffy offices hunched over a computer terminal for eight hours a day. That's the scenario for people being overweight and suffering strokes and heart attacks. Look around you. Everyone's tanned and nobody's carrying any surplus pounds of fat. My only worry was the restricted diet we had for the first couple of years. Now that our food intake is properly balanced there's no reason everyone here shouldn't live to a ripe old age. My guess is that there is going to be a high percentage of centenarians within the future population."

Dave resigned from the committee nearly five years ago. He had been showing an increasing interest in poultry farming over the previous year and expressed a desire to spend all his time in developing our flocks. Dan built him a cabin on the south side of the bridge over Broad River, where he, Fiona and their three children were soon joined by three like-minded families. They called the new community Bridgegate and took over all the turkeys and geese. Each of the other four settlements donated half a dozen ducks and two dozen chickens of assorted types to the new township. Dave and his helpers have since been conducting experiments in cross-breeding.

In Dave's place Riverside elected a young woman in her mid twenties, Michelle Gillespie. Hailing from Edinburgh and of Italian descent, Michelle had just passed out as a lawyer when she decided to emigrate to Paladia. She brought a new dynamic to the committee. As befitting her chosen profession she had a sharp, incisive mind and an awesome command of the English language. She also brought in a raft of new ideas, some useful, others impractical, and at one time or another found herself at loggerheads with each of us. Committee meetings became much more heated after she arrived, but in a dignified way. We all had too much respect for each other to descend to verbal slanging matches in the way that politicians did back on Earth. We have just reached the point where the age gap prevents our having a member for the under sixteens, but the present incumbent will stay on as the voice of the young ones until a suitable replacement can be found.

There have been times when I considered leaving the committee myself. Two things stopped me. One was my wife, who insisted that I was needed to, as she expressed it, 'provide a calm and sensible middle of the road approach to matters'. The other reason was that I had no clear idea of what I wanted to do in its place. I had an overriding interest in everything that went on at Landfall and in our new world generally, but no desire to specialise in any one thing.

Colin was a surprise visitor to Landfall last night. He arrived in time for the evening meal with the excuse that he thought it was appropriate to be here on this special day. Of all of us Colin seems to have aged the most. His hair is turning grey and there are lines etched in his face. Thankfully he is still as dedicated to the task of building our new world as he always was and is still looking far into the future. After supper we strolled out to a grassy knoll from which we could get an extensive view of the surrounding countryside. An uplifting sight filled our eyes. The orchard was in flower and the crops were showing green in the ground. Herds of cows and sheep grazed contentedly in the middle distance and from the camp behind us we could hear the grunting of pigs and the clucking of chickens.

We stood in companionable silence for several minutes. Then Colin sighed and turned to me.

"It's a heartening sight," he confessed. "But do you ever get the feeling we should have been able to do so much more?"

"For heaven's sake, Colin," I replied. "What did you expect after ten years: four lane motorways, supermarkets, high speed rail links and bingo halls? We've done wonders to get this far. Admittedly it was a major stroke of luck that George was able to salvage the wreck of the *Sunrise*. Without that we wouldn't have been nearly so far ahead. But we've done what we set out to do. There's a basis now for the generations that will follow us and it will be up to them to decide on further development."

He sighed again. "I suppose you're right. I guess I've always wanted to do too much too quickly. But it saddens me when I look around me. We've regressed to where civilisation was five hundred years ago. We're nearly all tillers of the soil, living in wooden huts with no sanitation and no running water."

"These things will come," I consoled him. "And it won't take us five hundred years this time. There must be coal, metal and minerals somewhere on this continent. Sooner or later we'll find them and then we'll take a giant leap forward. We have the technology and the knowledge already so we won't have to take it one step at a time as our forebears did."

We were joined at that moment by Dan Dunn and Paul Cooper. The two of them had been deep in discussion as they approached and it didn't take me much effort to guess what they'd been talking about. A couple of months previously the committee had looked at plans for setting up two new communities on the south side of Broad River. Though neither Riverside nor Junction was over populated as yet both sites had used up most of the ground in the vicinity that was suitable for cultivation. In any case, within ten years or less the new generation would be looking for homes and living space and it seemed sensible to provide these earlier rather than later. Timber was also becoming scarce in the existing four areas.

Paul brought the subject up immediately. "We've worked out a method of putting another couple of bridges across Broad River," he told us. "It's Dan's idea really, so I'll let him explain."

"It's quite simple really," Dan began. "We make a number of rafts and float them out, tying them together until we have enough to span the river. Then we anchor them at each end. That will enable people to cross on foot straight away. Once the rafts are in place we can drive piles into the river bed and construct a second bridge on top of them which will take the lorries and the altabs. Once the main bridge is in place we move the rafts to the next point at which a bridge is needed."

"Will you be able to get the poles in firmly enough to support the weight of the bridge?" I asked.

"That's the one point that I'm not sure about," Dan admitted. "I've tried driving one in near the bank and that's rock solid: whether the same will apply in the middle of the river will have to be discovered by trial and error. One good thing is that the river is only around four metres deep. What we can do is drive enough piles so that even if one or two collapse the others will hold the bridge up. But even if we find that we can't build a permanent bridge we'll still have the rafts. It will just mean that heavy loads will have to use the main bridge."

"There is an alternative," I pointed out. "We can increase the size of Bridgegate and put the sixth township about halfway between Riverside and Junction. That way we'll only need the existing bridge."

Colin laughed. "Once more I'm looking farther ahead than you are, Matt. If we do what you suggest in twenty years we'll have used up all the land between Riverside and Junction and then we'll have to expand south of the river anyway. Let's do it now. I'm going to propose that at least one, if not both of the new sites should be some miles from Broad River. There are enough streams in the vicinity to ensure a supply of fresh water and we've enough metal left to make additional wind and water turbines. We still have the generators from the lifeships that we scrapped. They'll operate just as well from a cabin as they do from the lifeships that we've retained."

As we walked back to camp Colin asked me if I believed in reincarnation. I told him I had no hard and fast views one way or the other and asked why he'd brought the subject up.

"It would be nice to think that we can come back sometime in the future and see just what becomes of this world," was his explanation.

"I'm not sure I'd like that," I said after a moment's thought. "Think how disappointed we would be if no progress had been made. Maybe in two hundred years' time it will simply be a matter of ten times the number of people doing exactly the same as we are now."

After Colin had gone and we'd put the children to bed Nicola and I sat up and talked far into the night. It seemed a suitable occasion for reminiscing over the previous ten years and making some plans for the future. Among other things we discussed whether we should add to the family. Nicola was keen and I would have loved another child but her last pregnancy had been difficult and I didn't want her to go through it all again. In the end we deferred making any decision on the matter.

Just before tiredness drove us to bed she asked me a question. "If a ship came to rescue us tomorrow would you want to go back to Earth?"

I had to think carefully about that one. Finally I replied: "I'm really not sure. I'd certainly like to go back for a visit. I still miss my family and friends. And I must admit that the thought of things like hot baths, proper sanitation, real soap and toothpaste and gourmet meals would be an overwhelming attraction. One change I would make, though. I wouldn't pursue my career in space. I'm too happy and contented with family life to want to leave you and the children for months or years at a time. I'd probably opt for a farm or a smallholding somewhere on Earth or one of the newly settled planets. But it would be a wrench to leave here after all this time and all we've done. What about you?"

"Like you, I'd like to be able to go back for a short while," she replied. "But I could never live there again and I could never take up the old way of life. Right now I've got everything I ever wanted and I've never been happier. If I couldn't come back here I wouldn't go."

When I gave the matter a little more thought I realised that I felt exactly the same. New Britain is our real home.

THE END

Printed in the United Kingdom
by Lightning Source UK Ltd.
123302UK00002B/24/A